CONQUEST

A LA RUE FAMILY CRIME THRILLER

RICHARD WAKE

MANOR AND STATE, LLC

PART I

SUNDAY AT VINCENT'S

The back table at Vincent's had been reserved on Sunday afternoons for the La Rue family for as long as Henri La Rue could remember, even if they only made it about once a month. He had been there as a kid when it was three tables pushed together and his entire goal had been to hit his brother with a spitball before the end of the paper straw got too wet to produce the necessary blast of air. He had been there, too, when it had become necessary to separate his children, Guy and Clarice, in order to avoid a full-scale war. But Guy and Clarice were grown now and only occasional attendees on Sunday afternoons. These days, it tended to be all old people.

Gérard, Henri's uncle, always sat at the head of the table. The food was always the same — either roast pork or roast chicken on alternating weeks, mashed potatoes, green beans, green salad, bread and butter, all served family style. Desserts were the only menu items that were ordered individually. And, as Sylvie said, "It might be different if it was extraordinary chicken. If it melted in your mouth. If it brought you to a culinary orgasm."

"Do we have to—" Henri said.

"Be nice to have an orgasm," Sylvie said. She was Henri's wife.

Aside from orgasms, the main topic of conversation among the men at the table was the story in that morning's Le Parisien, the story of René Morel, a man who was being sought by police after he was identified as a collaborator with the Gestapo during the war. Fifteen years after VE Day, this remained a big deal, a crime punishable by imprisonment or even death, depending upon the extent of the collaboration.

"I always suspected," Gérard said. He had a copy of the newspaper at the table with him, and waved it indifferently in front of his face.

"Based on what?" Martin said. Martin was Henri's younger brother, the spitball target.

"Intuition," Gérard said.

"Did you know him back then?" Henri said.

"I knew who he was, but I didn't know him," Gérard said. "I didn't get over to the 10th very much back then. Still don't."

The La Rue family was from Montmartre, the 18th arrondissement. The Morels were from the neighboring 10th. They shared a geographical boundary in Paris, north of the Seine, but little else. The La Rues ran their business and the Morels theirs, and they only interacted when there was a dispute — which there almost never was because of the boundary. The last time had been five years earlier, when Henri heard about a brothel that was two blocks into the 18th and that he did not control. It took exactly three minutes with the proprietor and one pair of brass knuckles to discover the Morel family connection. It took exactly one cup of coffee in the days after that to extract an apology and the signed-over lease to the brothel from René Morel. And that was the last time.

"He always was weak," Gérard said. He had ordered the Peach Melba and was in the process of inhaling it. Sweets were the only vice of his uncle's that Henri knew about.

"The paper said a woman is giving the testimony," Henri said. "An old mistress, maybe?"

"A woman," Gérard said, digging his spoon back into the dessert. Gérard had never married.

"All these years later, I don't get why anybody cares," Martin said.

"How can you say that?" Henri said, although he knew why.

But he couldn't help himself, and his voice rose, and he said, "The goddamned Gestapo, they killed—"

"Enough," Gérard said, his voice even louder than Henri's, his hand raised like a traffic cop. Then he stood up, and the man next to him stood up, too. He was Gérard's oldest friend, Maurice. Behind his back, everybody in the family called him Silent Moe, mostly because he almost never said anything to anyone other than to Gérard, and only then in whispers.

The two of them carried their port into the back room of Vincent's, which also had been reserved for the La Rue family every Sunday afternoon for as long as Henri could remember. The lunch was always just a prelude to the real ritual. After about five minutes, Henri went first. He was the oldest, and he always went first — with the port in his hand and the envelope in his breast pocket. Gérard had a small crew, and they still had some money out on the street, but that was about it. For the most part, all Gérard did was collect envelopes based upon his seniority — and he was a master at it. He could tell by feel if it was light or heavy, and by how much. If it was light, you got a question. If it was heavy, you got a nod. Actually, the envelope got a nod — Gérard's eyes were always down, looking at it in his hand. The one who handed it over never received so much as a "good job" or, God forbid, a "thank you." On that day, Henri's envelope was just right. On days when it was just right, there was no reaction at all, just a quick handing of the envelope over his shoulder to Silent Moe, who was sitting just behind him.

What followed would be a few minutes of conversation — about pending business, or staffing issues, or whatever. That day, though, Gérard began with a warning.

"Forget Morel," he said. "Forget about the 10th."

"I don't know what you're talking about," Henri said.

"Don't kid a kidder," Gérard said. "You forget I've known you since you were born. I've wiped your ass."

"My ass is clean and so is my conscience," Henri said. "I'm not thinking about the 10th."

The truth was, the 10th was all that Henri had been thinking about since he opened the newspaper that morning. With Morel out of the way — and he was either going to jail or disappearing for good — the 10th arrondissement became an open question, mostly because Morel had no children and there were no other Morels in the line of succession. Instead, there was just his half-assed organization led by three captains whom Henri had met along the way and referred to as Opie, Dopey, and Really Dopey.

The 10th was not a wealthy arrondissement — much of it was pretty run down, to be honest — and it wasn't particularly big, either. But what it had were train stations, two of them: the Gare du Nord and the Gare de l'Est. Train stations, with so many goods coming and going, were the Parisian gangster equivalent of gold mines. Through an accident of geography, the La Rues controlled two arrondissements — the 18th and the 9th — but had no train stations, while the 10th had two. Those stations were what Henri was fixated on most of all.

"I mean it, Henri — don't," Gérard said.

"I know, I know," Henri said, and then he put on Gérard's voice and began, "The historical sanctity—"

"Don't mock me," Gérard said. "But it's true, and you know it as well as I do. The historical sanctity of the boundary lines keeps the peace and keeps all of us wealthy. Don't be a hog. Hogs get slaughtered."

He had said it a hundred times over the years, and Henri knew that the old man wasn't wrong. The boundary lines had kept the peace, and the peace had made all of them wealthy. At the same time, the old man had evolved into a boss who was somewhere between risk-averse and calcified. And "wealthy" was a relative term. And it wasn't as if two train stations became available every day — and with Morel in hiding, and only Opie, Dopey, and Really Dopey to run the operation, the stations might very well be available. And it wasn't as if Gérard would be the one collecting the envelopes in Vincent's back room forever.

When Henri returned to the main table, it was Martin's turn. He waited about two minutes though, because that was how it had always been done — to give Gérard a chance to take a sip of port, and exchange a word or two with Silent Moe. When Martin got up and left for the back room, Sylvie turned to Henri and asked, "So what did he say?"

"About what, dearest?"

"About the 10th," she said. "About the Morels. About the damn train stations."

They had not discussed the matter that morning, but Sylvie read the same newspaper that her husband did and had been married into the La Rue family for more than a quarter-century. She knew how it worked. She also had enough ambition for both herself and Henri and always had.

"You know what he said," Henri said.

"That old fossil."

"He might not be wrong."

"Of course, he's wrong," Sylvie said. "My God, he's the walking dead. What was the last thing about him that moved, other than his bowels?"

Gérard was 72 years old. He had run the thing since Henri's father, Jean — Gérard's brother — died eight years earlier. When Jean was alive, he was the oldest and in charge, but he had an ability to allow Gérard enough authority that led outsiders to believe that it was an equal sharing of power between the brothers. It wasn't, though, and everyone inside the family knew it. When it became Gérard's turn, however, there was no appearance of power sharing with Henri, his oldest surviving nephew. Gérard's authority was undisputed as, year by year, it rusted over.

"That old man," Sylvie said. She poked at her slab of vanilla cake.

"Dried out, like him," she said. She tossed the fork onto the little plate. The clatter startled Father Lemieux, who was sitting two seats away on Sylvie's right, next to where Silent Moe had been.

"It can't be that bad, Sylvie," Father Lemieux said.

"I should have had the ice cream," she said. "I'd ask for a bite of yours, but you appear to have licked the dish clean."

"Growing boy," Father Lemieux said. He patted his stomach, which was non-existent.

Sylvie turned her back to the priest and half whispered to Henri, "And why exactly is he around so much these days?"

"He's become friends with Gérard," Henri said. "From when he was an assistant at St. Pierre's."

"And where is he now?" she said.

"You know, you could turn, and face him with a friendly smile, and ask him yourself," Henri said. When she gave him the same you've-got-to-be-kidding-me look that she gave him when they were 16, and he had begun to reach his hand under her blouse, Henri said, "He's downtown now — good with figures or something. He works for the archdiocese in some office."

"So he's a briefcase priest, probably in some fabulous rectory downtown that has a cook with a Michelin star, but he keeps coming back up the butte for the Sunday slop at Vincent's?"

"They became friends," Henri said. "What can I tell you?"

"I bet he goes to the house," she said. Then she picked up her fork and stabbed at the vanilla cake.

The house where Gérard lived was on the very top of the butte, just a block from Sacré Coeur. It was, without question, the thing that most bothered Sylvie about Henri's uncle. Gérard had the top two floors of a classic old building that had been updated with an elevator and tight windows along the way. It was enough space for eight, but Gérard lived there alone among his antique furniture and his fabulous views — neither the cook nor the maid lived in. On the wall in the living room hung a Van Gogh that was said to have been painted during the artist's short, wild stint in Montmartre.

"A minor work, but still," is what Gérard said every time he pointed it out. And if Henri had been in the living room 20 times over the years, Gérard had pointed it out 20 times.

"Just once, he could have the lunch at his house," Sylvie said. She was by then eating the vanilla cake without making a face.

"This is tradition," Henri said.

"He's a cheap old bastard," Sylvie said, "I mean, have we ever eaten in that palace?"

"Come on, he has us over every year for a Christmas drink," Henri said.

"That's not eating," she said.

"Last year, I think there was pâté," he said, and immediately regretted it. On the list of no-win arguments, this had to be at the top. No. 1: Gérard was a cheap, old fool with a fantastic house on the top of the butte that he did not deserve. No. 2: When are you going to buy me a house on the top of the butte? Even at the worst times, the mistress didn't rise above No. 3.

"Pâté?" Sylvie said. For a second, as she gripped and then re-gripped the fork, Henri wondered if she was subconsciously considering stabbing him with it. Then she sputtered the word "pâté" two more times, louder and then louder still. Henri looked over and saw Father Lemieux slightly raise an eye from his ongoing task, which involved scraping the last drop or two of ice cream smeared on the dish. Just as quickly, though, his eye was back down and the priest was back at it.

"If you would just show a little backbone in your dealings with him," Sylvie said. Then she went quiet. There was no way to have this argument without the appropriate decibels. Nobody he had ever met could reach a righteously indignant crescendo like Sylvie could, and she knew that Vincent's on a Sunday afternoon would rob her of the full range of her powerful instrument. So she stopped and picked at the vanilla cake, and then reached over and picked at Henri's untouched chocolate cake.

"But still," Sylvie said, and then she stopped as abruptly as she had started. Martin's return from the back room, and his taking the seat on Henri's other side, shut her up and allowed Henri to extricate himself from the unwinnable argument. Sylvie understood that business always took precedence.

Martin sat, and leaned into Henri, and said, "Got a problem."

"And, what, I'm the solution?"

"You could be, if you could keep an open mind for once."

"Always me," Henri said, adding a theatrical sigh that often became a part of his arsenal of punctuation in such conversations.

The sigh, all of it, was the essence of the relationship between older brother and younger brother. It was all there in a single short exchange. The ask from the kid brother. The resistance from the older brother before he'd even heard a single detail. The reply from the kid brother that said without saying that the older brother was a stubborn ass. The reply from the older brother that said without saying that the younger brother was a lazy, pathetic piece of crap.

With those time-honored territories thus marked, Martin began to lay out the issue. He stopped just as soon as he started, though, as their cousin stood and walked toward the back room.

"You ever wonder about his envelopes?" Martin said. He watched as Michel closed the door to the back room behind him.

"They must be pretty damn fat, I guess," Henri said. He watched Michel, too. He watched and wondered how someone who wasn't 10 years older than his son could be making at least as much money as he was, if not more.

"I can't believe there wasn't even a consultation," Martin said.

"When was the last time Gérard consulted about anything?"

"But it's just bull—"

"He brought the contacts, he got the business," Henri said. Then he shrugged.

"Heroin's too important just to shrug off," Martin said.

"So you go try to change Gérard's mind," Henri said. "And good luck with that. There's only one thing that would change the old fool's mind, and that's if the envelopes were light. But if the envelopes were light, he'd make the change without you asking."

Then Henri shrugged again. Michel grew up in Marseille, the son of one of Gérard's cousins. So he was a La Rue, but really? Anyway, Marseille was where everyone — including the cops — knew that all the French heroin arrived for processing from Turkey. So when Michel approached Uncle Gérard with a plan to add heroin smuggling to America into the La Rue family's Paris portfolio, Gérard gave him the business without any consultation with anyone. Michel got the product, and he got the product to the United States, and Gérard got the fat envelopes, and Henri and Martin got nothing — nothing but jealous and suspicious. It was about the only thing the brothers bonded over.

"So, tell me, what's your problem?" Henri said.

"It's really an opportunity," Martin said.

"Problem, opportunity — it kind of depends on where you're sitting, I think," Henri said.

Then Martin laid it all out. He ran the alcohol side of the family business. Most of it was muscling bars and cafés to be their beer, wine and spirits clients, and to take exclusive delivery from the La Rue family warehouses. A small piece of the business was a legitimate import/export operation of fine wines, just to keep the tax man happy.

Most of the money just came from the markup the bars and cafés paid — but a slice came from the highjacking of trucks from the big distilleries, as well as other thefts. In this case, Martin had developed a source who would give him access to a warehouse outside Reims and enough time to lift two truckloads

— mostly of real Scotch from Scotland, and vodka from somewhere to the east. The problem was the trucks.

"You must have—" Henri said.

"I don't," Martin said. "Everything's committed. This is all last-minute. I only found out last night."

"And when—"

"Tomorrow night."

"You've got to be—"

"Tomorrow night or we lose it," Martin said.

Henri thought for a second and said, "So I guess you steal the trucks. You've done it before. Why do you need me?"

"I don't need you to steal them, but I need your permission," Martin said.

"Permission for what?"

"To steal the trucks from Gus."

"No," Henri said, reflexively. Then, after a second, he said, "Why Gus?"

"Because it will be easy, and we need easy," Martin said.

Gus Parent was Henri's oldest friend. They didn't see each other all that much anymore, but they lived on the same street as eight-year-olds and stayed best friends until they were married in their early twenties. Put another way, they stayed best friends until Henri joined his family's business and Gus joined his. The Parents owned a small trucking firm and did deliveries for all manner of businesses, including the school uniform manufacturing company that supplied Henri with enough legitimate income to keep the tax man away from his door. The last time Henri asked, Gus was up to four trucks.

"There has to be another way," Henri said.

"We need a sure thing," Martin said. "We don't have time to scout out other locations. We know Gus, we know where he is, we know that when he shuts off the lights, that's it. No big security, nothing like that. He probably hangs the keys on a hook inside the office door."

"But, come on — it's Gus," Henri said.

"There's no risk to Gus," Martin said. "We can play it a couple of ways. We can just abandon the trucks when we're done, and he'll get them back. Or, we can repaint them and keep them ourselves, which is probably what I'd do — and Gus would just collect the insurance money. He comes out whole either way."

"I don't know," Henri said.

"What's not to know?"

"He is my oldest friend, after all."

"He owes you, and you know it," Martin said. "Didn't you always tell me that when you were 16, you convinced Marie What's-Her-Name to go down on him after she was done with you?"

"I'm not sure a 30-year-old blowjob exactly qualifies as a debt," Henri said.

"He's going to get the insurance money," Martin said.

Henri thought, but not for very long after Martin added, "And don't worry, you'll get your cut."

Guy arrived in time for a glass of port. It did not appear to be his first drink of the day. He was wearing a suit, but he had not shaved.

"Rough night, little man?" Martin said, standing to give his nephew a hug around the neck with one arm, and a punch on top of his head with the other. Then Sylvie stood and gave her son a peck on the cheek and a playful massage of the scruff on his cheeks. Henri stayed seated, settling for an exaggerated look at his wristwatch.

"Look, I got here," Guy said.

"Barely," Henri said.

"I can get some food from the kitchen," Sylvie said.

"I'm not staying," Guy said.

"Of course not," Henri said.

Silence descended on the table until Martin managed to begin a conversation about Stade Saint-Germain. He and Guy were supporters of the club, and they managed to fill five minutes with a series of denunciations of the goalkeeper and what Guy called, "his three fucking left feet."

"Easy with the language," Henri said.

"She's heard it before," Guy said.

Sylvie's eyes dropped to Henri's piece of chocolate cake as father and son stared at each other. Then Guy stood up and said, "All right, I'm out of here."

"You have to say hello to your uncle," Henri said.

"Who's in there?"

"Michel. Shouldn't be long."

Martin tried again with some more football talk, this time about the coach, the man he always referred to as "that imbecile." Guy listened, but he didn't engage. He was antsy in his chair.

"Why do you have to go?" Sylvie said.

"Business, mom," he said.

Guy was 25 and, despite Henri's misgivings, had joined the family business. He had a small crew — who, behind his nephew's back, Martin referred to as "knuckleheads on parade." Guy had a small amount of money out on the street, and was managing to earn a little. He was learning the business and always professing his independence, but the truth was the initial stake had come from his parents, and he still lived under their roof — on the nights he managed to make it home, anyway.

The deal was that Guy would pay back the money in a year. Until then, there would be no envelopes for Henri. And if it seemed a little odd — the notion of a son kicking up to the father — Henri's reasoning, delivered to Sylvie in a volume equal to her objections, was direct: "He works for me. He enjoys my protection and assistance. He pays me just like anybody else, and that's it." Henri was so unusually loud that Sylvie never brought it up again — and, for whatever it was worth, neither did their son.

As soon as the door to the back room opened, Guy was on his feet. He brushed past Michel with nothing more than a nod. Henri looked at his watch, and his son spent exactly 44 seconds in the back room before the door opened again.

There were no goodbyes. Sylvie went back to Henri's chocolate cake. Henri got up to refill his glass with port. He did not give his son another thought except in passing. Not for days, not for all of the time that he debated in his head, and then did his research, and then plotted out how he wanted things to play out. The deciding and the planning — the whole thing — took 10 days, all together.

The office was at Place de la République. It was on the second floor of a building that looked out on the vast square. Specifically, it stared directly at the monument upon which stood the statue of Marianne. It was erected in the 1880s to represent all that was France — liberty, fraternity, equality, reason, the whole thing.

As Morel told them, more than once, "She's the goddamned Goddess of Liberty. She's a national symbol. You look at her, and you're supposed to see everything that embodies this great country."

When Cyril, Luc and Muggs shrugged in reply, Morel said, "Don't you clowns know any of this? You did have to go to school for at least a few years, no?"

The office was above the luggage store that provided all of them cover from the tax man. They must have sold more valises than the rest of the shops in Paris combined, given the salaries listed on the accounts.

When they left for lunch, Cyril said to the luggage guy, "Busy today?"

"Not a soul," came the reply.

At precisely 12:30, they walked to the restaurant because that was the way Morel always did it. As they passed the statue, they offered a little salute to the old girl and then walked across the square and down the street. They passed a half-dozen perfectly acceptable restaurants, but they kept going and walked to the canal. Average people on the street, people doing their shopping or just passing through, did not know who they were, but the shopkeepers did. Most greeted the three of them enthusiastically, as usual. A couple were even more enthusiastic than normal, almost theatrical. They were the ones who knew who was in charge now that Morel was, as Muggs liked to say, "absent."

A few others, though, were different — the man from the patisserie, most notably. There was no greeting. If there was a smile, it was a straight-across face.

"What's with that asshole?" Luc said.

"Think about it," Cyril said.

When they got to the canal, they walked two more blocks to the left and stopped at the café at the corner of Rue Dieu. There were always two tables for them, on the left, in the sun because Morel liked the sun even in the summer. Cyril, Luc and Muggs preferred the shade, but none had the gumption to make a change. They picked up the signs that said "Reserved" and placed them to the side behind the sugar bowl. Then they sat and no one spoke. Morel was the one who always spoke when they came to the café at the corner of Rue Dieu — or, anywhere really.

At least once a month, Morel would tell some tale about the canal, about its history or about how hard it was for the city to keep it properly dredged, or some such thing. He would tell the story, and he would sense from the faces that they had no idea, just like when he was talking about the Marianne statue.

As the waitress brought the order, he would finish with, "It amazes me, your lack of education. No history. No culture."

And then, as the waitress walked away, Morel would say, "You know, I fucked her in the ass when we were both 19."

At which point, Cyril, Luc, and Muggs would guffaw, and elbow each other in the ribs, and wait for Morel to lift his fork. Then they would follow. But seeing as how it was just them, the other two waited for Cyril to pick up his fork. The three were technically of the same rank, but that really was only a technicality. Cyril would be in charge whenever he decided the time was right, and the others knew it and accepted it.

That succession was what they talked about when they sat in the office all day. It came down to a single question: when? And if Luc and Muggs were anxious for him to take over, Cyril was hesitant.

As he said, pretty much hourly, "Things are running fine. There hasn't been a blip. There's no hurry."

As Cyril also kept saying, almost as often, "What's a decent interval?"

And then, "Pretend it wasn't... this. Pretend that Morel wasn't a collaborator, wasn't on the run. Pretend he was dead. What's a decent interval? It's easier when you know for sure that he isn't coming back."

A few seconds after the waitress put down the plates, Cyril picked up his fork. And as the three of them sat there, tucking into some ordinary salmon croquettes — Morel ordered the salmon croquettes every Wednesday, and it was Wednesday, after all — the black Renault pulled up on the street between the canal and the café on the corner of Rue Dieu, and the man with the machine gun stuck the barrel out the window, and the subsequent burst of bullets killed all three of them. It didn't take five seconds, and then the Renault sped away. The first policeman to arrive, amid all of the death and the gore, for some reason fixated on a spot of blood on the little sign that said "Reserved."

PART II

OFF THE MODEL'S BACK

Henri and Marina walked over to the Lido from her apartment. It was a nice night, and it took only about 10 minutes. Marina couldn't handle even that distance in her heels, though, so she did it barefoot. Barefoot and bitching.

"I told you, we could get a taxi," Henri said.

Marina's reply was a hand waved in disgust.

"Really, the rank is at the next corner," he said.

"We're almost there," she said. Then, another wave, more disgust.

The club was beneath a shopping arcade on the Champs-Élysées. Outside the door, there was the usual hubbub — well-dressed men, better-dressed women, all of them just a bit louder than you would expect, excited by the anticipation. Inside, Jean-Pierre was working the reservation desk. He saw Henri, and the grin on his face grew to a size just this side of cartoonish.

"Mr. La Rue, it has been too long," he said. "And mademoiselle, may I say that you have never been lovelier. The dress is exquisite. Is it—"

"Dior," Marina said, with a conspiratorial whisper.

"The show just—"

"Just last week, Jean-Pierre," she said.

"I'd heard a few whispers, but this is beyond...But so quickly?"

"I bought it off the model's back," she said.

The dress was stunning — red, backless, sleeveless. The color set off Marina's blonde hair. The design revealed enough to shame a nun but not quite enough to cause a traffic accident. Henri was afraid to ask what it had cost, and Marina had not volunteered the figure. It would be an end-of-the-month surprise in the mail at the office, which was where all of Marina's bills were sent.

"Come, come," Jean-Pierre said, and he led them to the big ringside table, a table for 16. Everyone else was already there. Henri palmed a hundred to Jean-Pierre after he pulled out the chairs. Anybody who could make Marina smile, a skill that had seemed to evade Henri lately, was worth the money.

It was Friday night at the Lido, which meant it was girlfriends' night. Henri was with Marina, Martin with Helen, Michel with Lorraine, and the rest with women whose names Henri either forgot or never knew. Girlfriends on Friday, wives on Saturday — it had been that way for Henri's father, and for his father's father, and probably before that, too. It was a practice understood by everyone, including the girlfriends and the wives. On Fridays, the wives often got together in smaller groups to play cards or see a movie. On Saturdays, the men didn't know what the girlfriends did — although it likely involved the expenditure of their money.

Bottles of champagne already dotted the table when Henri and Marina sat down. The show was supposed to start in about 15 minutes, which meant that half of the women got up to use the facilities. Lorraine, Michel's girl, was one of the ones who stayed. Henri couldn't help but stare at her, and only partly because she was stunning. Mostly, he stared because she was so young. His daughter was 22, and he was pretty sure that Lorraine was younger. It was one of the dozen reasons why he didn't like Michel.

The men were all friends, or at least acquaintances, but they still gravitated into groups around their bosses. As such, Pascal, Timothée and Willy were in a cluster at Henri's end of the table. With the women gone, it was Pascal who raised a glass and toasted.

"To the 10th," said the man known universally as Passy.

Part of Henri wanted to stop any celebration before it started, but the room was noisy and no one else could hear the toast. Even Martin and his two guys at the other end couldn't hear, although they undoubtedly knew from the body language what it was all about. It was two days after Henri's crew — led by Freddy and his machine gun — had wiped out Opie, Dopey and Really Dopey. Freddy was missing the impromptu celebration because he had only a wife, not a girlfriend.

The Morel territory — the 10th arrondissement, and the Gare du Nord, and the Gare de l'Est — was theirs. The office above the luggage shop on the Place de la République had been secured, and Opie, Dopey and Really Dopey's crews had been given new leadership, and the men in the crews seemed fine with the arrangements — especially seeing as how Henri had decided that they could keep two percent more of their proceeds. When his own men questioned this bump, Henri said, "Come on, now. There will be plenty for everyone from those two stations alone. And we need Morel's men. And remember: hogs get slaughtered."

They toasted again, and then the girls came back from the ladies' room as a single squadron and reclaimed their seats. It was a noisy squadron, noisier than it had been, and Henri knew why. He knew even before he saw the grains of white powder still clinging to the rim of Marina's nostril.

Henri leaned over, as if for a kiss, but instead licked away the tiny smudge of cocaine from Marina's nose.

"Starting early," he said, trying not to sound like her father.

"Don't worry, daddy," she said. Obviously, Henri had failed.

"Who—"

"Does it really matter?" Marina said. And then she pivoted on her lovely ass, sheathed in red Dior, and turned to talk to Timmy's girl, whatever her name was. She was new, in his usual range — she 35, he 55 — and her makeup appeared to have been applied extra heavy on her right cheek, likely the result of Timmy and his left-handed backhand.

Then the lights blinked, which was the two-minute warning before the start of the show. Rather than quieting the room, the blinking lights just made it louder as conversations were wrapped up with some urgency and other remarks anticipating the show were exchanged. It just got louder and louder, it seemed, until the lights were doused to an "oooohhh," followed by the first few notes from the overture. And then came the girls.

There wasn't a covered breast among the dozen women, or much covered skin at all, and each was bathed in her own spotlight — but the Lido was not a striptease place. This was different. It was sensual, not crass. It was art. The costumes for the opening number that night, what there were of them, were a kind of teal color. The headwear — which sometimes could be so tall and heavy that you wondered how the girls could stand up straight — was understated, tiaras with just a couple of feathers. And the bodies, the breasts — let's just say that there was a definite Lido type of breast, taut but full, and never so heavy that you wondered how the girls could stand up straight.

They came out as a group, and they paraded and kicked, and then four of them would pose on pedestals of various heights as the rest continued to dance. One sneaked out in the blackness between the spotlights and emerged on a trapeze from the ceiling. That brought the first of several roars and rounds of applause.

As the clapping rose and died, Passy leaned over to the rest of us and said, "Standard bet?"

"Standard bet," the rest of the men all replied in unison.

The standard bet was 500 francs to anyone who spotted even a single hair between any of the girls' legs. In all the years they had been coming to the Lido, no one had ever won the money.

After the girls the acts came in rapid succession — a crooner for two songs, and then a blindfolded juggler, and then the damndest thing you ever saw, a German marksman who shot apples off the heads of showgirls. Then there were more girls in different revealing costumes, and then more acts, and then more girls, and on and on. As the night wore on, and people got up to use the toilet, the seating tended to rearrange naturally with the women closest to the stage and the men gathered at the farthest reaches of the table. It was there that Henri found himself next to Martin.

They were civil for about 30 seconds before Henri couldn't help himself and said, "Well?"

"Christ — what now?" Martin said.

"Gus's trucks, same as always."

"What about them?"

"What's new?"

"Nothing's new, okay?" Martin said. "Nothing's fucking new."

"Gus can't get screwed on this."

"I'm doing everything I can."

"Meaning what?" Henri said. The music rose and Martin did not answer. Of course, it could have been a silent room and Martin would not have answered because Henri knew that Martin was doing nothing to make sure Gus was made whole.

It had been over a week, but there was still no resolution from the entire mess. Martin was competent enough, except when he wasn't — and when he wasn't, the splatter seemed to get all over everybody, and all over Henri especially.

The way Martin told the story, the beginning of the operation had gone as expected. "Couldn't have been smoother," he said, about a hundred times in the days that followed. He would say it, and then he would swipe the palm of his left hand over his upturned right hand, and then he would say, "Silk." He would say it in a soft tone of voice, and elongate the S just a little, as if that made it all better somehow.

The trucks had been stolen from Gus's parking lot without a hint of a problem. Martin hired a couple of specials for that part, and for the drive to Reims, and there were no issues along the way.

"Not a hint of an issue — they checked from the phone box a half-mile from the warehouse," Martin said.

At the warehouse, the loading of the merchandise was quick and undetected by anybody who mattered.

"My guy in the warehouse called as they drove away," Martin said. "Again, nothing. Easy." Then he did it again, the bit with his left hand swiping over his upturned right hand.

"Silk," he said.

But about halfway back to Paris — and this is where it got murky, seeing as how there were no more telephone updates on Martin's flawless mission — the two trucks were somehow stopped and forced to the side of the road. How it happened, none of them knew — but the results were plain. The drivers were both shot in their seats. The cargo was stolen. Then the trucks were set on fire. They had burned, they along with the bodies, and then the gas tanks had exploded, and then they had burned some more, burned until the fuel was expended. Given the time of night, the road was quiet and police were not called for at least an hour, by their own reckoning.

Martin's first thought was that he had been betrayed by his man at the warehouse outside Reims. He followed up that thought the next day with a bullet to the temple, delivered by one of the kids who worked for him. When Henri made him explain why he thought it was that guy, he stumbled around verbally for a minute or two and concluded, "It had to be him."

"No it didn't," Henri said.

"He just needed somebody to steal it, so he could re-sell it himself," Martin said.

"Why not just have the guy who burned Gus's trucks and

killed your men steal it in the first place and eliminate the middle man?" Henri said.

"Because he needed our trucks," Martin said.

"They had their own trucks," Henri said. "Where do you think the Scotch went? And the vodka? You think the crates grew legs?"

Then Henri paused and muttered, "Idiot." And then Martin stopped trying to explain himself.

When the whole mess at the side of the road cooled down, the cops were able to decipher a truck serial number off of one of the engine blocks. That was how they knew the trucks belonged to Gus Parent. The La Rues had eyes on the police station, and their people had seen Gus being questioned before being allowed to leave — but that was all anybody knew.

"It's going to be fine," Martin kept saying. "Gus will put in for the insurance, and he'll get paid, and that will be the end of it."

"You'd better be right," Henri said.

Just then, their conversation was interrupted by a pushy magician who had decided that he wanted Marina and her red Dior dress to participate in his act. She had been to the toilet at least twice more with the girls and was in a mood to say yes. That the magician was handsome enough and thirtyish, about her age, likely didn't hurt. When he had her stand, and the spotlight caught the full cut of the dress, the laughter in the room shifted to a widespread "ooooh." There were also two or three wolf whistles as grace notes.

The trick involved Marina picking a card from a deck, looking at it, memorizing it, showing it to a few people behind her, and then putting it into an envelope. The magician asked her if it was the 10 of hearts, and Marina said it wasn't. He asked again, and she shook her head. He asked a third time, and she shook her head and made a face.

"The magician said, 'If it isn't the 10 of hearts, what is it?'"

"Two of clubs," she said.

"Okay, open it," he said. The card inside the envelope was, in fact, the 10 of hearts. Marina and the people she had showed were laughing, applauding disbelief.

Then, the magician said, "Open your handbag, mademoiselle." When Marina did as instructed, she found another envelope. Inside of it was the two of clubs.

It was, Henri had to admit, a neat trick. As for Marina, she melted into the magic asshole's arms in a mock faint.

Henri, though, turned back to Martin, and locked eyes with him, and stared him down. It was a look that Henri had perfected over the years, a look he used mostly on his underlings and only occasionally on his little brother. But when he did, they both knew what it meant. Words were unnecessary.

Martin reached into his pocket and put an envelope on the table. Henri scooped it up and got it into his own pocket in two seconds, while the room was still fixated on Marina untangling herself from the magic asshole. Because even though the whole thing fell apart so spectacularly on the road between Reims and Paris, Henri was still entitled to an envelope for his counsel and for his trouble.

After the girls the acts came in rapid succession — a crooner for two songs, and then a blindfolded juggler, and then the damndest thing you ever saw, a German marksman who shot apples off the heads of showgirls. Then there were more girls in different revealing costumes, and then more acts, and then more girls, and on and on. As the night wore on, and people got up to use the toilet, the seating tended to rearrange naturally with the women closest to the stage and the men gathered at the farthest reaches of the table. It was there that Henri found himself next to Martin.

They were civil for about 30 seconds before Henri couldn't help himself and said, "Well?"

"Christ — what now?" Martin said.

"Gus's trucks, same as always."

"What about them?"

"What's new?"

"Nothing's new, okay?" Martin said. "Nothing's fucking new."

"Gus can't get screwed on this."

"I'm doing everything I can."

"Meaning what?" Henri said. The music rose and Martin did not answer. Of course, it could have been a silent room and Martin would not have answered because Henri knew that Martin was doing nothing to make sure Gus was made whole.

It had been over a week, but there was still no resolution from the entire mess. Martin was competent enough, except when he wasn't — and when he wasn't, the splatter seemed to get all over everybody, and all over Henri especially.

The way Martin told the story, the beginning of the operation had gone as expected. "Couldn't have been smoother," he said, about a hundred times in the days that followed. He would say it, and then he would swipe the palm of his left hand over his upturned right hand, and then he would say, "Silk." He would say it in a soft tone of voice, and elongate the S just a little, as if that made it all better somehow.

The trucks had been stolen from Gus's parking lot without a hint of a problem. Martin hired a couple of specials for that part, and for the drive to Reims, and there were no issues along the way.

"Not a hint of an issue — they checked from the phone box a half-mile from the warehouse," Martin said.

At the warehouse, the loading of the merchandise was quick and undetected by anybody who mattered.

"My guy in the warehouse called as they drove away," Martin said. "Again, nothing. Easy." Then he did it again, the bit with his left hand swiping over his upturned right hand.

"Silk," he said.

But about halfway back to Paris — and this is where it got murky, seeing as how there were no more telephone updates on Martin's flawless mission — the two trucks were somehow stopped and forced to the side of the road. How it happened, none of them knew — but the results were plain. The drivers were both shot in their seats. The cargo was stolen. Then the trucks were set on fire. They had burned, they along with the bodies, and then the gas tanks had exploded, and then they had burned some more, burned until the fuel was expended. Given the time of night, the road was quiet and police were not called for at least an hour, by their own reckoning.

Martin's first thought was that he had been betrayed by his man at the warehouse outside Reims. He followed up that thought the next day with a bullet to the temple, delivered by one of the kids who worked for him. When Henri made him explain why he thought it was that guy, he stumbled around verbally for a minute or two and concluded, "It had to be him."

"No it didn't," Henri said.

"He just needed somebody to steal it, so he could re-sell it himself," Martin said.

"Why not just have the guy who burned Gus's trucks and killed your men steal it in the first place and eliminate the middle man?" Henri said.

"Because he needed our trucks," Martin said.

"They had their own trucks," Henri said. "Where do you think the Scotch went? And the vodka? You think the crates grew legs?"

Then Henri paused and muttered, "Idiot." And then Martin stopped trying to explain himself.

When the whole mess at the side of the road cooled down, the cops were able to decipher a truck serial number off of one of the engine blocks. That was how they knew the trucks belonged to Gus Parent. The La Rues had eyes on the police station, and their people had seen Gus being questioned before being allowed to leave — but that was all anybody knew.

"It's going to be fine," Martin kept saying. "Gus will put in for the insurance, and he'll get paid, and that will be the end of it."

"You'd better be right," Henri said.

Just then, their conversation was interrupted by a pushy magician who had decided that he wanted Marina and her red Dior dress to participate in his act. She had been to the toilet at least twice more with the girls and was in a mood to say yes. That the magician was handsome enough and thirtyish, about her age, likely didn't hurt. When he had her stand, and the spotlight caught the full cut of the dress, the laughter in the room shifted to a widespread "ooooh." There were also two or three wolf whistles as grace notes.

The trick involved Marina picking a card from a deck, looking at it, memorizing it, showing it to a few people behind her, and then putting it into an envelope. The magician asked her if it was the 10 of hearts, and Marina said it wasn't. He asked again, and she shook her head. He asked a third time, and she shook her head and made a face.

"The magician said, 'If it isn't the 10 of hearts, what is it?'"

"Two of clubs," she said.

"Okay, open it," he said. The card inside the envelope was, in fact, the 10 of hearts. Marina and the people she had showed were laughing, applauding disbelief.

Then, the magician said, "Open your handbag, mademoiselle." When Marina did as instructed, she found another envelope. Inside of it was the two of clubs.

It was, Henri had to admit, a neat trick. As for Marina, she melted into the magic asshole's arms in a mock faint.

Henri, though, turned back to Martin, and locked eyes with him, and stared him down. It was a look that Henri had perfected over the years, a look he used mostly on his underlings and only occasionally on his little brother. But when he did, they both knew what it meant. Words were unnecessary.

Martin reached into his pocket and put an envelope on the table. Henri scooped it up and got it into his own pocket in two seconds, while the room was still fixated on Marina untangling herself from the magic asshole. Because even though the whole thing fell apart so spectacularly on the road between Reims and Paris, Henri was still entitled to an envelope for his counsel and for his trouble.

Sylvie's dress was from Galeries Lafayette — Henri didn't know the designer, but it was a notch or two below Dior, and months behind the runway show where Marina bought the dress off the model's back. It was a deep blue, and it had half-sleeves, and it more than flattered Sylvie's figure. He made sure to whistle when she came out of the bedroom, and she couldn't suppress a little smile as she did a turn for him in the doorway. So far, so good. Henri had managed to sell the you-look-great whistle, so it did not come off as you-look-great-for-a-45-year-old.

Rexy drove them from the apartment, dropped them on the Champs-Élysées, and was told to be back at 11:30. By then, the girls would have retired for the evening and the only part of the show remaining be the walk-out acts, generally terrible comedians. Jean-Pierre had once told Henri that they were an industry unto themselves, the walk-out comedians, who worked earlier gigs in lousier clubs around the city and then hustled over to get in the queue for a walk-out spot at the Lido. But all of that was still three hours away.

"Madame La Rue!" Jean-Pierre said when he saw her. It was actually more shrieked than said, the words accompanied by kisses on her cheeks, and then a step back, and then an exaggerated look up and down her body in admiration.

"Fabulous," he said. "Just spectacular. And the color, it suits you..."

Then, an exaggerated chef's kiss. When it came to Jean-Pierre, exaggerated was the only way.

"The two of you, it has been so long," Jean-Pierre said. "You stay away for weeks and weeks and weeks — I'm going to get a complex."

Sylvia giggled — Henri wondered if she'd had a couple

while getting dressed — and Jean-Pierre took her arm and led her to the same table for 16 that Henri and the boys and their girlfriends had sat at the night before. Only it was wives now, not girlfriends. And seeing as how Freddy had a wife but not a girlfriend, and Timmy had a girlfriend but not a wife, the numbers worked out splendidly.

"You must make sure to stay until the end — the magician is the final act, before the bad comedians, and he is—"

Jean-Pierre offered up another chef's kiss to the room. Sylvie told him that she loved magicians. Jean-Pierre's eyes met Henri's, and then the man offered another of the grins that was just this side of cartoonish. At which point, Henri palmed him another hundred.

The dynamics of the evening were the same, minus the cocaine in the ladies' toilet — and the standard bet. For some reason, gambling about stray pubic hairs seemed more appropriate for the girlfriends' night. So, people left and came back throughout the dozen or so acts, and the men tended to rearrange themselves toward the back of the table while the wives clustered near the stage in the front. It was in the back where Henri sat down next to Freddy and immediately regretted it.

Earlier in the day, Henri had decided that Willy would oversee the new operation in the 10th. It was a plum, and Henri felt certain that Willy was the best fit overall. He didn't even think it was a tough call.

Everyone was in their appropriate slot. Passy was the clear No. 2 in Henri's crew. His burden was that he had to run the school uniform business, a complete pain in the ass that was only barely profitable but an absolute necessity because it gave the rest of them employment documents for the benefit of the tax authorities. As a reward for the bullshit, Passy also got the casino in the 9th, the organizational cash cow.

Timmy was older than all of them — older than Henri by a decade — and a bit lacking in the ambition department. It wasn't that he was lazy or a bad worker — he just never had much interest in climbing any ladders. He'd had the good whorehouse — the one in the 9th that shared the building with the casino — for the better part of a decade, and that was plenty for him. Other than a belief that it was his God-given right to bang every girl who ever worked for him, Timmy had no other long-term goals or firmly held principles.

Then there were Willy and Freddy. Willy was 35, Freddy 32. Willy had the middling whorehouse on Rue Lepic, Freddy the skank place on Boulevard de Clichy. Willy worked hard and was the most organized of all of them — he actually took a business class at some point, Organizational Something-or-Other, and his books and records were meticulous, and he never seemed to have the scheduling problems that the rest of them did. As for Freddy, he was just, well, younger — even if he was physically fearless and by far the best of them with a gun. Henri admired that physical courage, admired it a lot. But adding the two train stations, and all the men who used to work for Morel — that was an organizational challenge. It was obvious that Willy made the most sense — obvious to everyone except Freddy.

"It was good that you gave the congratulations, the toast," Henri said.

"I still think it's bullshit," Freddy said.

"The toast was the right thing."

"Fuck the toast."

"Watch your mouth," Henri said. "This isn't a goddamned democracy. It was my decision, and it's final. And, you know, if it was a goddamned democracy, you would have gotten one vote — yours. So just knock it off."

"Boss, I'm telling you, I'm ready," Freddy said.

"Are you not hearing me? Willy is more ready."

"But, Boss…"

"He almost has a business degree."

"But…"

"No buts," Henri said. "We're done. You know you're valued by the group. You also are getting a damn big raise out of this yourself — the house on Rue Lepic to go along with the house on Boulevard de Clichy, that isn't nothing. Just try to be patient."

With that, they turned 45 degrees and listened to the woman singing a solo, and then Freddy got up and left. The singer was good, as long as you didn't have to look at her. She was, to put it as accurately as possible, an operatic tugboat swaddled in yards of light green fabric. Or, as Sylvie muttered as she took the empty seat next to Henri, "How many chiffons did they have to kill to make that tent?"

He liked Sylvie when she was like that — a little drunk, a lot snide, especially when he wasn't the target. But then Henri turned and looked at her, and he knew there was more trouble. She must have heard about the 10th. The women must have been talking.

"When were you going to tell me?" is how she revealed her knowledge.

"I don't know. What's the—"

"You know what the issue is," she said. "Guy is the issue. Guy. Your son. Remember him? That would have been perfect for him."

"There's no way," Henri said.

"He's your son, for God's sake."

"He's not ready. It's too big. He isn't even ready for something small."

"You could have guided him," she said. "You could have mentored him, taught him."

"This is stupid," Henri said. "It's inconceivable. It's an enormous job, and it means a lot of money to a lot of people, not just me."

"Not just us," Sylvie said.

"This isn't just daddy taking junior to the office for the day," he said. "It wasn't even a consideration."

And it wasn't. Henri had not thought about putting his son in charge in the 10th arrondissement for even a nanosecond, for all of the reasons that he had told both Freddy and Sylvie. The job was primarily about stability and organization, and Guy couldn't organize a piss most days without splashing his shoes. There was just no way.

Henri knew he was right. But he did wonder why he hadn't considered his son even for that nanosecond, why the notion had not even entered his head.

PART III

BLUE RENAULT CARAVELLE

The six of them were in two cars, both black Renaults. Rafael was driving one of the cars, and Guy was riding next to him. Rafael was still new at the whole business, and while his driving skills were unquestioned, his gastrointestinal system needed some work when the kid was under pressure, like in the minutes before a job. As the car idled a block from the bank, he farted three of four times in five minutes.

"I'm sorry, Boss," he said. "I'm just so fucking..."

"Don't worry about it," Guy said. He cracked a window and lit a Gauloises to cover the stench. Nothing could cover the noise, though, and Rafael's face grew redder with each blast.

Guy looked at his watch. Five minutes.

The first time they robbed a bank, Guy and his crew got their information the old-fashioned way: by buying off a guard. Guy and one of his men followed the guard home after work — the bank branch was in the 6th, on Rue du Four — stood next to him at the bar where he stopped, got drunk with him, talked to him about the setup, and then made the offer. It would have to be at lunchtime when the other guard was taking his break, and he would have to suffer the embarrassment of being locked in the toilet while taking a piss, but that would be it. The envelope full of cash would more than make up for it. The whole thing went as smoothly as they had planned, too.

They wore balaclavas and, the next day, the newspapers speculated that Algerians were the culprits, which infuriated Guy. And after he had spent an entire morning in Sally's drinking and occasionally shouting the phrase "fucking Algerians," Rafael, all of 18 years old, said, "Explain to me why the 'fucking Algerians' is a bad thing?"

"Because it was me — it was us," Guy said.

"But we don't want them to know it was us, right?" Rafael said.

Guy didn't answer, except with another pour from the bottle that Sally had left at his place.

Guy looked at his watch again: three minutes.

"Two minutes," said Michel. He was sitting in the back seat.

"Three minutes," Guy said. His was the official watch.

The second bank they had robbed was in the 16th, way out by Roland Garros. Guy liked that one more because, instead of bribing a guard for information, in this one, he slept with a teller instead. Her name was Marie, and what she lacked in looks, she more than made up for in enthusiasm. After a couple of exhausting weeks, Guy was able to get the key information — the timing of the armored car arrivals — without having to involve Marie directly. It just came up in conversation one night, pillow talk, and he didn't even have to ask. Add in one more nugget of information — that one of the armored car guys spent the entirety of each visit trying to talk Marie into bed — and the numbers began to work in Guy's favor.

Again, the whole thing went as planned — the armored car was on time, the horny guard was occupied with Marie, and all it took was the wave of a couple of pistols and a few shouted commands. The next day, the newspapers did not speculate on the identities of the robbers, although a witness was quoted as saying, "Young, tough guys, it seemed like to me."

"That's what I'm talking about," Guy said, poking at the quote with his index finger and reading it out loud. Young, tough guys.

Guy had sworn all of them to secrecy. No one was to know about the robberies, not even Henri — especially not Henri — until he had enough money to pay back his father, months ahead of time. Fuck-you money. Until then, silence.

Now came the third bank robbery. His watch again: one

minute. The information for this one came from the owner of another bar, a place in the Marais, a place with no name over the door. It was a bar that catered to an all-male clientele, and one of its customers was the married vice-president of the branch of the Bank of France on Rue des Abbesses, and he was pretty easily blackmailed into providing the information Guy needed. Of course, the owner of the bar with no name over the door was getting five percent of the take for his trouble, and Sally — whose real name was Salvatore, and who slept many nights in the same bed as the owner of the bar with no name over the door — was getting five percent for making the introduction.

And if the money in the vault was a little light — it was a small branch — the ease with which it was obtained was a benefit unto itself. The total population of the bank when Guy and his crew entered was one guard, one teller, one customer, and the married vice-president from the bar with no name, which meant that there was a pistol aimed at all of them, with two to spare. The vault was open in a minute, and empty about two minutes after that. On the way out, Guy bashed the vice-president on the back of the head with the butt of his gun, just to make it look good. The truth was, the guy was begging for it.

Then it was into the cars waiting out front, with Rafael behind the wheel. He drove easily, without any hurry or alarm. They all listened for a police siren, but nobody heard anything — two minutes, three minutes, four minutes, nothing. The six of them, and the valise full of the money — with the clown masks they wore as disguises also stuffed in with the cash — decided to take a ride and go to lunch at Les Deux Magots on Boulevard Saint-Germain and celebrate.

The lunch turned into bottle after bottle after bottle at Sally's. The hours after all three of the bank robberies were unlike any that Guy had ever experienced — the high that he felt, the absolute floating. The closest comparison was after his first sexual experience, but even he knew that it wasn't as if he had accomplished anything he hadn't managed a thousand times by himself. The robberies were different — conceived by him and executed by him, evidence of his skill and daring and smarts most of all, evidence of everything that his father believed he lacked.

Guy spent the better part of an hour dividing up the money in the back booth. He pocketed his share, the biggest share, and leaned back in the booth and did the calculation in his head. One more job and he'd have enough to pay back the stake his father had given him. He couldn't wait to see the look on the old man's face, and he wanted to reply with what he came to refer to as a nonchalant sneer. He actually practiced the look in the bathroom mirror, the fuck-you look after handing over the fuck-you money. He found himself practicing without the mirror when the front door banged open and Rafael ran in, holding a newspaper.

"Holy shit, Boss," is what he managed to blurt out as he handed the copy of France-Soir over to Guy. Rafael was a kid, and he was the only one who ever called him Boss — everyone else in the crew was Guy's age or older, and most of them had known him since they were in school, and none of them was going to call him Boss under any circumstances. But from Rafael, it seemed right — and Guy tried not to grin whenever he did it.

"Holy shit, what?" Guy said. Then he unfolded the paper

and saw the headline: "A Clown Caper." It was an enormous headline, and the story — including a photograph of the bank about halfway up the butte — took up almost half of the front page.

He scanned the story, and then he didn't mind if anybody saw him grinning, and then he yelled, "Shut up, shut up," and then he cleared his throat and began reading aloud:

"A daring afternoon robbery by a half-dozen gangsters wearing clown masks as disguises emptied the vault at the Bank of France, 11 Rue des Abbesses.

"An alarm was called into police at 12:48 p.m. When they arrived, they found the tiny branch bank had been cleaned out. Witnesses said that all the robbers carried pistols, but no shots were fired. One bank employee received a rap on the back of the head from a gun butt after he was slow in opening the vault, according to police. The man, a vice-president of the bank, was examined by an ambulance driver. No hospitalization was required.

"Two witnesses, a customer and a bank teller, described the disguises worn by the thieves as rubber clown masks. The customer, Anne Ratelle, 58, of Rue Lepic, said, 'You know the kind — big red lips, red hair, wicked smile. They were all the same.'"

Guy stopped reading. He beamed.

"Wicked fucking smile," he yelled, and the rest all cheered.

The rest of the story was about what the writer called "the epidemic of bank robberies" in Paris in recent months. According to sources, the belief of the police was that most of them were perpetrated by Algerians looking to fund their terrorist activities. Everyone in Sally's booed when Guy read that part.

"Then it's more blah, blah, blah," Guy said. "But here's the ending."

He cleared his throat again and read:

"If nothing else, this particular robbery sparked additional interest among observers. As Mrs. Ratelle said: 'All these robberies, no arrests. Who exactly are the clowns in this saga?'"

Again, the bar filled with cheers. It was only Guy and his men, but they made enough noise for dozens. The robbery, the newspaper — it truly was a high unlike Guy had ever experienced. When the girls showed up later, he banged two of them in the storeroom, the second undressing as he finished with the first.

Henri checked his watch for the fourth time. Martin was supposed to meet him at 11, and Henri made a point of not leaving his apartment until 11:10, and now it was 11:16. He looked down Rue Caulaincourt, and did not see the big black Citroën coming. It would not arrive until 11:18.

The driver, real name Maurice, jumped out of the car and opened Henri's door.

"Good morning, Mr. La Rue," he said.

"Little late, aren't we, Sir Winston?" Henri said. Maurice was the only family associate of any stature — who didn't clear toilets or make food deliveries — who called him Mr. La Rue. So, in turn, Henri called him Sir Winston, because of his shaved head and slight paunch. It embarrassed Maurice, which was an added benefit to the real purpose, which was that it embarrassed Martin.

"Ridiculous traffic for a Saturday," Martin said, as Sir Winston pulled away from the curb and headed the Citroën toward Saint-Lazare. "And tell me again why we can't just drive the whole way to the stadium?"

"You know as well as I do," Henri said.

"Screw the tradition," Martin said.

"You're welcome to tell him yourself."

"He listens to you."

"Christ, what world are you living in — he listens to no one," Henri said.

The ridiculous traffic was non-existent, and they made it to the meeting place outside the station with a few minutes to spare. When Martin started to reach for the door, Henri grabbed his arm and then leaned forward and said, "Sir Winston, go get yourself a newspaper. Five minutes."

When they were alone, Martin said, "What now?"

"Does he have the new trucks yet?" Henri said. There was no need to identify the "he," or to elaborate on what it was all about. Because it was all they talked about now, Gus and the two trucks that burned along with Martin's two hired thieves in the middle of the night on the road to Reims.

"You have to think the insurance came through by now," Martin said.

"I walked by his yard two nights ago — no new trucks," Henri said.

"Maybe they're on order," Martin said.

"Fuck 'maybe.' Why don't you know? You have a responsibility. He's a dear old friend of both of us."

"Not my friend," Martin said.

"The hell he's not."

"Tortured me in school."

"Harmless pranks."

"He tied me to a tree and pissed on me with Rebecca Levine and that other Jew girl watching from the bushes."

"You were 12 — how long are you going to hang on to that?" Henri said.

"I was 12, you and him were 15, and I bet you put him up to it," Martin said.

"That's bullshit, and you know it," Henri said. And the truth was, Martin never knew that Rebecca Levine and the other Jew girl had removed their shirts and were both available to Henri in the bushes as Martin was being humiliated by Gus a hundred feet away. It was only when Martin was untied and had run away that Gus joined them in the bushes to partake of Rebecca's availability.

Henri smiled at the memory and then said, "You need to stay on top of this. We owe the man."

"Not as far as he's concerned."

"Meaning what?"

"Meaning that we've fucked over plenty of people who don't know it, and Gus might just end up being another one. And if you have a problem with that, you can pretend that you didn't approve the whole thing."

"Now wait a minute..."

"And you can return the envelope," Martin said. "I mean, what the fuck? Honestly — it's a couple of goddamn trucks. Nobody got killed."

"Except for the drivers, and the guy..."

"Nobody you knew got killed," Martin said, correcting himself. "Hell, I didn't know them, either." And then he muttered again, "A couple of goddamn trucks."

"It's a man's livelihood," Henri said.

"The insurance will come through."

"So you say."

"You could throw him some extra work."

"So could you — and you will, goddamn it," Henri said. "But he needs the trucks. He's my oldest friend..."

Sir Winston interrupted with a tap on the window. When Henri and Martin look, the driver pointed to another black Citroën parked in front of them. Uncle Gérard had arrived.

It was two trains to the stadium, an entire pain in the ass, but Uncle Gérard insisted because, well, that's the way it had always been, ever since Henri and Martin were kids, and their father and brother were still alive, and the five of them went to a handful of games every season.

The train from Saint-Lazare was crowded enough, and more crowded with every stop. But the change of trains at Nanterre was always a riot, even when the crowd was down because of the weather, or because the team was dreadful. The last part of the tradition always took place on the tiny platform at Nanterre. Gérard removed the silver flask from his breast pocket, and then Henri and Martin followed suit, and then came the toast: "To victory." The flasks were birthday gifts when each of the boys turned 16, and God forbid you forgot to bring it.

They ran extra trains on game days, but they were all still jammed for the ride to Saint-Germain-en-Laye. Then it was the short walk to the stadium, the crowds filling both of the side-walks and spilling into the middle of the street. They sang, and Uncle Gérard joined them. Whenever the old man died, Henri always said he would hold two visions of Gérard: singing in the middle of those crowds, and holding out his hand for an enve-lope in Vincent's back room.

And while Gérard seemed to see himself as a man of the people on those game days, there were limits. The La Rue family seats were reserved and under cover, protected from the weather and from the supporters in the terraces who stood out in the rain, drank beer to excess, and pissed where they stood into newspapers rolled into funnels that they dropped at their feet.

They got to their places and the two empty seats for the

departed — father and brother to Henri and Martin, brother and nephew to Gérard, Jean and Jean — remained empty. The thought of inviting Cousin Michel to fill one of them had never been considered, apparently. As for Guy, he lost interest soon after he received his birthday flask and hadn't been to a game in at least three years. It was really about the original five of them and always would be. Gérard said he never had the heart to cancel the extra tickets, and the places where they sat were as if the five of them were still alive. Left to right, it was Martin, empty seat for Big Jean, Gérard, Henri, empty for Little Jean. None of them could remember how the arrangement started, but it was as much a part of the tradition as the train rides and the flasks.

One of the byproducts of the seating was that Gérard and Henri tended to chat more with each other, and Martin tended to feel left out. Sometimes he didn't come back right after the half-time toilet break, running into an acquaintance or two and lingering with them at the bar rather than returning to his exile on the end of the row. It was right after the interval, with just the two of them in the row, when Gérard turned to Henri and said, "Are you ever going to tell me about it?"

He was talking about Henri's takeover of the Morel territory in the 10th. Henri knew this, of course.

"I thought I was pretty clear," Gérard said.

"You just weren't seeing—"

"I see everything," Gérard said.

"But it went fine," Henri said. "It went fine, it's going fine. They were a teetering shack. A loud fart would have knocked them down. It had to happen when Morel disappeared. And you don't get that kind of opportunity—"

"Hogs," Gérard said. "Hogs get slaughtered."

"Nobody's getting slaughtered."

"Metaphorically."

"Metaphorically or actually — nobody's getting slaughtered," Henri said.

"Look to your right," Gérard said. "Just casually. Maybe 100 feet and two rows in front of us. You know where."

Henri knew exactly where. He had looked a half-dozen times already. Still, he faked a yawn and stretched out his arms and stole a peek. In their own row, as always, were the Levines — Joseph, and his son Daniel, and another of his men.

"I've caught Joseph looking at us twice," Gérard said. "So, what do you think they're talking about?"

Joseph Levine was older than Gérard by about a decade, and his family had run the 2nd and 3rd arrondissements for as long as the La Rues had run the 18th and 9th. The 10th, along with its two train stations, was the buffer between them — except that there was no buffer anymore, not since Freddy and his machine gun had splattered salmon croquettes, among other bits of animal flesh, all over the front of the restaurant along the canal at Rue Dieu.

"They seem to have accepted it," Henri said.

"You're not that stupid," Gérard said.

"They make deals — they don't fight," Henri said.

"Don't kid yourself — they get their suit jackets made one size bigger, just like we do," Gérard said. Bigger for the shoulder holsters, which Gérard still wore even though he likely hadn't drawn his gun since the 1940s.

Right then, Menou was tripped in the box and the referee blew his whistle and pointed to the spot. Everyone stood as Anut deposited the penalty into the top right corner, and with that, Stade Saint-Germain scored the only goal of the game.

Afterward, the car with Sir Winston driving was waiting outside the stadium. The man of the people would be chauffeured home — you can take the symbolism only so far. They dropped Martin first, and then it was just the two of them in the back being taken to Montmartre. It was only then that Henri handed his uncle the first envelope containing proceeds from the 10th. Gérard might have been mad, but he also must have felt the envelope's heft — not that it showed on his face.

The top of the butte in Montmartre was home to some of Paris's wealthiest people, but Montmartre as a whole was a hodgepodge — seedy down near the base and then, as you began to climb, the home of artistic types, bohemians, people like that. So even the richest people at the top enjoyed the eclectic mix of the place, the energy and the unpredictability, or they wouldn't have chosen to live there in the 18th.

But the La Rues also controlled the 9th arrondissement, which ranged from the flesh of Pigalle to, well, to the goddamn Opéra. There was real money down at the end of the 9th, the Opéra end, real money and privilege and stature — and those kinds of people, the ones who wore black capes when they went to see Verdi, were not fans of the eclectic or the unpredictable and were not going to hike all the way up to a casino or a whorehouse on the butte for their other entertainment needs. From this knowledge — or, rather, insight — was Trinity One born.

It was Henri's great uncle, also named Henri, who came up with the idea. As Gérard said, "He saw a need, and he filled it. Sometimes life and business are just that simple."

There was a big risk involved, though — a financial risk. Because when the whole thing came together in 1910, the La Rues were not nearly as well established as they were later, and the cost of purchasing two floors of the building at 1 Place de la Trinité was an enormous gamble. Every cent of the family's financial reserves went into the purchase and into the renovations. But within months, they all knew it would be a success — the casino on the second floor, the whorehouse on the third floor, one-stop shopping with plenty of room to hang up the black capes.

When the Nazis came in 1940, the decision was made — by

Gérard and Jean, given that they were the oldest by then — to cater to German officers even as both of them worked in the Resistance during their down time. Business is business, et cetera. When the city's brothels were closed by decree after the war, the La Rues noticed only a blip in that business — doubling the police payoffs saw to that. When the name of Place de la Trinité was changed to Place d'Estienne-d'Orves to honor a Resistance hero after the war, the family all still called it Trinity One. And through all the decades, and all the millions of francs they had raked in, the La Rues still argued about which was the greater irony — that the windows of the casino and the whorehouse looked out at the magnificence of Trinity Church, or that the tenant below them on the ground floor of the building at 1 Place d'Estienne-d'Orves was a branch of BNCI bank. Or, as old uncle Henri used to say, "When I am leaving the casino, I drop to my knees and look out at Trinity Church and ask forgiveness every night for being an even bigger thief than the men who work on the first floor."

Decades later, Henri liked to stop in — not every night, but maybe twice a month. These were cash cows for the family, and they were very predictable besides. The money from the casino fluctuated downward only twice a year, during the August vacations and around the holidays in December. As for the whorehouse, the only dip was in August, proving perhaps that gambling was a vice that could be forgone around Christmas — but sex, not so much.

On that Saturday night, Henri made a five-minute visit to the whorehouse first. It was about 9 p.m., and Timmy was putting on his coat to leave when Henri was arriving.

"All good," he said, when he saw Henri.

"Quiet?" Henri said.

"No, normal Saturday night," Timmy said. Then he patted

his breast pocket and said, "The early take might even be a bit heavy."

They stood and chatted for a minute or two more. At one point, they both turned and looked down the hallway as one of the girls, in a lime green negligée, took a stroll toward the barroom. Marcella was her name, and her red hair was her trademark. She was the newest girl in the house.

"And it's real?" Henri said.

"Drapes and carpet, absolutely," Timmy said. "She even paints her toenails red."

"And is she—"

"A goddamned tiger," Timmy said. "You should see the waiting list. It's actually starting to piss off some of the other girls."

"That's fixable enough," Henri said.

Timmy nodded. "One thing about Paris — there's no shortage of ass," he said.

The casino was a different operation, run by Passy. He always wore a tuxedo on the casino floor, and he always stayed until the last gambler left around midnight. Henri gave his men the latitude to have their own management styles — and while Timmy spent more time worried about the carpet and the drapes, and was willing to leave early and allow his men to take custody of the second envelope overnight, Passy always stayed to the end and did his books and pocketed the full night's take when he left.

There were about 15 gamblers on the floor when Henri arrived. He knew almost all of them by sight and by name, seeing as how you had to be a regular, or vouched for by a regular, in order to gain entrance. Throwing dice at Trinity One, or sitting at a card table, was not a young man's pastime. The stakes were prohibitive, for one, but there was just something about the longevity of the regulars that was somewhere between impressive and uncanny. There were two card games going on that Saturday night, and the youngest player at one of the tables was probably 65. The oldest was probably 80. Henri offered them all a hello by name, and then walked away to find Passy, wondering for the hundredth time if they should bring in researchers from the national institute to try to figure out the longevity statistics of their customers.

Passy saw Henri and walked over and, reading his mind said, "It would be the goddamndest scientific paper of all time. And I would be all for it, as long as they quoted me as saying, 'The secret is in the La Rue water, especially when it's mixed with the La Rue Scotch.'"

The two of them walked over to the craps table. There were a half-dozen men arrayed around the perimeter and, given that you had to stand, it tended be a younger game. By Henri's estimation, two of the players were in their forties.

The man with the dice was Julian Broussard — mid-fifties, lot of dough, a twice-a-week kind of player for as long as Henri could remember. Won some, lost some, good streaks, bad streaks, certainly down over his gambling lifetime but not a ton. When Henri asked him about it once, Broussard shrugged and said, "Cheaper than a villa on the Riviera."

Passy called people like him "B&B," which had nothing to do with Broussard or bed-and-breakfasts. B&B was his shorthand for bread-and-butter, which is what the gamblers like Julian Broussard meant to Trinity One and the La Rues. They had some fun and provided the family with a steady income in return, one that never varied. And so, the family stocked the wine Broussard favored, and got the charcuterie plate he liked from Perreault's, and made sure he had a chauffeured ride home if he wasn't stopping for some additional entertainment on the third floor.

Henri wasn't paying attention, but Broussard threw a four,

and the six men around the table erupted in cheers, and Broussard punched the air with his fist.

"Good for him," Passy said. "It's been a dry couple of weeks for him."

Then he turned, and snapped his finger to get the attention of one of the waiters, and then motioned toward Broussard. Within seconds, a bottle and a fresh glass materialized, and Broussard took a sip and punched the air again.

The night was cooler than Michel had expected, and he was shivering as he kneeled amid the shrubbery that framed the car park of the Renault assembly plant in Boulogne-Billancourt. Between the nerves and the cold, he'd had to piss twice among the bushes. It was easy enough to accomplish from his knees, the only worry being a stray bit of poison ivy that he had noticed before the moon had hidden behind a cloud. He thought he was far enough way, but his mind would sometimes play tricks on him in situations like that, nervous situations, shivering, waiting. And then as the dawn came, he saw the poison ivy again and it was closer than he remembered. And then all he could think about was scratching his crotch.

There were two cars left in the lot. It was the executive lot — the real workers parked on the other side of the massive building. Michel was waiting for the man who drove the blue Renault Caravelle, not the one who drove the black Renault Caravelle. The blue Renault Caravelle belonged to Mario Laperrière, the manager of the third shift. The black Renault Caravelle belonged to René Primeau, the assistant manager. Primeau was the recipient of a weekly envelope, Michel's eyes and ears inside. Laperrière was the concern.

As it got to be about 7:30, Michel caught himself doing the same routine, over and over. Stare at the door of the plant, pat his breast pocket to feel the revolver, scratch his dick. Stare, pat, scratch. Stare, pat, scratch.

The Renault assembly plant had been good to Michel La Rue. There were lot of ways to smuggle heroin into the United States, but inside of the Renaults had proven to be the best. They varied the locations — wheel wells, spare tires, behind the car's radio, others — and raked in the cash. The maintenance man who brought in the heroin with the custodial supplies had to be paid, and the workers on the line had to be paid, and Primeau had to be paid because he was in charge of paying the rest of them, and making sure the whole thing ran properly, and most of all, seeing to it that his boss never found out.

Except that Primeau made an emergency phone call to Michel the previous morning, telling him that Laperrière was more than suspicious. He said one of the men on the line, about to be fired for drinking on company time, tried to bargain for his job with the story of heroin smuggling beneath the rear bumpers of the latest shipment of Renaults to New York.

"I think I convinced him it was bullshit," is what Primeau told him. "But I'm not positive."

At which point, they made a deal. If Primeau sensed that Laperrière was about to act on his suspicions, he was to come out to the parking lot and tell Michel, who would be hiding in the bushes. But that never happened. It was 7:45, and the shift was over in 15 minutes, and maybe Primeau was right. Maybe he did convince Laperrière that it was bullshit. Of course, that wasn't a chance Michel could take.

At 7:50, the door opened and Primeau looked into the morning sky. But he didn't walk over to the bushes. Instead, he just got into his black Renault Caravelle and drove off in a roar.

Five minutes later, the door opened again. It was Laperrière. The day bosses would not arrive for another half-hour, at least. It was just the one man and the one car. Michel stood and waited until Laperrière turned to open his car door and then emerged from the bushes. Because his back was turned, Laperrière did not know where the shouting man had come from.

"Sir, sir," Michel shouted, smoothing his coat and hurrying toward the blue Renault Caravelle.

Laperrière turned. Michel got closer.

"Sir," Michel said. "You'll have to excuse me. But I have an 8:30 meeting with Jean Richler."

That was the name of the accountant.

"So?" Laperrière said.

"I know I'm early — is there a place to wait, maybe get a cup of coffee?"

"Employee canteen on the other side," Laperrière said, not even looking at Michel as he waved vaguely to his right. Prick.

It was when he turned to reach for the handle of the door of the blue Renault Caravelle that Michel shot him in the back of the head — once, then twice. Prick. Then Michel reached into his hip pocket and took out the envelope that contained the message written in a hurried scrawl, all capital letters and in a shaky hand.

It was only five words:

STAY AWAY FROM MY WIFE!

Michel looked at the torn-open envelope, crumpled it once more for luck, and shoved it into the dead man's jacket pocket, careful not to step in the growing pool of blood. A crime of passion, then. Such were the stories of Paris, both dramatic and tidy at the same time, both crazy and universally understood. The fellows at the police precinct would be laughing about it over an extra beer at lunch, speculating about the attractiveness of the wife whom they would never find — partly because they would never really look for her.

And then Michel was gone, back through the bushes and then the several hundred more feet to his own car, also a blue Renault Caravelle. They could have been twins.

PART IV

THE TROUBLE WITH CLOWNS

Henri waited for Uncle Gérard outside Sacré-Coeur. It was two minutes before 7, and the old man was never late. Every day but Saturday, he made the walk from his house to the basilica for early Mass. If Henri wanted an impromptu meeting, this was the way to get it. The understanding, though, was that Henri would have to sit through the service before they talked.

When Gérard saw him, Father Lemieux was walking alongside. Shit. Whatever. The priest offered his hand, while Gérard offered what might be described as a constipated nod as a greeting. Henri nodded back and, without a word, the three of them were up the steps and inside. They walked up the left aisle, never the right. They sat down in the fifth row on that aisle, never the sixth, never the fourth, never anywhere but the fifth.

"I'm not a show-off," Gérard said, when Henri asked him years earlier why he didn't move to the very front, especially considering that only one person sat closer. That guy was in the second row, right aisle. The band on his hat changed colors with the seasons. That was Gérard's definition of a show-off.

On the altar, there was a cross sculpture with two women at the feet. A little lower, there were six men on each side. Apostles? There were 12 of them.

On the back wall, there was a huge mural where Jesus was posed with his arms extended to the ceiling. Near him at his feet were holy people of his day. Scattered around the perimeter, farther back, were people dressed as from a relatively modern vintage. It was all very involved, like a drunken dream through the centuries.

"Father Drinan says he misses you," Father Lemieux said, after they sat. The priest wasn't out on the altar yet. He always started at 7:01. The only reason that Henri even knew Father Drinan's name was because Sylvie told him.

"Tell Father Drinan that I'll be back when he changes his 6:30 Mass back to 7, where it always belonged," Gérard said.

"He says it made no sense, two churches, close enough to spit on each other, both with a 7."

"Made perfect sense to me."

"You know, that's still really your parish, Saint Pierre's," Father Lemieux said. "Sacré-Coeur isn't a parish. No wedding, no baptisms — and when the day comes, many decades from now, St. Pierre's is where you will be buried from."

"At that point, the difference between 6:30 and 7 will probably be less important to me than it is today," Gérard said. "Probably."

A bell rang, just a quick tinkle, and the priest and an altar boy emerged from the sacristy door to the right of the altar. It wasn't like Sunday — no procession up the main aisle, no music. This was down and dirty and quick, much of the Latin still resonant out of Henri's boyhood. He checked his watch at the end and the whole thing took only 16 minutes.

"His record is 13," Gérard said. "I think he had the runs that day."

Henri nodded, and the three of them genuflected in the aisle before leaving. As he kneeled, Henri saw the words on the ceiling that always hit him: JESV GALLIA POENITENS ET DEVOTA ET GRATA. Roughly translated, it meant that France was penitent and devoted and grateful to Jesus. At least, that's what Henri thought — schoolboy Latin had been a long time ago.

"So?" Gérard said. Father Lemieux had said his goodbyes and the two of them were standing outside the basilica, down the steps and over to the fence that you could lean on and take in one of the great views in all of Paris, what seemed like the entire city waking up at their feet, lights clicking on in the houses, traffic starting to emerge from its garage slumber.

"Just this," Henri said. He reached into his breast pocket for a second unscheduled envelope, also from the 10th.

Gérard accepted it, weighed it almost imperceptibly — really for just a blink — and then slipped it into his breast pocket.

"Electric mixers, believe it or not," Henri said. "And men's suits."

Gérard stared at him, as blank as a morning chalkboard.

"A shipment from the Gare du Nord," Henri said. "A whole boxcar full of them. Meant for the Galeries Lafayette. We took half. Not hogs, after all."

Gérard stared on.

"The newest model," Henri said. "The mixers, I mean — eight speeds, I think, and some kind of refrigeration element that keeps the bowl cool while you work. I could send one over to the house."

Gérard turned from the fence, from the view, and began walking home, all without a word. Henri stayed at the fence, waiting until he saw at least one more light flick on in the distance.

"Henri," Gérard said. He was 20 feet away by then. Henri turned, and the old man said, "My size hasn't changed. Dark blue or gray."

And then he turned again and continued walking. In suits, Gérard's size was a 44 regular in the jacket and 42 regular in the pants.

There were days when the business kind of ran itself, which meant that Henri relaxed at home after church and then took Sylvie to lunch. She always chose Café du Mont-Cenis — not because the food was anything special, but because she could bitch about the view from the sidewalk tables, and one part of the view in particular.

"Those goddamned stairs," she said, as if she was surprised they were there, and then exhausted by their very presence.

Their apartment was at 70 Rue Caulaincourt, and the café was about a five-minute walk down what Henri believed in his heart was a beautiful Parisian street. For most of the year, the canopy of trees covered the roadway and the sidewalks in blissful shade. It was busy enough with traffic but not overrun — not quiet but not loud, part of the city but not suffocated by it.

"I've never seen the trees look better, fuller," Henri said, ignoring the stairs that led up to the top of the butte. It was easily 100 steps, probably a lot more, with streets and landings along the way. He had not walked it in three decades and likely never would again — but it really was a charming walk.

"It's Rue Caulaincourt, not Boulevard Saint-Germain," Sylvie said, dismissing Henri's comment about the trees with a wave. As for Boulevard Saint-Germain, it was on the Left Bank. Sylvie would never consider living on the Left Bank.

"On this street, you can get all of your shopping done in one block," Henri said. "All the errands, just like that."

"Trust me, I would walk away from that convenience in a minute."

"Even Jackie Quillette? You told me you'd never serve a roast to company that didn't come from Jackie Quillette."

"He delivers," Sylvie said.

Henri suspected that Jackie Quillette did, indeed, deliver — and that what he brought to Sylvie was not always just a roast beef, and that this was not a new service. Sylvie never shoved it in his face, though — so, whatever. But Henri enjoyed the hint of a blush whenever he brought up the butcher's name.

Jackie Quillette's butcher shop. François' bakery. The Mernier Brothers' fruit and vegetables. Rue Caulaincourt. Henri once spent an entire morning with two different maps and a draftsman's ruler that measured down to 1/32nd of an inch. The one map showed the standard distances in Montmartre. The other, which he sent Willy to find in the geography department of the bookstore at the Sorbonne, was a map that showed elevations. Henri's project, with the maps and the ruler and the Pythagorean Theorem, was to determine the exact distance between Gérard's home on the top of the butte and his home. If you walked it on the streets, it was just about exactly a half-mile. But if you flew there like a bird, it was half that distance, only about 1,300 feet. That was the reason Henri's balls were perpetually in a state of breakage, those 1,300 feet — and, more specifically, the 118 feet in elevation.

"That poor woman," Sylvie said. She raised her martini glass and used it to gesture toward the steps. A woman with a string bag full of vegetables from her shopping was taking her first steps up.

"At least she has sensible shoes," Henri said.

"She's saving the nice ones for the casket, after she has a heart attack," Sylvie said. Then she took a big slug from the martini.

The apartment at 70 Rue Caulaincourt was where Henri raised his children and built his success. In recent times, though, it had become the house that Sylvie had decided was somewhere between unbecoming and uninhabitable — even after they bought the apartment above them on the third floor and combined the two places when her mother needed to stay with them. Even a massive renovation after the old lady died, a do-over that took the better part of six months to complete, did little to silence Sylvie's whining.

Or, as Henri liked to tell her, "You started complaining again before the paint was dry."

The martini softened the roughest edges of Sylvie's complaints, and it turned into a reasonably pleasant lunch, all things considered. Sylvie still couldn't get over the magic act from the last time at the Lido, and the good fortune that she had been chosen as the woman in the card trick. She didn't need to know that it had cost Henri another hundred to Jean-Pierre to make that good fortune happen.

So, Henri was in a pretty good mood when they returned to 70 Rue Caulaincourt — for a few seconds, anyway, until he saw the message that the maid had left next to the telephone in the hallway.

It said, "Mr. Brown, 3 p.m."

They always met at the little park on Rue Burq, a little park on a little uphill street that led nowhere. There was a playground in the back of the park, and there were six benches around a dirt square nearer to the front that was perfect for boules. But nobody played. It was a public place but with very little chance of them being seen or recognized. Back in the playground, there was a woman — a grandmother, probably — pushing a little girl on a swing. Henri didn't know the old woman, and she likely didn't know him. And even if she did, so what? On a quiet afternoon, Henri was just a man sitting on a park bench, taking a bit of sun, eating an apple. He was nearly finished when Inspector Chrétien arrived.

"We have a problem," Chrétien said.

"So much for the pleasantries," Henri said.

"La Rue, I'm serious — we have a problem," Chrétien said.

Henri knew this intuitively. The man did not ever call just to say hello. He was a bit of a nervous sort, Chrétien was — but, to be fair, what cop on the take to the local mob family wouldn't be nervous? Henri never gave it a second thought. Given what he paid Chrétien, the cop could afford the antacids.

That day, Henri brought the quarterly envelope with him, raiding the shoe box in the back of his closet at the apartment. It was a few weeks early, and he normally took the payment from the safe in the back of the uniform store, but whatever. The envelope sat on the bench next to Henri when the inspector arrived. After saying his opening lines, Chrétien noticed it, scooped it up, and slid it into his breast pocket. No thank you. No nod. No fucking manners.

"Okay, what do you mean, we have a problem?" Henri said. When he was dealing with Chrétien, or especially with less-friendly police officers, Henri knew to follow the rules — and the first of those rules, from time in memoriam, was to admit nothing. To play dumb. To say as little as possible. To turn the normal cop trick back on the cop. The normal trick was for them to say little and wait for you to say something during the prolonged silences. The cops assumed that the person they were questioning was nervous, and that the silence would freak them out, and that they would just start talking to fill the void. The reason they did it was because it often worked. Not with Henri, though — or with anybody who had been around the same blocks that he had been around. In this case, the silence would unnerve the cop. Henri knew that more than anything. Even if he had known what Chrétien was talking about, he would have played dumb.

In this case, though, Henri wasn't playing. He had no idea what this was about. The only thing he could think of, in the time between the phone message and Chrétien's arrival, was the business with Gus Parent's trucks. All that did was raise the level of acid in Henri's stomach and the level of disdain he held for his brother. He thought about calling him — actually picking up the phone in the apartment — but then decided to wait.

When Chrétien did not answer, Henri kept as placid a face as he could manage and asked again, "What's the problem?"

"The clown masks," Chrétien said. "That's the fucking problem."

Henri didn't get it at first, but then he remembered.

"The bank robbery — I thought the papers said it was the Algerians. That wasn't..." Henri said.

"It's the fucking clown masks," Chrétien said. "The newspapers — you've seen. They're eating it up. That's the problem."

Henri listened, nodded, said nothing, then started again to say that he had nothing to do with the bank robbery.

"Look," Chrétien said, "I know it's your son, and you know it's your son."

Henri said nothing, showed nothing. Guy? It didn't seem possible. He was just a kid. A bank robbery took some planning if you were going to get away with it. You needed to know when, and how, and how many if you were going to get away without using your guns for anything but pointing. Guy? Really?

"I don't know," Henri said, after a long pause.

"You know," Chrétien said. "Come on. I know and you know. But I'm worried about who else might find out."

Henri attempted to gather his thoughts in the ensuing silence. Guy? Really? Part of him was mystified. Part of him was, surprisingly, proud. He desperately wanted to ask Chrétien how he knew, but he didn't want to acknowledge to the cop on his payroll that he didn't know what his son was doing.

But then he just blurted out, "How did he give himself away?"

"The fucking clown masks," Chrétien said.

"But... what?"

"They're sold in exactly two stores in the city, costumers," Chrétien said. "The witnesses said they were high-end, not some cheap paper mask for kids. I took it upon myself to check. No one else knows that I made the call. Fake name on the phone. 'Hello, this is Sergeant Person from the 18th precinct...' The clerk at the first store told me all about the three kids who bought a half-dozen clown masks last week. How they were all drunk at 3 in the afternoon. And how one of them tried on his mask and shouted, 'I am Guy Fucking La Rue, king of the clowns.'"

Henri listened, trying for something softer than a stone face, something more placid. He was silent for 30 seconds, and then he said, "Two shops?"

"They're top-of-the-line fucking clown masks," Chrétien

said. "The clerk gave me the name of the other shop. I called, just to be thorough. They haven't sold a clown mask in six months."

Then, more silence. And then Henri reached over and, with his extended index finger, tapped on the breast pocket of Chrétien's uniform jacket, the pocket where his quarterly envelope currently resided

"Listen," the cop said. "You know how successful our, our... arrangement has been. But this is different. This is just about over my head now. I think it's about here," and then Chrétien raised his flat hand, palm down, and touched his forehead. "But it could be higher. When it gets above your eyes, you don't really know anymore, not for sure. And there is only so much I can do when it gets over my head. That's the problem. That's what I needed to tell you."

Henri said nothing.

"You have to understand," Chrétien said. "I mean, I have to make you understand how this could get away from us. Right now, the only people who know I made those phone calls are you and me."

"You think someone will find out? How could they?" Henri said.

"I'm not worried about that," Chrétien said. "I'm not worried about me. What I'm worried about is that someone else will think to make the phone calls. Like I said, this is over my head now. Important people will be using their own investigators, at least part-time. If nothing else, they'll pick their brains. If I thought to check on the masks, it's only a matter of time until someone else does. And then it's out of my hands. That damn newspaper — it was like the whole front page."

Henri nodded. The way Chrétien explained it, this was a real problem for Guy — and the whole concept was nothing that Henri didn't already know. You can buy a policeman. You can even kill a policeman in extreme circumstances. But you cannot taunt, or embarrass, the entire police force in the newspapers without paying a price in the end.

"You have to stop," Chrétien said. "You have to stop your kid. It's gone too far."

Henri stood up. There was nothing to say. He tossed his apple core in the bushes and walked away.

"Fucking clown masks," Chrétien said, half to himself.

Henri went to the office — the uniform store — to try to figure out what to do about Guy, and also to dip into the safe and replenish the money he had given Chrétien out of his personal funds. When he walked in, he must have been wearing what Passy called "the boss's leave-me-the-fuck-alone face," because other than a wave from Passy as he walked by, and a few muttered hellos as he headed to the back room, no one made any real attempt to engage with him. The door slam told them all that they had read the situation, and the boss's mood, correctly.

Into and out of the safe in about two minutes, Henri paid himself back for the Chrétien money and then sat back in the chair behind his desk and closed his eyes. He didn't even know where Guy was. His son had not slept at home in close to a week, and Henri had no idea if there was a new living arrangement, or just a temporary... whatever. With the rest of his guys, he either knew where they were most of the day or where he could leave them a message. Guy was different, as free a free agent as Henri had ever tolerated. It was all a part of his plan for the kid. Guy would receive no help unless he asked for it. He would be under no supervision unless he sought out someone's advice.

"Sink or fucking swim, huh?" Passy said, back when Henri laid out the rules for his son.

"My money's on sink, but maybe he'll surprise me," Henri said. "But either way, it will be his doing. Better for all of us that way."

"I don't know," Passy said.

"You telling me how to run my business?" Henri said.

"This isn't about the business," Passy said. "It's father to

78

father. If he does sink, and you just watch, what does that do to your relationship? What does it do to your marriage? Because we all know what sinking means in this business."

"Stale baguette for breakfast, followed by a shit in a bucket, followed by a few laps around the exercise yard — yeah, I know," Henri said. "I know."

"That, or worse," Passy said.

"I know," Henri said. "I know."

Guy was spoiled, in Henri's mind. He was temperamentally unsuited for the family business. It would be better if he flamed out early — and then Henri could set him up with something small but legitimate, maybe a little bar. He would do everything in his power to cushion Guy's fall, and to do it covertly, but he would not prevent it.

But how to cushion this? Chrétien was right — it was too big. If the cops above Chrétien figured out the masks were better than dime store kids' masks, if they started snooping around the costume shops, there was nothing his man would be able to do about it, quarterly envelope or no quarterly envelope. At that point, there would be nothing for Guy to do but run — and you had to believe that Chrétien would be able to tip him off before an arrest and give Guy the time to run. But short of that, it was clear that Guy had to get out of the bank robbing business. The risks were just too great.

That was what Henri was thinking when he got up and opened the back office door. What he did not expect was to see Gus Parent walking in with his son, Gus Jr.

"Mr. L — good to see you," Gus Jr. said.

"Little G, it's been too long," Henri said.

Gus Jr. walked over for a handshake and then pointed out the obvious — that he was now at least two inches taller than Henri.

"You might need to call me something else," Gus Jr. said.

"You've been Little G to me since you were drooling, and you'll be Little G to me until I'm drooling," Henri said.

"Sorry, you're stuck," Gus told his son, as he shook Henri's hand and then leaned in for a hug. "Been too long, Henri."

"Too long," Henri said.

"Just came for this pickup," Gus said, pointing at four boxes stacked against the wall.

"I've got it, Pop — you visit a minute," Little G said. He began to load the boxes onto a hand truck, and Gus and Henri sat down on a couple of folding chairs.

After the obligatory discussion about their families, and the knocking on wood about their good health, there was a moment of uncomfortable silence. Some old friends seemed to pick up previous conversations seamlessly, almost exactly where they left off, even given the months in between. But that wasn't Henri and Gus.

Into the silence, Gus finally blurted, "Henri, I have a problem."

Henri hoped his face did not betray that he already knew. He looked at Gus's face for any hint of that, but he saw nothing, mostly because Gus was having a hard time looking him in the eye as he told him the story — about how his two trucks were stolen, and apparently used in a robbery, and then burned with the robbers inside.

"But the insurance?" is all Henri could manage during a pause.

"They say they won't pay," Gus said. "The bastards. They say that until the police absolutely clear us — they think I was involved. And until the police clear us, they say they won't pay."

"So the police..." Henri said.

"The police say I'm still a suspect, and until they definitively find who did it, I will remain a suspect."

"But the dead guys — they're the obvious suspects," Henri said.

"Which is what I have told the cops a hundred times, like a skipping record," Gus said. "But it does no good."

"They'll come around," Henri said. "They have to. It might just take some time."

"But I don't have time," Gus said. "I only have the two trucks left, and one of them is shot — it barely runs. I've got two drivers I can't pay. I've got customers I can't service as quickly as before. The first cancellation was this morning. It's only a matter of time..."

Gus looked at his watch, and then he stood up.

"You wouldn't believe what we have to get done in the next couple of hours," Gus said. Henri muttered a "hang in there, old buddy" when they shook hands. As he watched Gus walk away, the rage that Henri felt for his brother, and his bullshit disaster of a scheme, grew to the point where he could feel the heat rise in his face. He wondered how red it was.

"Passy!" Henri shouted, and then waved from across the room. When his trusted No. 2 arrived, he said, "Guy — do you know where he is?"

"Boss, you said—" Passy said.

"Old friend, don't bullshit me," Henri said.

"I have an idea," Passy said. "There's a bar—"

"I don't need the details," Henri said. "Just tell him, or find someone to tell him, that I need to talk to him — soon. Like, no later than tomorrow morning."

"Urgent? Serious?" Passy said.

"As a heart attack," Henri said.

PART V

FATHERS AND SONS

The thought of keeping this all bottled up through a dinner with Sylvie seemed more than Henri could bear. The idea of an evening with Marina, or even an unzip/re-zip half-hour, didn't seem very appealing, either. He needed to think, and he needed to drink, and he figured that Trinity One was as good a place as any. Besides, Passy would be there, and he would get the word first-hand if they had managed to contact Guy.

When he got there, the number of gamblers was typical — maybe a little lighter than normal, maybe not. The business really did run like clockwork — maybe not as reliable as the sunrise in the east, but close. If you kept your cops paid off properly, and you kept your amenities stocked and the decor regularly refreshed, and you kept the clientele comfortable and exclusive, the money just flowed — and the availability of the ass on the third floor didn't hurt.

Henri made the rounds and then sat in the back with a bottle of Pernod and his thoughts. He alternated between being worried about Guy and being furious with Martin. Worried because Guy, in the end, was just a kid who didn't know any better; furious because Martin was just an idiot and always would be. Worried because Guy was in real jeopardy; furious because Martin was going to skate away as always while Gus, a true innocent, suffered. And the problem was, Henri didn't know what to do about either situation.

In this midst of all of this, Passy poked his head in the door.

"Anything?" Henri said.

"Not yet," Passy said. "But we think we're about to find him. We know the girl he left the bar with an hour ago."

Henri nodded, then said, "Well, what?"

"Small issue out here on the floor," Passy said. "I think we could use your touch on this one."

"So, what?"

"Julian Broussard."

"Fuck. How bad?"

"Not a disaster, but getting there."

"He won the last time I was in here."

"Blind squirrel," Passy said. "He's really on a bad run, and the bets are getting bigger, and he's here almost every night lately, and he's drinking more, and then upstairs."

"Problem at home?"

"Maybe. But he needs more credit."

"Well, you handle that."

"I think he needs the talk," Passy said. "You know, the fatherly arm around his shoulder."

"Fatherly? He's older than I am," Henri said.

"You know what I mean."

Henri did know. It was all a part of the business. Sometimes you broke legs. Sometimes you did worse. But especially in Trinity One, sometimes a calmer approach was required. You wanted these people coming back. B&B and all that. You didn't want their lives turned upside down by the losses — marriages ended, jobs lost, all of that was bad for business.

So, Henri sat with Julian Broussard. He approved the increase in his credit line, but not before he offered a fatherly lecture on the importance of keeping this whole thing under control. But it was a kindly fatherly thing, not the stern fatherly thing that Henri was going to have to do with Guy. And there was a condition that Henri placed on the line of credit: that it wouldn't begin until the next night. Broussard accepted happily and then took the stairs to the third floor.

"Well?" Passy said when he saw Broussard leave.

"Credit's approved, starting tomorrow."

"How was the talk, Dad?"

Henri shrugged and said, "Not sure. He's going upstairs either to celebrate or to forget."

"Works either way, I guess," Passy said. "And we got to Guy. He'll be at your house at 10 tomorrow morning."

Guy walked into the kitchen at about 10:30, looking as if he hadn't slept. He certainly hadn't shaved or combed his hair with anything but his fingers. His suit was creased in many of the wrong places, and he wasn't wearing a necktie.

"What a nice surprise," Sylvie said. She got up to hug her son and then began to pour him a cup of coffee.

"It wasn't a surprise," Guy said. "It was a command."

He slumped into his chair at the kitchen table and then leaned forward and held his head in his hands. Henri walked into the room and had no idea why Sylvie was staring him down when she saw him. He said, "Right on time, as usual."

"Christ, I'm here," Guy said.

"Business?" Sylvie said. She set the coffee in front of her son. Henri knew that the question was one that went to the established boundaries of their relationship. Because while Sylvie had better business instincts than most of his men, including when it came to the messier parts of the La Rue portfolio, she was not a participant and never would be a participant. Whatever Henri told her, it was in private conversations. When business was being transacted, her place was in the other room — and that included the business related to their son.

But Henri told her, "No, stay. You need to hear this."

"Hear what?" Guy said.

"That you've put yourself in a box with the police," Henri said.

"How?"

"Clown mask? Ring a bell?" Henri said.

At that very instant, it was as if the hangover had been slapped out of Guy's system. His eyes brightened — no, they burned. Sylvie looked confused but said nothing. Henri turned directly to her and told her what Chrétien had explained: that Guy had masterminded the bank robbery on Rue Lepic, the one where the thieves all wore clown masks.

"But how?" Sylvie said. Guy also said it, the same two words, about a half-second after his mother. Henri again ignored his son and, looking directly at Sylvie, said, "Did you know your little boy now identifies himself as, and I quote, Guy Fucking La Rue, king of the clowns."

Sylvie still looked confused, but Henri could tell that the coins were starting to drop. Guy had screwed up, but she still didn't know how. Meanwhile, Guy looked both horrified and bewildered.

"The costume store, idiot," Henri said, and then he saw the bewildered part of the expression falling away from his son's face. "Top-of-the-line masks — Jesus. They only sell them in two costumers in the city. The cops have talked to the guy who sold them to you and your boys. And how you tried on the mask and announced, 'I am Guy Fucking La Rue, king of the clowns.'"

Guy's head fell back into his hands. Sylvie said, "But, Henri, can't you contain this? You have a man in the precinct—"

"My man is the one who made the call to the costumer," Henri said.

"So, what's the problem?" Guy said. "Your money's still fucking good with him, I assume."

The kid's look was almost defiant, the implication being that this was on Henri now, that it was his problem to fix, and that the blame would be his if he didn't fix it. All with a look. Henri just shook his head, but he saw that Sylvie was sort of, kind of trying to screw her face into the same defiance.

"The newspapers are the problem now," Henri said. "My guy, he's the only one who knows about the masks. But because of all the publicity, the police commanders are all embarrassed, and they're up in arms, and they're starting to get involved in the investigation. People above my guy in the precinct are taking over, and they don't ask him what he thinks."

"Why not?" Guy said.

"Jesus Christ — they're his bosses," Henri said. "And as my guy said, if he thought about trying to trace the masks, maybe one of his bosses will think of it. And then you're done for."

"God, just take care of the guy in the costume shop," Guy said.

"Meaning what, exactly?" Henri said.

"Take care of him. I don't know, pay him," Guy said.

"Pay him once, and you'll be paying him for life," Henri said.

"Then, you know..." Guy said.

"Kill him?" Henri said. "Are you out of your mind?"

"Well, then just beat him up," Guy said. "Persuade him. Isn't that the term of art?"

The truth was, that was the first thing Henri considered when Chrétien dropped the news in his lap. Persuasion. The problem was, it didn't always work. Sometimes, a kidney punch just led to defiance.

"There's time for that," Henri said. And by "that," Henri meant killing the guy, although he didn't say it.

"Any contact with the guy would lead to potential complications, and we don't need any more complications," he said. "Look, my man in the precinct thinks he would have advance warning if they were going to arrest you — like, if somebody else got to the costume guy. Other than that, you're okay — as long as you don't rob any more banks."

Henri looked at his son. He stared, waiting for a nod of acknowledgement, but none was forthcoming.

"It's a small hurdle, but this is something I've been successful at," Guy said.

"How many times?" Henri said.

"Three so far," Guy said. And then he ran through the other

two jobs. Henri had vague memories of them, but Sylvie, who read the newspapers much more closely than her husband did, nodded enthusiastically. She knew. And she half smiled in a sign of pride — a pride that Henri also felt, at least a little, but that he was determined not to show. Because in Henri's mind, Guy Fucking La Rue, the king of the clowns, was still an idiot.

"Tell me again why we can't just take care of the costume guy now," Guy said.

"Because leaving broken bodies strewn along the streets is bad for business," Henri said. "This isn't a little boy's game, it isn't something out of a cheap novel — it's business. If we need to — if they arrest you — we can take care of the man from the costume shop. He'll never be able to testify, and that will be that. No testimony, no court case. We would do it then because it would need to be done. We wouldn't have a choice, and so, we would accept the risks. Now, though, we do have a choice. And to do it before it's absolutely necessary, it's like I said. It's bad for business."

Guy stood up. Henri said, "Where do you think you're going?"

"I've got work," Guy said.

"No more banks," Henri said.

Guy did not answer. He just walked toward the kitchen door, and then he turned and said, "You're just jealous."

Henri wanted to chase after his son and hit him, but managed to control himself. He sat and fumed in silence, him and Sylvie. One minute. Two minutes. And then his wife stood up to wash her son's coffee cup and said, "You never got the whole top half of France-Soir for anything you ever did."

Apparently figuring that a shitty mood should never be permitted to go to waste, Henri drove straight from home to Martin's office. Just walking through the front door of La Rue Importers raised his blood pressure. Henri, the older brother, the operational head of the family, worked out of the back of a uniform supply store on Avenue de Clichy with the clatter of sewing machines supplying the ambient noise. La Rue Importers, on Avenue Fucking Victor Hugo, where the import and sale of fine wines and liquors was nominally the business at hand, had music playing softly in the background. Classical music. Christ.

"Brother," Martin said, walking over to greet him. "To what do I owe the honor?"

"Stop with your happy horseshit," Henri said.

"So it's going to be like that, huh?"

"Your office," Henri said, leading the way. When the door was closed, he unloaded on Martin about Gus Parent and the stolen trucks and the police refusing to clear him and the insurance company refusing to pay him.

"He could lose the goddamn business," Henri said.

Martin, who was picking at the crud beneath his fingernails with a gold letter opener, said, "Not my problem."

"The hell it's not," Henri said.

"They're going to pay eventually," Martin said.

"I'm telling you, he's worried about losing the business," Henri said. "It's his whole fucking life. And you... you..."

"Me?" Martin said. "Me? You okayed the whole damn thing — or have you forgotten? Without your say-so, it doesn't happen — or don't you remember how this works, big brother?"

"You have to find a way to make him whole," Henri said.

"The fuck I do," Martin said. "I can throw him some more business, but that's it. Make him whole? Me? Fuck no. Your decision. Your friend. Your problem. Besides, don't you have that cop on the payroll? Can't he?"

"Don't you think that was the first thing I tried?" Henri said. He had called on Chrétien right after it happened, but the investigation was not operating out of his precinct and he had no control or influence. He did manage to tell Henri where and when Gus was being questioned, but that was it.

"Well, whatever," Martin said. "I'll say it again: your decision, your friend, your problem."

When Henri stood up, he knocked over the chair he had been sitting on, and then he kicked it rather than righting it.

"Your decision, your problem," Martin shouted as Henri stormed out, the slam of the office door providing the punctuation.

Back in Montmartre, his blood pressure ebbing, Henri made a phone call from a box on the street and then waited in the little park at Place Émile Goudeau. For most of his life, Henri had no idea who Goudeau was. It was Gérard who told him — or, rather, sneered the information at him — when Henri admitted to his uncle that he had no idea when they were walking through the park one day. Goudeau was a novelist and a poet, as it turned out. Whatever. The park was famous for another reason, too — for the Bateau Lavoir, which apparently housed an artist's studio where Picasso worked in the early 1900s. Henri didn't know which one of the buildings framing the park was the Picasso studio back then, and he really didn't care. For all he knew, it was the little hotel tucked into the corner, the little hotel where he always fucked Gina.

The verb was exactly the right one, too. He didn't love Gina and never would, not like Sylvie. Deep in his heart, Henri actually believed in the for-better-or-worse part of the vows. Whatever came after this life, Henri was prepared to experience it with Sylvie, at whatever hectoring tone or decibel level she chose. He didn't care for Gina in the same way that he cared for Marina, either. He would never show her off to the boys, or buy her extravagant gifts, or make the weighing calculation that he did constantly with Marina — proud of her as a bauble on the one side of the scale, intense dislike for her shallow and expensive bullshit on the other side. Gina didn't fit into any of those boxes. He didn't employ her, or lavish her with gifts, or even really talk to her very much. He just fucked her, and she was fine with the arrangement.

He first met her when he was working in the skank whorehouse on Boulevard de Clichy — although she wasn't a skank in the looks department, only in the cocaine department. She had a nice body, and short black hair, and a beautiful smile to go along with her drug habit. The first time, Henri offered her a ride home and instead took her to the little hotel at Place Émile Goudeau. He got her out of the whorehouse and arranged a job as a hostess at Louis' up the hill on Place du Tertre. If it didn't get her into a better apartment or cure her of the cocaine addiction, it at least was more respectable than the skank house — not that she really seemed to care. She was working at Louis' when Henri called, and it wasn't a five-minute walk down the hill to the hotel.

He stood when he saw her approach, and kissed both her cheeks, and was rewarded with that smile. Thinking back later, he wasn't sure she said anything as they walked into the hotel, grabbed a key from the manager, and made their way to a small room that was soon a riot of tossed pillows and disheveled sheets. It was fast and it was hard and uncomplicated. He liked it, she liked it, and it was no more than that. Lying in bed afterward, still entwined, trying to regain their breath, Henri felt content. It was a feeling he did not often experience, simple contentment. But he always did with Gina. Guy and the clown masks, and Martin and Gus Parent's stolen trucks, were banished from his mind — at least for a few minutes.

Gina dressed and left the room first, as always. Henri didn't offer her a late lunch or a drink, and she wouldn't have accepted if he had.

After a Friday night out with Marina and the boys — this time to the Moulin Rouge, which he despised but which nonetheless remained in the entertainment rotation — Henri always got home after Sylvie was asleep and usually left before she woke up. They had taken to sleeping in separate rooms on those Friday nights because, as Sylvie ultimately concluded, "Shit, whatever."

On Saturday morning, whenever he could drag his ass out of bed early enough, Henri played boules. His preferred game was at Square des Batignolles. It had two advantages. First, there were a couple of well-maintained places to play in the park. Second, and more important, the park was in the 17th, which was adjacent to Montmartre and the La Rue family territory in the 18th but still far enough away that he was not frequently recognized on the streets or feared by people he did not know.

It really was a nice little park, and there really was a sense of freedom about the whole experience, an untethering from the daily world, and Henri found the clichéd spring in his step whenever he entered the gates, especially when the weather was nice. As he walked along the cinder path, he passed the pond that was home to two swans — at least some of the time. Whenever they were there, Henri greeted them by the names he had given them, Heckle and Jeckle, from the American cartoon they used to play before the movies. After the pond there was a playground with climbing bars and also a little merry-go-round. Lots of people came to picnic and sun themselves on the lawns. Only on one side, at the very edge of the park, overlooking the railroad tracks that ran into Saint-Lazare, could you play boules.

It was a serious crowd, no kids — not that Henri had seen

many kids playing in his time. The men there knew him, but they didn't know him, if that made any sense. The La Rues had some small dealings in the 17th, consisting of a single whore-house that was somehow grandfathered into the family's terri-tory, likely by his grandfather's father. So, it was like the players knew him but really didn't give a shit. That was a better way of saying it.

Every week, it was somebody else's job to bring the bottle of Armagnac. After they played, they drank and talked, talked and drank. Henri felt oddly comfortable revealing bits of his person-ality and his hopes and his anxieties to these men whom he had never seen in any other context. They knew things about him that no one else did. They never talked business, though. So, they knew Henri's wife was an ambitious pain in his ass, but they didn't know about the hit on the Morels in the 10th. They knew Henri had a son who didn't listen to him or respect him but they didn't know he was running the gang that was knocking over banks and sometimes wearing clown masks, as they had read in the papers.

And about his old friend, Gus Parent, he asked them the last time, "Did you ever disappoint an old friend? Really hurt him?"

Marcel was the oldest guy on the bench. He said, "I slept with my best friend's wife once. Does that count?"

After Henri stopped laughing, the guy sitting next to Marcel, another Henri, said, "My friend, you could have her."

Then, they looked at my face and burst into laughter again.

"Long time ago," Marcel said. "Before the war."

"Well, I guess you win," Henri La Rue said.

"Maybe," Marcel said. "Maybe not."

"I just fucked an old, dear friend in a business deal," Henri said. "I thought there was little risk for him, but I was wrong. And I don't think I can fix it."

"Just apologize," Marcel sad.

"I can't."

"Why not?"

"Because he doesn't know I'm the one who fucked him," Henri said.

They held the reunion every three years and Henri had never missed one. The numbers did drop every time, though — Martin skipped the last one and was skipping this one, and he wasn't alone. What started as 14 men in the same Resistance cell was now down to seven of them around the table in the back room of La Mer, a bistro on Rue Lamarck. Martin and four others lost interest, and two of the 14 were dead — René Duguay from cancer and, of course, Jean La Rue, Henri's older brother.

Henri hated those days at the end of the war but, at the same time, could not let go of them completely. Fighting with those men was the best, purest thing he ever did as a human being — better than fatherhood, better than anything — and being reminded of those few noble millimeters in his heart every once in a while made the current days go better sometimes. That was especially true in that moment, with everything Henri was dealing with: the son who hated him, and the uncle who distrusted his instincts, and the brother who continually let him down, and the old friend who he screwed just because the alternative was inconvenient.

And besides, there was just this bond that still drew him close, invisible but ever-present, like a magnet with its pull. Because Henri La Rue might be a lot of things but one of them was a member of the Bastards of the Butte — and it always made him smile when he thought of the name.

"To the Bastards," was their standard toast at these reunions, and it was proclaimed several dozen times over the course of five or six hours in that back room at La Mer. It was their calling card back in 1943 and 1944, sometimes painted on a wall, sometimes just written in chalk. So, when they stole a German vehicle off the street near the Moulin Rouge, they chalked an outline of the vehicle and the word "Bastards" in its former parking place. And when they set fire to a German soldiers' barracks one night, the word "Bastards" was chalked on the front steps so that the men fleeing the flames in their drawers saw the words on the ground as they ran over them in their bare feet.

For their greatest success, though, there was no chalk memorial. It was Henri and his brother, Jean — Henri and Jean and two rifles perched on the sill of a darkened window on Boulevard de Clichy, across the street from a strip club that wasn't there anymore. The target was Carman, a general in the Wehrmacht, who was partaking in the nubile Parisian delights, just down the street from the Moulin Rouge.

The whole thing happened not three hours after a terrible argument between Jean and their father, also named Jean. The older Jean and Uncle Gérard were brothers, and they ran the family in 1943. He and Gérard had balanced their duty to resist the German occupiers with what they perceived as their duty to keep their families fed and the business intact. As the older Jean liked to say, "I can still be a patriot without being an idiot."

So, they balanced. They kept Trinity One open and catered to the German officer corps, both on the second floor and the third floor. Business, after all, was business — and there were plenty of Parisians of a certain level, the capes-at-the-Opéra level, who had no trouble handing the dice to the uniformed German officer standing immediately to their right. Deep in their hearts, the capes probably preferred the Germans to their own Communists — and, as Gérard liked to say, "Regardless of what's in your heart, the money in your wallet spends the same way."

So, for Jean and Gérard, resistance meant passing on dossiers of their customers' habits to those who took the risks, with the understanding that no action would be taken against said customers while they were on the Trinity One premises.

The other way Jean and Gérard contributed was monetarily. They funded the Paris Resistance at a time when money was scarce, when even the Allied Resistance based in England would not provide much assistance for fear that they were bankrolling Communists who would take over the city when the war ended. The formula for their contributions, Gérard said, was simple: "Two francs for La Rue, one franc for liberation."

But that, in their view, should be that. And when they found out that Jean's three sons were involved in actual Resistance operations, Jean was livid. Gérard tried to calm his brother down.

"You should be proud," he said. "If they were my boys, that's what I would be."

"Fuck proud," Jean said. "This isn't some game. I need them alive. The family needs them alive."

And while he said "they" and "them," he mostly meant Jean. Martin and Henri knew that. They were treated like family pets and little more by their father, especially after their mother died. It was a man and his firstborn, Big Jean and Little Jean, and that was all that mattered. Which meant that, when it came to the Resistance, Big Jean unleashed all of his rage on Little Jean, and Henri and Martin were barely mentioned. The truth was, Henri and Martin would follow their older brother anywhere, and their father likely knew that if he convinced Jean to leave the Resistance, they would leave, too.

The argument that night between Big Jean and Little Jean had been loud enough that Henri heard it all from down the hall of their house. Their father was adamant, and Jean was just as adamant, and the volume increased, and the language deteriorated, and the last thing Little Jean said to Big Jean was, "Fuck you, old man. Just because you have no life in you, I mean, you can't even remember what it's like to get your dick hard, so there's no way you can understand this."

Then there was a great thud. Little Jean said later that their father had thrown a book at him. At which point, the son said to the father, "Nice fucking aim, old man. Just sit here and count your money."

Jean told Henri the whole story as they made their way to the vacant apartment across from the strip club, their rifles disassembled and hidden in knapsacks. As they were perched in the window, waiting, Jean told him the last thing his father said, after the thrown book and the rest. "It was almost a whisper," Jean told him. "Like a growl. He said, 'You'll never know what a disappointment you are to me.'"

Then Henri saw a tear roll down Jean's cheek. He could not remember ever having seen his older brother cry. He looked up to Jean in the way that little brothers do, but it was more than that. Resistance fighting was a young man's game, and they were the two oldest of the Bastards — Jean was 31, Henri 27 — and so there were a dozen more little brothers who looked to Jean for affirmation on pretty much everything, from the jokes they told to the women they slept with. As it had always been with Henri, just a nod or a grin from Jean, that quick grin of his, meant everything.

And then, there he was in the window, one tear becoming two and two becoming a torrent. Jean was crying, and then the rifle was shaking and banging on the window sill, and then he was sobbing and curled up in a ball, the rifle on the floor next to him. Henri didn't know what to do as he continued to look through his rifle scope and focus on the door of the strip club. This was Jean, after all. He couldn't believe what he was seeing, and it scared him. But what to do? How do you comfort a rock?

And then it all happened in just a few seconds: the door opened and a couple of German officers were on the sidewalk. One of them whistled loudly and waved down the street for their driver. And then there was General Carman — shaved head, monocle, every bad stereotype in a single human form. The bald head was tinged red from the neon of the strip club's sign.

Henri looked down quickly at Jean, and he was hugging himself and shaking. Then he got a whiff. He was pretty sure his brother had pissed himself. And then it was back to the rifle scope, and the neon reflecting on the bald head, and then Henri squeezed the trigger once, a single shot, and then there was a deeper red. Henri was pretty sure he had shot Carman through the left eye.

"Come on, come on," Henri said. He got Jean to his feet, and they were down the steps and into the alley behind the apartment within 30 seconds. Louis was waiting there, and he had started the car as soon as he heard the rifle shot, and so the engine was already running and the three of them were out of there before the German officers and their men had a chance to react.

They were a few blocks away when Louis turned to the back seat and said, "You get him, Jean?"

Henri said nothing.

Jean grinned, just for a second.

"That fucking grin — remember it?" Louis said. It was 15 years later, and he was retelling the story for the thousandth time in the back room of La Mer.

The seven of them toasted to Jean's memory. In the days and years after that night, Jean never participated in the retelling of the story. He always just sat at the table with his arms folded and didn't react. He also never corrected the record — not later and not even on that night, after Louis had dropped them off and the two of them were making their way home, making their way up the butte from the back side, far from Boulevard de Clichy. He never thanked Henri for keeping the myth of his leadership alive. He never said anything to Henri about not telling their father the truth. That was just understood, big brother to little brother — at least, that's how Henri always felt. And as the rumors spread, and Big Jean heard the story — not the real story but the manufactured one — there was a different vibe between the father and his firstborn. It wasn't pride, not exactly, but maybe a bit more respect.

"To Jean La Rue, our leader," Henri said, and the six others in the back room of La Mer raised their glasses. And then Louis said, "And Henri, remember in the car when I said I smelled piss, and Jean said, 'Henri had to take a leak under the window while we were staked out, and I think I kneeled in the puddle.'"

"Speaking of which," Henri said, and they all laughed as he got up to use the toilet.

PART VI

A SPIRITUAL VISIT

Martin and Marie's open house was two hours of torture that Henri had been dreading for weeks, ever since the invitation arrived — black script and gold leaf printed on heavy cream-colored stock that felt a little like linen when you ran your finger across it. If you were going to be showing off a 10-room duplex on Avenue Montaigne, even the best pre-printed note cards from Galeries Lafayette weren't good enough.

Avenue Fucking Montaigne — pretty much directly across the street from the Dior salon, pretty much just around the corner from the Champs-Élysées. Henri heard about it on the entire ride over with Sylvie — walk to the shops, walk to the tea rooms, the elegance, the et cetera.

"Fine, look around," Henri said.

"You're not serious," Sylvie said.

"I'm willing to call your bluff."

"You'd never move."

"So you don't deny it's a bluff — because you'd never move from the butte, either," Henri said.

"Gérard would never let you go," Sylvie said.

Martin was allowed to go because of the wine importing business being located where, as he said, "the market demanded it be located" — as if rich people didn't drink wine in Montmartre. Unspoken was that Marie demanded they go. Understood by everyone was the real reason, though — Gérard didn't give a shit about Martin, not really, or his piece of the business. It was the smallest sliver, and Gérard thought Martin was the smallest character, and so, Avenue Montaigne or wherever. Just know that Gérard never had any intention of setting foot in the apartment.

Ten rooms on one of the wealthiest streets in probably the wealthiest neighborhood in the city — Henri could only imagine the cost. And when they walked in the front door, well, Sylvie actually gasped for a second and Henri almost did, too. They had just had their place on Rue Caulaincourt redone, and the work was all top shelf — Henri had the bills to prove it — but this, he had to admit, blew it away. The furniture, the window treatments, the oriental rug in the dining room — it really was something. When Marie's little poodle scampered by, sniffed them, and kept running, Sylvie said out of the side of her mouth, "Do you think the dog shits gold bars, too?"

Family friends, wine importer friends — the place was more crowded somehow than Henri expected. He found the bar, and then they tortured themselves further by taking a self-guided tour that ended in a master suite that Sylvie said was "big enough to put a basketball court."

"And the ceiling, it's high enough for a trapeze," Henri said.

Sylvie scoffed.

"You know, for Marie," Henri said. "She's got to be doing something to convince Martin to spend like this."

"If a trapeze is all it would take..." Sylvie said. Then she just shook her head.

They were there for 15 minutes before they ran into Martin and Marie.

"Such a location," Sylvie said.

"You know, just those few hundred feet from the Champs, it makes all the difference," Marie said. "It's so much quieter — both from the traffic, oh the cars on the Champs — and from the foot traffic, the shoppers. The boutiques on Avenue Montaigne are, how to put it, more selective. More discreet. It's just, just the perfect location."

Henri felt like gagging. After all the rest of the best-wishes bullshit had been exchanged, Martin steered him into what he said was his study — big desk, red leather chairs, library shelves that took up two of the four walls.

"Have you read even one of them?" Henri said.

Martin scoffed. "Apparently, you can buy books by the foot these days," he said.

They sat in the chairs and Martin said, "Look, I feel bad about how the other day went."

Henri didn't react.

"I have an idea," Martin said.

"About Gus and the trucks?"

"No, something better."

"Like what?"

"Like having a little fun at Cousin Michel's expense," Martin said.

"Is he here?" Henri said.

"No. Sent his regrets. Marie is furious. Peasant motherfucker."

"So?"

"So, listen," Martin said. "I've got a line on Michel's latest, shall we say, smuggling mechanism."

There was a bottling plant on Rue Le Course in the 14th. Because wine goes in bottles, and because Martin imported good wine and also distributed shitty wine — which was sometimes good wine that had been mixed with crap wine and diluted and repackaged — he had occasion to deal with the guy from the bottling plant. And during one of those dealings because the guy figured a La Rue was a La Rue was a La Rue, he laid out Michel's latest heroin smuggling scheme.

"Honestly, it's a beauty," Martin said. "We have to give him that."

"We don't have to give him shit," Henri said.

"Whatever — it's a good scheme."

"Hiding heroin in wine bottles isn't exactly nuclear physics."

"No, it's more... more... more elegant than that," Martin said. "If you do the math — I mean, I did it on the back of an envelope last night — he has a 97 percent chance of pulling it off."

"Ninety-seven?" Henri said. "Okay, Euclid, I'm intrigued. Tell me more."

At which point, Martin showed his work. Only one-third of the cases of wine were being touched at all. Of that one-third, only one of the 12 bottles was being filled with heroin instead of wine.

"So it's one-twelfth of one-third — those are the odds that a customs inspector would open one of the right cases and then lift out the heroin bottle and look at it," Martin said.

"So it's even a little more than 97 percent," Henri said.

"It might even be, like, 99 percent — because, really, what are the odds that a customs inspector bothers to open even one case out of a high-end wine shipment?"

"He's a smart fucker," Henri said.

"But here's the thing," Martin said. He walked over to the far end of the study where there was a drinks cart, fully stocked. He grabbed a bottle and walked it back to Henri and handed it to him.

"This is the wine," Martin said. He pointed to the label. "This same design is printed on the outside of the wine cases, same red ink. Now, see the name — Cardin. Look at the dot of the i — it's an open circle. See that? Well, they need to mark the cases so that the people on the other end in New York know which ones have the heroin bottles. Well on those cases, the open circle will be filled in, also in red. It's subtle, but you'll see it if you're looking for it."

"Okay, so?" Henri said.

"Well, if the customs inspector here knew about the dot of the i..."

"You can do that?"

"I have friends who can."

Henri thought about it for maybe a half-second.

"Fucking do it," he said. At which point, Martin walked back to the drinks cart for an opener and two fresh glasses.

The planning for the fourth bank robbery was more abbreviated than the others. All Guy did was have a couple of his guys sit in a car outside the BNCI branch on Rue Ordener for a week and note the time when the armored car showed up. It was easy enough, and the time was consistent enough — between 3:05 and 3:16, every day, every time — that Guy cut short any further surveillance or planning.

"Fuck it," he said. "This will be the easiest one of all."

Rafael, the kid with the farting problem under stress, asked him why.

"First, there's the street — it's wide-fucking-open then," Guy said. "People don't start going home from work for at least another hour. The consistency of the timing works for us, too — we like predictability. We fucking love predictability. Two guards, bank pretty quiet after lunch, street wide open — a goddamned cinch is what it will be. A goddamned cinch."

"Masks?" The question came from Georges, the closest thing to a skeptic in the crew.

"No masks," Guy said. "Fuck the masks. Just hats — normal fucking hats — and bandanas over our nose and mouth."

"Bandanas?"

"Just use a fucking handkerchief, I don't care," Guy said. "It'll be mostly deserted — after the lunch rush, but before the shop-keepers and shit bring over their daily deposits. Nobody's going to see us. We'll take whatever they have bundled for the armored car guys and we'll also take whatever the armored car guys were bringing to replenish the vault. Five minutes. No more."

"But what about the inside?" Georges said. "We had diagrams before."

"And they didn't mean shit," Guy said. "It's a fucking bank. You've been in a hundred of them. There's the counter with the girls behind it, and there's an office on the right for the boss, and the vault is behind the girls on the left. There's nothing to it. I'm telling you — five minutes."

Salvatore made the call at 2 p.m. the next day. It was the only way he could think of to get his bar back. Sally's was a neighborhood place, but the neighbors had become increasingly scarce since that La Rue kid and his crew pretty much took over the place. Sally didn't dislike them, not even the asshole kid in charge — they were good for a couple of laughs every day. But the tab they were running was big and their payments were slow — and even if their payments had been timely, it would not make up for the money they were chasing away, the neighborhood money. Sally had to do something.

"You know the clown bank robbers?" he said.

"Yeah, I know," said the voice on the other end. "What about them?"

"Their next job — I know the details," Sally said.

"Wait. What? Who is this?"

"BNCI Bank, the branch on Rue Ordener. In about an hour. About 3:15."

"Sir, who is this? What's your name?"

"BNCI Bank, Rue Ordener, 3:15."

Then Sally hung up. He could only imagine the scene at the precinct when the desk sergeant began shouting for his captain.

Rafael only farted the one time while they waited in the car outside the bank but it shook the windows. He was past apologizing, though, and the others in the car were past commenting. Guy lit up a Gauloises and rolled down the window on his side, and they waited. As 2:55 became 3:00, and 3:00 became 3:05, he was filled more by adrenaline than nerves. He had no doubt that this robbery would be a success, just as the other three had been. They had the timing down, and they had the guards and their guns outnumbered by 6-3. And those numbers alone, along with the element of surprise, were enough that they wouldn't even have to use their guns. If it was like every other time, the bank guard would be no issue at all, maybe with his head in the sports page and maybe even half sleeping off his lunch. The one armored car guy would be occupied with the hand truck carrying the delivery, and the other tended to be a social being more than a guard. Every time, the second armored car guy said hello and started chatting with some familiar face the minute he got through the door. This would be no different.

So, 3:05 became 3:10, and then, at 3:11, the armored car pulled up in front of the bank. They unloaded their shit onto the hand truck, and the second guard took a look around outside, and then he held the door open for the guard with the hand truck. Ten seconds after the door closed, Guy said, "Now," and the six of them in the two cars pulled up their bandanas and followed him inside.

And it went exactly as he predicted. They got inside just as the branch manager was opening the safe. There were only two customers, and two girls behind the counter, and they were no problem at all. The bank guard was showing the second armored car guard a picture of a dancer in the newspaper, and they were no problem. The guy with the hand truck might as well have had his dick in his hand, and the bank manager looked like he was going to wet himself. All told, it might have been the easiest of the four robberies.

As they got to the door, Guy looked at his watch. He had said they would be in the bank for only five minutes, but he had been wrong. It was only four minutes, 45 seconds.

"Only 4:45 boys," he shouted over his shoulder, seeing them all ready to follow him out.

It was only when they got to the sidewalk when the voice on the bullhorn said, "Stop right there or we'll shoot. You're surrounded. Put down the guns."

Startled, it took Guy a second to focus. The six of them were all on the sidewalk. He looked across the street and saw that the police had already cuffed Rafael and the kid driving the other car. Then he scanned and saw six, no seven police cars blocking Rue Ordener at both ends, and probably 20 cops arrayed behind the cars parked on the other side of the street.

A dozen things went through his mind in the next five seconds, including the words, "My fucking father." And then he placed his gun on the sidewalk, raised his hands, and turned to the rest of them and told them to do the same thing.

"Fuck it, boys," he told them. "I think the odds were better at Verdun."

And then they stood there, with their arms in the air, as the swarm of policemen approached from three sides.

It was another one of those days for Henri, one of those days without a lot to do. His diary was empty except for a lunch at Gartner's with Willy that further convinced him that he had made the correct decision about the 10th. The money was rolling in, especially from the two train stations, and Willy was more organized than the commander of a naval destroyer. The ledger he brought along to show Henri was not only meticulous, but written in a style that reminded Henri of something produced by one of those scrivener monks in the 12th century. Every number was perfect on every line, businesslike but still with a kind of flourish. And the numbers themselves — the La Rues were close to doubling their income in just the first months in control of the 10th. Gérard had never been so wrong about anything, as Henri reminded him at every turn — not with words but with the heft of the envelopes.

After lunch, Henri went home for a nap on the couch. Sylvie was reading a magazine in the comfortable chair across the room when the phone rang. She walked out to the hallway to get it and then came back.

"Mr. Brown," she said. "Sounds important."

Mr. Brown was Chrétien. Shit. When Henri picked up the receiver, he heard shouting in the background, a real commotion.

"What is it?" Henri said. "And where the hell are you, at a football game?"

"I'm at the station," Chrétien said. "You haven't heard?"

"Heard what?"

"The BNCI Bank on Rue Ordener."

"Fuck me."

"Yes, fuck you," Chrétien said. "I warned you. I told you. This is just about out of my hands."

"Wait, what happened?"

"We got a tip, and it got passed upstairs quickly. Very quickly. Like I said, bank robbery — it's over my head now. It goes straight to the top. Fucking clown masks. The brass got together and we sent an army, men from three different precincts. Eighteen cars overall. Forty men, I think — a lot of them with rifles."

"Wait," Henri said. Sylvie was listening over his shoulder, and she squeezed his arm. Hard. "Rifles? Don't tell me."

"No," Chrétien said. "Nobody fired a shot — not us, not them. Nobody's hurt. They saw how many guns we had outside and gave up. They're all fine. They're all in custody."

"How many?"

"Eight."

"And you're sure Guy is one of them?"

"He's in my fucking jail," Chrétien said. "He came in my fucking car, with me and my sergeant and my driver."

By then, Henri was holding the receiver far enough away from his ear for Sylvie to hear. She gasped at the news, but almost inaudibly and just for a second. She squeezed Henri's arm again.

"So, what—" Henri said.

"Look, it was a complete circus — and that could work for us," Chrétien said.

"What do you—"

"Just listen," the cop said. "Like I said — 40 men, three different precincts, a complete circus. The bosses were there, and the adrenaline was up — you know. Well, no, I guess you wouldn't know. Anyway, eight robbers were transported back to three different precincts in five different cars, or maybe six. All of that can work for us."

Sylvie wanted to say something. Henri held up his hand. He

needed more information.

"Like, right now, there is a question about the number of robbers," Chrétien said. "There is some confusion. I've been saying seven, and I'm not the only one — it really was chaotic. On the scene, the bosses were all fired up, and nobody was really doing anything to organize it, so I piped up and said that we should get the robbers out of there as fast as we could and get their paperwork in order, and then bring them all together at the 18th — we have the biggest, nicest building after the renovations."

"So how does that help us?" Henri said.

"We have a new cell block that we use every day now. But we still have the old cells, too — mostly we store paperwork in them now. Well, Guy is in one of the old cells as we speak. The only people who know are me and my sergeant — and you're going to have to take care of him if this works. But he's helped us before — I've taken care of him out of my end. The sergeant is fine. If it wasn't for the Boy Scout of a driver, I would have just dropped Guy on a street corner. The sergeant would have gone along with it. But the Boy Scout is just out of the academy, and I'm not sure he would get it, and I couldn't take the risk. I sent him back to the bank after he dropped us, though, so it's just me and the sergeant. If anybody comes across Guy in the old cell block, I'll just tell him it's for security reasons — so I'd be covered but you'd be screwed."

Henri listened and felt his heart racing. He turned and saw the anguish that was contorting Sylvie's face. She wasn't crying, not yet.

"But nobody's screwed yet," Chrétien said. "Me and the sergeant, we're the only two who know, for now. That won't be true in an hour. If your boy is still here when the rest of them come from the other precincts, and the bosses arrive for the interrogations, that's it. There won't be anything I can do."

"But can't you just hide him until—"

"If I could draw you a map of the precinct, you'd see why that isn't possible," Chrétien said. "The old cells are off by themselves, but not way off. It's just a different hallway. People use it all the time. I'm telling you — we can't hide him."

"Can't you just let him go? Now that the Boy Scout is gone?" Henri said.

"You don't get it," Chrétien said. "This place is... it's a madhouse. And the newspapermen — we usually let them in if it's only one or two, but there are about 20 of them, so we're keeping them all out on the street out front — and a couple are at the back door, too. Like I said, it's a madhouse. There's no way to walk him out through all of that. I couldn't get him through my own people without some sort of explanation that would be seen as bullshit in about three seconds. And then the press after that? No."

"So what are you saying?" Henri said.

"I'm saying that I don't know what the answer is, but that the window of opportunity closes completely in an hour when they all get here. At that point, it's going to be eight robbers, not seven, and your son is going to be one of them."

"An hour? No more?"

"No more," Chrétien said.

Henri hung up and asked Sylvie, "Did you hear enough?"

She nodded. They both were quiet for a second.

"What do you think?" Henri said, finally.

"I think we both know," Sylvie said.

At which point, Henri picked up the phone and called his uncle. He hated to ask, and Sylvie probably hated it even more, but he didn't feel as if he had another option. His mind was racing as fast as his heart, and he couldn't think of a play, of a way to get Guy out.

Forty-five minutes later, the scene outside of the police precinct was still as Chrétien had described it to Henri, only worse. The newspapermen — there must have been 30 of them by then — were hyper-aggressive when anyone had the misfortune to walk down the street. They accosted one and all. That included an old lady shuffling by, hunched over, carrying a string bag full of produce from the market at the corner.

"Anything to do with the bank robbers inside?" one of the reporters asked. He wasn't 25 years old, and while it took a lot to embarrass a pack of newsmen, even they were embarrassed that the kid would confront the old biddy.

When she looked up at him and said, "Go shit in your hat," the embarrassment turned to glee. For the next 15 minutes, they took turns imitating the old girl. Little did the kid know that he would be 30 before he stopped running into colleagues in the office, or out in the field, or in the bar after work — especially in the bar after work — who would tell him to go shit in his hat in an old lady's voice.

Every cop who went in and out of the precinct was badgered by the pack, even jostled, and seeing as how it was getting near the end of the day shift, there was a decent amount of coming and going, badgering and jostling. Most of the cops were as rough as the reporters, though, including the one old sergeant — he was 61, and had seen action at Ypres — who bellowed, "Out of my way, pencil dicks." They made a ready path for him.

But when the two priests showed up and attempted to climb the steps to the front door of the precinct, it was the definition of a gauntlet. One of the priests was dressed in most businesslike attire — black pants and jacket, black shirt and white clerical collar. The other priest wore the outfit of a parish priest, and one likely from the country — black cassock, white clerical collar, and the wide-brimmed hat that looked like the model for a flying saucer out of the Buck Rogers comics.

The newspapermen closed in on them as they tried to make their way up the steps. The priest in the cassock was more physical than his companion, bigger, stronger, as if he had been bred to work on a farm and not to sit behind a desk. He cleared the path, using his left arm as a makeshift battering ram, as he held the hat in place with his right hand. He just cleared bodies and said nothing. The business priest kept repeating, "Excuse us, gentlemen. Excuse us, gentlemen." As they neared the top step, and the shouted questions from the reporters melded into a cacophonous din, the country priest managed to pry open the door and the city priest turned to the pack and said, "A spiritual visit, gentlemen. I'm sure you understand."

Once inside, the door slammed behind them and the roar of the reporters was replaced by the loud hum of the police station. The country priest fixed his hat back into position and turned to Father Lemieux and said, "All right, let's get this fucking done."

Lemieux walked up to the desk sergeant and asked for Chrétien and, after a quick phone call, they were pointed down a hallway to Chrétien's office. The door was open, and they walked up to his desk, and the cop stood up out of respect for the clergy, and then he waited for an explanation.

"Fucking tell him," said the country priest.

"Guy La Rue," Lemieux said.

"What about him?" Chrétien said.

"Just go fucking get him," the country priest said.

Chrétien thought about arguing, or at least questioning, but it clicked soon enough. He looked at his watch. They had 10 minutes, maybe.

He hustled Guy La Rue out of the old cell and into his office. Upon arrival, he found Lemieux as he was and the country priest standing in his underwear.

"What the—" Guy said, looking at the half-naked guy. But then he looked at the priest and saw that it was Father Lemieux, and started to understand, too.

"Come on, come on," the undressed man said.

"I can't wear that," Guy said, when he saw the cassock.

"Why not?" Chrétien said.

"I'm not wearing any underwear," Guy said.

"Then you better button it tight," the undressed man said. "And you," he said, pointing at Chrétien, "I need parking tickets, five or six."

"I'm not a goddamned meter maid," Chrétien said.

"Then go find some," the country priest said. He was buttoning Guy's dress shirt. The whole costume change didn't take three minutes, at which point Chrétien was back, and they were ready to go. Guy had the priest's hat on the back of his head, thinking of fashion more than camouflage. The man now wearing his clothing walked over and yanked the front of the hat down until it was almost over Guy's eyes.

"Out the front, same as before," he told them.

"The back will have fewer reporters," Chrétien said.

"Same as before," the man said. "Exactly the same. You fucking say nothing and just make sure the hat doesn't fall off. And you," he said, pointing at Lemieux, "just keep repeating that same bullshit about a spiritual visit to a prisoner. And then make a right at the sidewalk and keep walking — down the hill and all the way to the fucking Seine if that's what it takes to shake the last reporter. But it won't. They'll give up in 10 seconds. You'll see."

And that's what they did. The precinct door opened, and Father Lemieux and Guy were engulfed by the newspapermen. Guy reflexively adopted the same posture that the other country priest had — battering with his left arm, holding the hat down low over his eyes with his right hand. Lemieux drew most of the attention because he was the only one of the two saying anything. Ignoring all requests for names — either their names or the name of the prisoner they were visiting, Lemieux just kept repeating in a shout, "Just a spiritual visit, gentlemen. Just a spiritual visit to a prisoner."

And it was true, once they reached the sidewalk and turned to the right, the last of the reporters quickly gave up and returned to the front steps. The newsmen didn't know exactly what to expect, but if one of the captains was to come out and give them a briefing, that is where it would be, on those steps. None of them could risk leaving for long, which is why they were all taking turns pissing in the alley on the side of the precinct, pissing into the void but still leaning backward to see the crowd at the front steps.

As it turned out, they would be there for hours before the

brass came out and told them about the seven bank robbers they had arrested, and how one of them had suggested under interrogation that this was the same bunch that had worn the clown masks at the previous robbery on Rue des Abbesses. In those hours, there were only two or three flurries of activity, including the man in the slightly too tight navy blue suit who offered a bewildered look at the crowd of reporters, and then a shrug, and then a fistful of parking tickets.

"But they're all paid now," the man said. The newspapermen all laughed and backed away to create a path for him to walk through. His name was Marc Theriot, and he was a part-time actor and a part-time bartender at Le Cenis, the place down the street from Gérard La Rue's house, his local. Theriot had owed Gérard a favor.

PART VII

INTRAMURALS

Two hours later, the little gathering at Gérard's house was equal parts celebration and exasperation. Because they got Guy out of the police station, and because Guy was such a goddamned arrogant idiot to have gotten himself caught.

Marc Theriot was gone by the time Henri arrived, so he went unthanked — beyond the envelope from Gérard, that is. Guy said nothing, choosing instead to concentrate on emptying the decanter of whatever Gérard had been decanting, drinking while alternately complaining about the cassock and proclaiming, "I would have done the fucking time. None of this was necessary."

When Henri arrived, he held his tongue as he handed over some clothing from Guy's closet. The father had hoped for some acknowledgement from the son that he had been an idiot to ignore the warning about robbing another bank, even a tiny hint of regret or remorse. Instead, what Henri received from his son was a single exasperated word: "Finally." And then he snatched the bundle of clothing from his father and left the precious sitting room with the Louis XIV furniture.

Which left Henri to join Gérard and Father Lemieux, who were sitting by the fireplace and pretending not to watch the youthful insolence. He poured himself a drink from the cart — brandy of some sort — and sat next to the priest on the sofa.

"Both of you, I can't thank you enough," Henri said. He was actually just a bit choked up, even though his son had been a fool and an asshole besides, and even though he had been exposed as dependent on his uncle's wisdom as well as his operational reach.

"Just glad it worked out," Father Lemieux said. "I have to

admit to being afraid the whole time. Not my usual line of work."

"You turn water and wine into the body and blood of Christ on a daily basis," Gérard said. "This was but a minor miracle by comparison."

"Well, to the wise man and the holy man — Henri and Sylvie La Rue are forever in your debt," Henri said. He raised his glass and the others joined him. The whole "wise man" bit was something he had practiced on the drive over, and he watched Gérard's reaction as he said it, the quick smile that the old man could not hide. It was the reaction he had sought. As he told Sylvie on the way out the door, "When you're in this situation, the only move is to kiss his ass on both cheeks. Anything else turns the debt into a debt wrapped around a resentment — and those are the kinds of debts you can never repay."

"It's just lucky Father was here trying to whip my books into shape when you called," Gérard said. "I don't think we could have made it work in time otherwise."

The three of them went quiet for a minute, savoring their drinks and the fire. The silence was broken by the return of Guy, who stood next to his father with his hand out and said, "Keys?"

Henri fished them out of his pocked, handed them over, and said, "You know—"

"Yeah, yeah, Uncle G told me," Guy said. "Straight to the house in Normandy, no stopping."

"I filled the tank on the way over," Henri said.

"Yeah, whatever," Guy said. "Straight to Normandy. Any cop calls or shows up, I've been there since yesterday, just a regular off-season look-see, that we all take turns in the family checking on the house, that this time it was my turn."

"Straight there," Gérard said.

Guy nodded and left.

"Sometimes..." Henri said, half to himself. And then he

looked directly at Gérard and said, "He's such an idiot sometimes. Such a know-it-all. Won't listen. Appreciates nothing.
Never says 'thank you.' He's just..."

"I know," Gérard said.

Then, Henri told them about the warning from Chrétien,
and the clown masks, and how he had told Guy his bank-
robbing career had to be over, and how the police brass had
been embarrassed and how they were gunning for the robbers.
Gérard's only reaction as he listened was a theatrically raised
eyebrow at the mention of the clown masks he had read about
in the newspaper. Meanwhile, it dawned on Henri that he was
spilling all of this angst, and these family secrets, in front of
Father Lemieux, something he never would have done in the
past but which now seemed natural.

When Henri had finished, Lemieux seemed about to say
something, but then he stopped and sank back into the couch
cushions and sipped his brandy. Then it was quiet again, save
for the occasional crackle of the fire.

"You know who he reminds me of?" Gérard said.

"Who, Guy? Not me, I hope," Henri said.

"No, not you," Gérard said. "Your brother, Jean. Little Jean
and Big Jean — that was quite a dynamic in its day, and for a
long time. I know that you know — you watched it, lived it. But
you also saw Little Jean grow out of it eventually."

"If you say so," Henri said. He gulped down what he had and
brought the brandy over from the cart and refilled everyone's
glass.

"Really, he did grow out of it," Gérard said. "And Guy will,
too. You'll see. Women think mothers and daughters have the
most complicated relationships in the family, but my money is
on fathers and first sons."

"The expectations of the father projected on the son?"
Father Lemieux said.

"That's part of it," Gérard said. "But it's more than that. The complicated part is the fathers having to deal with the living, breathing embodiment of all of their worst traits being transferred to their sons."

This was bullshit, Henri thought. He had never been the walking, talking pile of insolence that Guy had become. He also had never been anything but grateful when his father paid any attention to him, grateful and eager to please. Bullshit. Total bullshit.

"You have a lot of theories for a guy who never had kids of his own," Henri said.

"I read a lot," Gérard said. "And I have eyes."

Without a car, Henri walked home from his uncle's place — down, down, down the butte. Sylvie was on him as soon as she heard his key turning in the lock. When he told her about Guy, that he was fine and on his way to Normandy, she blessed herself. And then she said, "So you kissed the ring?"

"The ring and both cheeks — twice on each," Henri said. He smiled weakly and made a smooch with his lips.

"And?" Sylvie said.

"I think it worked," he said. "I owe him, but I don't think he's going to be an asshole about it."

Laurence Perrault owned the bottling company on Rue La Course. He was eating lunch with Michel La Rue, finalizing the details of the smuggling scheme, collecting his final envelope. Because Perrault's terms were clear: cash up front, whether or not the heroin actually reached New York undetected. As he said, after sucking the broth out of a snail shell, "My risks end at the warehouse door."

Michel disliked Perrault, disliked the smarminess that oozed from the man's every pore. In business, Michel had come to believe that you could smell a weasel before you saw the actual evidence, and Perrault reeked. But he needed him, and so there they were at Le Stube.

The waiter had served the plates of sausages and mustard and pretzel bread, but Perrault would not let the snails go. As Michel worked on his entrée, the bottler was determined to get the final drops of juice and broth, and he didn't seem to care how loud he was in the process, or if the repeated licking of his fingers was causing to two women at the next table to make faces that were half disgust and half pity.

"Nice place," Perrault said, between sucks and licks. "Even if it's not quite the Martin La Rue Special."

"You know Martin?" Michel said, and then he immediately realized. "Wine importer, bottling company — of course, you know him."

"Funny fucker," Perrault said.

"But what's the Martin La Rue Special?"

"Drinks and a light snack around the bar at Tangerine," Perrault said. "Then, we dive into the main course in the back room."

The bottler guffawed and half choked on some snail broth

that went down the wrong pipe. Tangerine was a strip club in Pigalle. The light snack was likely a bowl of nuts or a hard-boiled egg and toast. The main course was likely more substantial. Michel wondered why Martin took his client to Tangerine and not to one of the family's places. But then again, he didn't really wonder, based upon the age-old principle that you really shouldn't shit where you eat.

It took Perrault about 10 seconds to stop coughing, at which point he took a big swallow of wine and picked up the next snail.

"Really a funny fucker," he said. "And good company. He always lets me take the first pick at Tangerine, even though we both favor the big asses. Just good people. He really thought our little scheme with the wine bottles was genius — he was very complimentary of you."

Perrault sucked and Michel suddenly fumed, although he couldn't let it show. He camouflaged his feelings with a throw-away line — "That Martin, he does love the big asses" — but he hated that his cousin knew that much about his business. Michel didn't trust Martin or Henri, not as far as he could throw them. They couldn't hide their jealousy of him, and if truth be told, Michel couldn't hide his disdain for them and their old-fashioned gangster bullshit. Heroin was going to drive the business into the future, into the 1960s and beyond, and he knew it and they knew it. They could run their little casino games and their broken-down whores, and they could strong-arm bar owners to buy their liquor, and they could hijack train cars full of women's girdles every day of the week, but the brown powder was going to overtake the whole enterprise, which meant that Michel La Rue was going to overtake the whole enterprise. The only question being whether it would happen before or after Gérard kicked off.

"So, he liked the plan, huh?" Michel said.

"Fucking loved it," Perrault said. "And what isn't to love?

When I showed him the bit about filling the i in Cardin on the label, he was so impressed. Ingenious — that's the word he used. Ingenious. He must have said it five times."

Ingenious. Shit.

"Well, here's the thing," Michel said. "One of the reasons for the lunch was, I want to change the plan."

"But why?"

"Look, I have a sense about these things," Michel said. "And I have contacts with the border police. And while I'm probably being paranoid, well, better paranoid than incarcerated, right?"

"So what are you saying? It's all set," Perrault said. For the first time since the snails were put in front of him, he stopped sucking and licking.

Michel didn't know what he was saying. He was making the whole thing up on the fly, which was beyond dangerous. And maybe he was being paranoid, but Martin — and, likely, Henri — knowing his business was a risk he wasn't interested in running, not if he didn't have to run it.

"I want to change to olive oil," Michel said. He had done his homework before approaching Perrault in the first place, and he knew that they had a regular bottling contract with the Tartine Olive Oil Company. The sense he got, in fact, was the olive oil bottling contract was Perrault's steadiest deal — that it was the deal that kept the lights on while the wine and other bottling jobs provided the profit.

"I don't know," Perrault said. "We were all set with the wine."

"It's the same process," Michel said. "And, remember, I've been to your place. I know how big it is, and how big it isn't. Wine, olive oil — it's the same workers, the same palms to grease."

"I don't know."

"Yes, you do," Michel said. "It's the exact same thing — one bottle per case. And instead of filling in the i in Cardin, you fill in the e in Tartine."

Perrault went quiet and stared hard at Michel. He was still holding the little fork from the snails, and he pointed it at Michel and said, "Last minute change like this, it's going to change the agreement." And then, with the fork, he tapped the outside of the breast pocket where the envelope from Michel was nestled.

"I don't think so," Michel said, and the look on his face was severe for one second and then relaxed in the next. He smiled and continued.

"Look," he said. "We could have a good, long relationship here. You know how much money we're talking about."

He leaned over the table and tapped the envelope in Perrault's pocket with his index finger.

"It's a simple swap," Michel said. "It'll take the exact same amount of time. You'll be running the exact same amount of risk, which is minimal. And then, when the work is done, you can take that envelope out of your pocket and pick up that cute little daughter of yours at that school of hers on Boulevard Raspail and buy her an ice cream cone and a balloon."

Perrault began coughing again, but not from some snail broth that went down the wrong pipe. He agreed to the swap from wine to olive oil without any additional compensation. Then, he begged off the rest of the lunch, saying that he needed to get back to the bottling plant and plot the changes that Michel had ordered. In the taxi ride back to work, Perrault looked down and saw his hands shaking. He had no idea how Michel La Rue knew he even had a daughter, let alone where she went to school.

Henri was in his office in the back of the uniform store, sitting at his desk, filling envelopes. Business in the 10th was so good, the money from what he euphemistically referred to as "merchandise transfers" at the two train stations so big, that he decided that bonuses were in order, bonuses for everyone — employees, not family — from Passy and Timmy on the top end to the girls who ran the sewing machines for the uniform company at the bottom. The envelopes contained different amounts, but they all contained something. There were 22 of them on the desk in front of him, filled and sealed and identified by name on the front. It would take him several days to make the rounds and give them out, but it was a task that thrilled Henri. Because while he liked money as much as the next guy — and, truly, a lot more than the next guy, with his Italian suits and his Rolex and the rest, not to mention a wife and a mistress who tended to shovel out the cash as quickly as he could shovel it in — what was the point of having it if you didn't share at least some of it?

He had pocketed the envelopes that would go to the girls out front, and was putting the rest in the safe, when he heard a knock and a shouted hello from his open door. It was Gus Parent.

"I've got some news," Gus said. Behind him, Henri could see his son loading a hand truck with the first three of six cartons of uniforms to be shipped.

"Sit, sit," Henri said. He motioned to the chair next to his desk. "Good news, I hope."

"Not the worst news, I guess," Gus said.

Henri didn't react, other than to squeeze the arms of his desk chair. He didn't think Gus could see him, see the white of his knuckles, which was what he hoped was his only outward sign of rage. Fucking Martin. Fucking Martin and his fucking schemes.

"The police don't believe me and the insurance company still won't pay without their absolution," Gus said. "But I'm not going to lose the business."

"But, how—"

"I have some money put away," he said. "We can make it work — buy another truck second-hand, repair the shitty truck. We can make it go."

"Your retirement money?" Henri said. "You can't leave yourself naked!"

"Retirement?" Gus said. Then he laughed. "I'm not sure retirement was ever on the cards for me, but I'm also not sure I'm the retiring kind. Besides, that's years off."

"I'm sure those boxes are getting heavier all the time, though," Henri said.

"No lie there," Gus said. "The money was really for Gus Jr. He met a girl, and she grew up on a farm, and they're talking about getting married, and Gus wants to buy a little place for them."

"A farm?" Henri said.

Gus nodded and smiled.

"Little G, who has spent his whole life on the butte, walking in pig shit?"

Gus shook his head and laughed.

"He met her at a club on the Left Bank," he said. "It's not like when we were kids, when if you married somebody who lived more than a mile away, they acted like you were bringing an alien into the family. But, you know, young love."

Henri looked at Gus and their eyes met and each understood what the other was thinking — because they were both fathers. Gus was a good man, a good man who owned a small business and made an honest living and had no great visions or desires other than an occasional vacation in the sun and the ability to provide for his family.

Henri, without really thinking, said, "You know, I might be able to help Little G."

At which point, the soft, sad smile on Gus's face froze. Henri could see the fear in his eyes, although he didn't react to it as quickly as he saw it.

"We couldn't," Gus said.

"It could be a loan, if you insist," Henri said. "I'd prefer it to be a gift. How much are we talking about?"

Gus's face remained frozen. His eyes darted. He seemed almost panicked, and the whole picture registered now with Henri. If Gus's pride was the issue, he would not be reacting like that. He would not be panicked. He would just tell Henri, old friend to old friend, that he couldn't possibly accept such a generous gift — and Henri would offer again, and Gus would repeat that he couldn't, and Henri would tell him the offer remained open if he changed his mind, and that would be that. There would be no question of mentioning it to Gus Jr. This was between them. Old friends, pride — something men understood.

But this, this panic? No. This wasn't Gus's pride. This was Gus's horror at the idea of accepting Henri's money, La Rue money. This was about the one boy who chose one life, and the other boy who chose another — and the first boy not approving of the choices of the second. And even if they both probably thought of themselves as passengers on the highway of predestination — both Gus and Henri went into their family businesses, after all — this was a moment of judgment. For the first time in their lives, Henri sensed that Gus was judging him and his mistress and his Rolex and the rest. And now, Henri was angry — not that he would let it show. Judge me? This fucking truck driver is going to judge me? He looked behind the father and saw the son loading the hand truck for a second time.

"Little G, come say hello," Henri shouted. And then he saw Gus sink a little in his chair.

"Mr. L, how goes it?" the kid said. He was leaning on the hand truck.

"Good, good. I've been talking to your father here."

"No, Henri," Gus said, half under his breath.

"He tells me you've met a girl," Henri said.

"Yes, Paulette. Thank you."

"Farm girl, your dad says," Henri said. "Do you even know which end of the cow supplies the milk?"

Little G laughed. "Milk from the tit, shit from the asshole — nothing to it," he said.

"A born farmer," Henri said.

The kid waved and pushed his load back to the truck. Gus stood up and said, "Thank you for the offer — most generous, but I couldn't," and then he turned on his heel and walked out before Henri could say anything else.

On the morning of the shipment, Michel went to a pay phone a few blocks from his apartment and called Laurence Perrault at the bottling company. He spoke in generalities, just to make sure everything with "the order" would go as planned. Perrault answered back in generalities, with several variations on the phrase "good to go."

"Good, good," Michel said. "I've added to my order. The invoice should be in your morning mail. Have you gone through the stack yet?"

Perrault lifted the pile of about 20 letters and riffled through it until he saw the one from Michel La Rue. It was an order for a shipment of three cases of the Cardin wine — the wine that was supposed to have carried the heroin in the original plan. The cases were to be shipped, one each, to Gérard, Martin and Henri La Rue. A handwritten note in the margin of the typewritten order said, "Make sure to fill in the i in Cardin on the outside of the cases with a red pen. Thanks, MLR."

The call from Passy about Julian Broussard came right as Henri sat on the bed and began getting undressed. One shoe on, one off, he leaned over and picked up the ringing telephone on the night table. It was on his side of the bed because nobody ever called Sylvie after dark. She was reading a book on her side.

"Boss," Passy said. Henri hated when Passy called him Boss because it was always the prelude to him having to act like the boss. Passy called him Henri whenever the news was good — an unexpected windfall, say, or a funny joke or anecdote from the casino. But Boss, that was different — and Henri didn't even know if Passy did it on purpose.

"What is it, Pass?" he said. Then he sighed loud enough for Passy to hear it.

"It's Julian Broussard," Passy said.

"Shit, again?"

"Again, and worse."

"And?"

"And I think it's time," Passy said.

"Why do you need me?"

"It'll come better from you — I think he sees you as almost like a father, or maybe an uncle."

"He's fucking older than I am," Henri said.

"Metaphorically speaking, Boss."

Again with the Boss. Henri hung up the phone and sighed again, this time for Sylvie's benefit. She seemed unimpressed, and even uninterested, as he put his shoe back on and tightened the knot on his tie and headed over to Trinity One. She didn't say goodbye or even look up from her book. He didn't say goodbye, either.

At that time of night, the drive didn't take 10 minutes. When he reached the casino floor, he did the obligatory meet-and-greet with the gamblers he knew well. It was a fairly slow night, and it didn't take long.

"Where is he?" Henri said, when he reached Passy's office.

"The alley," Passy said. "The usual place."

"You got somebody who knows what he's doing?"

"No worries there. No visible marks."

Henri looked at his watch. "I'll be down in three minutes," he said. Passy scurried out toward the back entrance.

Three minutes later, Henri reached the alley. Under the single overhead light bulb, he could see Broussard seated on an empty crate, doubled over. His hair was a mess, and when he looked up, Henri could see that the old fool had been crying. There were no visible marks on his face or his hands. What Henri noticed most was Broussard's eyes — the hope he sensed when Broussard looked at him, the hope and the pleading.

"Half in a week, the other half in a month," Henri said. "Understand."

Broussard nodded.

"No more access to the casino, ever," Henri said.

Broussard nodded again.

"Failure to meet these terms will result in significant repercussions," Henri said. "Understand?"

Broussard hung his head.

"Understand?"

His eyes still down, Julian Broussard nodded.

The case of wine arrived at the apartment without a note attached. Henri saw it, and saw the i in Cardin filled in with a red pen, and figured that Martin had sent it to celebrate their little victory over Cousin Michel. It was only the next morning, when Gérard called to invite him to his home for a celebratory lunch, that his senses began twitching.

"Celebrating what?" Henri said.

"You'll see when you get here," Gérard said.

When he got there, after walking between Sacré-Coeur on his right and St. Peter's on his left, between the churches and then down Cité du Sacré-Coeur to Gérard's place, he saw that he was not the first to arrive. Silent Moe had lifted a bottle from another case of the Cardin wine and was uncorking it, preparing to pour for Gérard and Martin.

When he got close enough, Henri could see that the i on this case was filled in, too. At which point, he became convinced that none of it made sense. Because there was no way that Martin would tell Gérard about their bit of fuckery with their cousin, if for no other reason than the money it was taking from Gérard's pocket. It certainly was no cause for celebration.

Henri's eyes caught Martin's, and he asked without asking. Martin answered with the slightest of shrugs.

"Damn good wine," Gérard said, after they had all been served. They were mid-sip when Michel bustled in. He apologized for being late.

"At least somebody's working," Gérard said. Henri was pretty sure that it was just a conversational throwaway without any deeper meaning.

"How's the wine?" Michel said.

"Damn excellent," Gérard said.

"Did you get your cases?" Michel said, looking at Henri and Martin.

They both said that they did, and then Henri said, "But there was no note. I didn't know who it was from. I figured I had a secret admirer."

At which point, Michel plastered on a hard smile and stared down both of them. He knew, Henri thought. Of course, he knew. Fucking Martin and his fucking schemes.

Then Gérard toasted and revealed the reason for the celebration. Michel had just managed the family's biggest heroin smuggling load to date. Word had arrived from New York of the successful delivery, and the final payment had arrived promptly from Marseilles.

"Fellas, fellas, just a great day," Gérard said. He was borderline giddy, patting backs and then hugging Michel. And why wouldn't he be? In the byzantine financial structure of the family, Gérard received two percent off the top in his envelopes from Henri, Martin and Michel. The three of them received 10 percent off the top from each of their individual enterprises. Then, after the men and the other expenses were paid, the rest of the money went into a pot from which the four of them each received an equal share.

The truth was, the heroin business was good for all of them — but it was best for Michel and Gérard, and Michel had done nothing to earn the fattest of the family's cash cows. Even with the addition of the two train stations in the 10th, heroin was still going to be a slightly bigger piece of the business, especially if there were more scores like this one. And the reason Michel controlled it was... it was just an accident of geography, of where he was born.

When Gérard took Michel to the library to show him some antique globe, Henri cornered Martin and said, "So, what the fuck?"

"I don't know," Martin said. Only later would he receive a call from the guy he had paid to tip off the customs inspectors. They said the wine cases were not marked as expected, that none of the i's in Cardin had been filled in with red ink, and that a random inspection of the cases revealed nothing but wine. So, they had no idea how the heroin had been smuggled out of Paris.

"You and your fucking schemes," Henri said.

"You will recall that you endorsed me and my fucking scheme — 100 percent," Martin said.

Henri actually felt himself ball up his hand into a fist, but then he unclenched it. Martin didn't see any of that, though. He said, "So, do you think—"

"Do I think that Michel knows it was us?" Henri said. "Of course, he knows. He sent us the wine. The i's are filled in. And did you see his face? Of course he fucking knows."

"I didn't mean him," Martin said, half to himself. That, of course, was the real question. Had Michel told Gérard what the two of them had done?

PART VIII

TO WAR

The Pink Flamingo was a new place on Place du Tertre that people were talking about, and so it was the place where Sylvie met some of the wives for lunch. She couldn't abide the other women who had married into the La Rue family, mostly because they thought his brother and cousin were Henri's equals, and she could never accept that. They weren't friends except when they had to be, at bigger family functions when people were watching, when the kisses were entirely fake and the conversation was especially vapid. So, the wives she tended to invite to lunch were married to Henri's employees — Passy's wife, Hélène; Willy's wife, Sandra; Freddy's wife, Lorena, and Marc's wife, Genevieve. Marc worked directly for Willy, and Sylvie liked Genevieve the best of all because she was a hoot after her second glass.

Or, as she said that day after pouring No. 3 and raising her glass, "To the high-titted legion."

This is what she called the mistresses.

"May they never droop or sag — because I'll be damned if I'm going to spend both Friday and Saturday night with Marc."

They all roared, even Lorena. Freddy didn't have a mistress, and they all knew it and all secretly hated Lorena for it. Not that they allowed it to show.

The specialty at The Pink Flamingo was what they called "American diner food" on the menu — hamburgers, chicken pot pie, club sandwiches, pot roast, meatloaf, biscuits in gravy. It was crap, in Sylvie's mind, but it was all anybody was talking about — there had been a big story in France-Soir the previous week, with pictures of much of the food. That the biscuits and gravy looked awful to her, she kept to herself. After all, when a plate of the stuff went by, on the way to another table, Genevieve said, "What was that? Chunky vomit?" There was no way to top that.

"The hamburger's very good," Sandra said. "Although I don't care that the menu says to pick it up like an American. I mean, really."

Sylvie felt as if Sandra's nose had begun pointing a little more up in the air, subtly but noticeably, since Henri put Willy in charge of the train stations in the 10th. And why not, she figured? If Henri was making more money than he ever had before, then Willy was undoubtedly doing well, too. And Willy was doing all of the work, so, whatever.

The conversation worked around to fashion, then makeup, then ungrateful children, then around again. Sylvie listened more than she participated and observed most of all. While the wives never talked business, not to each other, she knew that they were all plugged in. And from what Sylvie had been able to notice — from a rolled eye here, or an uncharitable grimace there — the rest of the wives had noticed the recent elevation of Sandra's nose, too. What that meant was, the men had noticed the money that was now flowing through Willy's hands from those train stations — flowing through his hands and falling into his pockets. The jealousy was something that Henri might have to manage in the future. Anyway, it was something she would tell him that night.

"Sylvie, tell us about the apartment — it must be finished, no?" Lorena said.

"Not quite," Sylvie said, even though the renovation had been finished for months. She just didn't feel like having people over to see it. She couldn't be bothered.

"Just little things, but you want it to be perfect, right?" she said. "And the tradesmen, well, you know. When they have their money, it's hard to get them to come back to make the little fixes. But, slowly."

"Tell me again what you did?" Lorena said. She seemed more interested than the rest.

"Well, with Mama gone, the third floor — I thought, why?" Sylvie said. "I mean, we could have just sold it, I guess — and gotten a nice price, too. At least, that's what Henri said. But I took some time, and really thought about it, and I've completely reimagined the space. The entrance is now on the third floor, in the apartment where my mother lived. We gutted the whole thing, and what was a three-bedroom apartment is now just a massive living room and the master suite — that and two bathrooms. So, you get off the elevator on three, and you come right into the living room. It has a working fireplace on one wall that is six feet tall and floor-to-ceiling windows on the west exposure with a balcony. The master has two walk-in closets, plus a small dressing room for me and bathrooms for the both of us. The walls in the master are done in a rose-colored fabric. The carpet is champagne. It's really striking. Really spectacular.

"Then, downstairs, is the old apartment — it's bigger than the third floor. Kitchen, dining room, den for Henri, sunroom for me, three bedrooms, three baths. So, Guy and Clarice have their own entrance on two. It's really a fabulous setup."

Which she really hated, of course — not that the wives would ever know.

"How is Clarice?" Sandra said.

"Still in Switzerland," Sylvie said. "One more year of school after this one. Our little banker — she already has a job promised at Credit Suisse. I just wish we saw her more."

Or even talked to her. Because while Guy was insolent, Clarice was invisible. Given her druthers, Sylvie preferred insolent. But the distance between Clarice and Henri was greater than the distance between Paris and Zurich, which meant that the telephone conversations were perfunctory at best and the visits home were only for the holidays and then the summer —

although she was making noise about spending the upcoming summer working at a bank branch in Basel.

"We'll have a big open house when it's finished," Sylvie said, and they all said pretty much simultaneously that they couldn't wait. And then the dessert came for the table — something called S'mores, which involved marshmallows, chocolate, little cookies and a pit of fire that sat in the middle of the table. The waiter handed them instruction sheets that showed them how to melt the mess, then assemble it.

To which, Genevieve picked up one of the skewers, studied it, dropped it on the table, looked the waiter directly in the eye, and said, "Screw the Americans and their diarrhea on a stick. I don't know about the rest of them, but I'll have another bottle for dessert."

Tuesday afternoon and Friday night, followed by Tuesday afternoon and Friday night, and on and on. The boredom of the routine was palpable, but it was boredom interrupted only by sex with the tightest body he had ever seen. Henri actually laughed when he thought that thought, laughed out loud as he pulled on his underwear. Not Marina. Not a woman. Just the tightest body he had ever seen.

"Can I ask what's so funny?" Marina said. She was beneath the covers and would remain there until Henri left the apartment on the Champs-Élysées. Because that, too, was part of the routine. Henri dressed within two minutes of finishing, dressed without so much as washing his hands. Marina waited until he was gone, and then soaked in a hot tub accompanied by a bottle of Bordeaux.

"Nothing," Henri said. "Just something Passy said this morning at work."

"Well?"

"It wasn't really intended for mixed company."

"Oh, please," Marina said.

"Sorry," Henri said. "Well, okay. I'll tell you the punch line: 'the tightest body I've ever seen.'"

Which is when the honking started again. Marina's apartment was on the second floor, with windows facing the Champs. Honking and police sirens were, if not a constant, then certainly a regular companion during the day. Henri once asked her how she slept, and she said it was better at night — but she also opened the drawer of her bedside table and produced a pair of ear plugs. Still, from Henri's Tuesday afternoon experiences, well, put it this way: he heard some persistent honking when he was being driven to an appointment a week earlier, and his mind began to wander, and the honking and the wandering ended up leading to a stirring behind his zipper.

Rather than call ahead, Henri decided to walk over and get a taxi from the rank in front of The George V. He was thinking about Marina. He had known men in his line of work who ended up loving their girlfriends, loving them and half moving in with them and almost leading double lives. He knew one guy — one of the Ferrer brothers over in the 16th — who did the full double-life thing, who kept his real family and then a second family with his girlfriend and two more kids. Ferrer once reputedly said, "I'd like to shoot the fucker who invented Christmas — I need a nap for a week when that's over." He pulled it off for years without his wife finding out, and when she finally did, he was worried she would divorce his ass and get a big settlement. Instead, his wife said, "Don't mess it up with her because if you do, there's no way you're moving back in here seven nights a week."

As far and he and Marina were concerned, love was out of the question for Henri. He aspired, in fact, to merely liking his mistress — but he pretty much never did. He liked showing her off on Friday nights when they went out with the boys. He liked watching her undress on Tuesday afternoons — Henri liked that a lot. But like her? Like her as a person? No, and he was pretty sure that the feeling — or, rather, the lack of feeling — was mutual.

She had stopped asking to go to lunch on Tuesdays before returning to her bedroom. There had been a big blowout, maybe six months earlier, when he felt she was being too needy, and he shouted, among other things, "The last thing I want is two wives — don't you get it?" And if that put Marina in her place a bit too harshly, well, Henri had no regrets. It needed to be said. And if she was compensating for that shot of reality by going through the Bordeaux a little more than she had been, and heading to the club toilets with the girls on Friday nights a little more giddily than she had been, so be it. And if her level of spending on clothing and the rest had become almost punitive in his eyes, and if the recent raise in her rent in the doorman building on the Champs-Élysées had been nothing short of obscene, he would handle it. As Martin liked to say when he was talking about his girlfriend and her spending, "Cost of doing business, brother. Cost of doing business."

As he approached the taxi rank, there was another burst of car horns, one then two then five... three seconds... five seconds... more. And then Henri's mind began to wander again.

Back on his desk, the message said: "Call Mr. Brown."

Shit. Henri could only guess what Guy had done now. He knew that he was back from Normandy, and that he had actually spent a couple of nights in the apartment — not because he had seen much of his son, but from the late slam of the door on one night, and the mess his mother was left to clean up in the kitchen another morning.

There had been no further repercussions from the bank robbery fiasco — no repercussions for Guy, anyway. His men had kept quiet. No one had given up that Guy was the one who planned the robbery and organized the whole thing. It went without saying that Guy was going to have to take care of them financially. It was the only time he was actually proud of his son, the one time he saw him since Normandy, when Guy was heading out and Henri was heading in and Guy said, "I was going to pay you back early, you know. But now everything I have is going to the boys' families or their girlfriends."

But now, well, what?

"Henri La Rue, the pleasure is all mine," Chrétien said when he answered the phone.

"Cut the shit, Chrétien."

"No shit, Henri."

"What's the bad news?"

"No bad news."

"It's always bad news when you call, Mr. Fucking Brown," Henri said.

"Not this time," Chrétien said. "It's good news, actual good news. Remember your friend with the quote-unquote stolen trucks? Gus Parent?"

"Of course, I remember," Henri said. "You said you couldn't help me, that you had no connections in that other precinct."

"Well, things change," Chrétien said. And then he explained about a captain in that other precinct whose son had too much to drink, and then got behind the wheel of a baby blue Renault and drove it straight through the plate glass window of the baby store on Rue Lepic that sells the prams and such. And seeing as how it was 2 in the afternoon at the time, and the store was populated by a salesman and a woman who was eight months pregnant, and seeing as how the woman suffered severe cuts to her right arm, the police had no choice but to take the drunken kid into the station.

"Where he remains as we speak," Chrétien said. "His father, the captain, is on the way over. I'm sure we're going to lose the paperwork as a favor. I'm also sure I could get Gus Parent's paperwork straightened out as a favor in return, which will get him his insurance money."

Henri was quiet, thinking, for about 15 seconds — about the opportunity, and about Gus, and about the look on Gus' face when Henri offered him the money. But he really decided in the first three seconds.

"Forget Gus Parent," he said. "That's too valuable a favor for a couple of broken-down old trucks. Way too valuable a favor. Bank it for something better later on."

"If you say so," Chrétien said.

"I say so," Henri said.

The office above the luggage store at Place de la République just wouldn't do, Willy had decided about five minutes after he entered it for the first time. Morel had really let it go. The floors were a mess, the desk was shit, the stuffing in the couches and chairs was sticking out of cracks in the leather. And the safe! It was the first thing Willy noticed. It was a squat little thing, no bigger than a beagle, sitting by itself in the corner.

"Will you look at that thing?" Willy said to Marc and the others.

"Kind of a runt in the safe litter, I'd say," Marc said.

"It can't possibly hold what they bring in," Willy said. "We need a real safe — like the one in Henri's office. No, bigger. Those two train stations — a lot goddamn bigger."

The new carpet came first — dark red, deep pile, the kind that left footprints when you walked over it. The desk was the size of a baby battleship, made of polished mahogany. The couches and the chairs were re-covered in new black leather. Plus, a new pool table for entertainment, and a new bar and refrigerator for refreshments. And then there was the safe, which arrived last because it had to be shipped from the Schmid Company in Switzerland. If the old safe was the size of a beagle, the new one was as big as a Great Dane standing on its hind legs — four and a half feet tall, three feet wide, with two-inch steel all around and what Schmid described in its written guarantee as "a lock and tumbler system that has never been breached by an unauthorized intruder."

On the day it was delivered, Willy entered the expense for the safe in his new ledger as "new safe." And even though he was pretty sure that Henri wouldn't have cared about the office redecoration, well, there was no need to take that chance, especially given the decidedly un-palatial condition of the boss's office behind the uniform store. So, for the carpet and desk and the rest, that had gone into the ledger in stages as "information sources." Running the looting of two train stations took a lot of snitches, after all, and given the size of the envelopes Willy had been dropping off lately, he figured that Henri wouldn't bat an eye. And he was correct.

Thursday was collection day in the 10th. Willy's guys made the rounds of Morel's old guys to get their envelopes. Then they brought them to the office above the luggage store for Willy to count and catalogue and fill in the total in the ledger. After that was done, Willy prepared the envelopes for his men and paid them on Friday. He also paid himself and Henri on Friday. Henri's envelope contained Gérard's cut, which Henri paid to his uncle on a monthly basis. And thus were the wheels appropriately greased.

Willy got to the office at noon on Thursdays and took care of whatever legitimate invoices there might be — for trucks and gas and whatnot. Those were the only expenses he paid with checks, and they were from the luggage store's account. There were two sets of ledgers. From the cash that came in, deposits were made to the luggage store account, and that money was immediately paid out as medium-sized salaries to himself and his top men. Those salaries were taxed, but they didn't make up even a third of their total compensation. The rest was paid in cash — cash that was stored in the safe that was as tall as a Great Dane standing on its hind legs.

Willy's four main men were supposed to make their collections and be back to the office over the luggage store between 2 and 3 p.m. The Apostles — Peter and Paul — had the smallest piece of the business, the street money (Peter) and the two whorehouses (Paul). There was a crappy casino in the 10th and Willy ran that himself. It frankly wasn't worth his time. The business was already too complicated, and even if you airlifted The Flamingo in from Las Vegas and dropped it in the middle of the Place de la République — lock, stock and Sinatra — it still wouldn't generate as much cash as the two train stations.

Tito had the Gare de l'Est, and Marc had the Gare du Nord. Willy had no idea what to expect when they took over, but as it turned out, while they were both cash cows, the Gare du Nord had the biggest udders. Just more shipping came in that way, more goods to be pilfered, more stuff to steal. That was the one surprise. The other was that the shipping companies seemed to view theft by gangsters as just another cost of doing business. You had to pay off the right people, but that was it. There was very little danger of getting caught, even of being hassled — and for every dollar you spent in bribes, you got back 20 in profits. As long as you weren't too greedy, it was the scam of all time.

Starting at just after 2, Willy's men arrived in the order they always arrived — first Peter, then Paul, then Tito. It had been a good week for Tito, a big week at the Gare de l'Est, the week when some kind of fancy crystal arrived from Austria on Monday, and then a year's worth of caviar from some Baltic country on Tuesday, and then a bunch of silk from Lyon on Wednesday. This was high-ticket stuff, all of it, and Tito had been able to unload the goods almost as soon as he received them. The result was seven different envelopes stuffed with cash, bulging out of every pocket in his suit. When he handed over the last one, Tito said, "One more and I was going to have to stick it up my ass."

They poured drinks and waited for Marc. He was always last. The other three began to play a game of billiards while Willy went about the business of counting the cash and putting it in the safe and tallying the numbers in the ledger. He had thought about getting one of those cash counting machines that the banks use, but it seemed pretentious. Besides, he liked the feel of the cash.

At 3 o'clock, Willy looked at his watch and said, "Okay, what the hell?" He looked at the other three playing pool, and they all shrugged simultaneously.

What Willy did not know was that Marc was dead, garroted downstairs in the luggage store along with the store manager. He had walked into the shop with full pockets, as usual. He was whistling "The Marseillaise" for some reason when the customer looking at the black leather valise came up behind him with the wire. What Willy did not know, what none of them knew, was that in 30 seconds, three men with silenced pistols would quietly climb the stairs from the luggage store and walk into the office and fire 13 shots that killed Willy, Tito and the Apostles where they stood — or, in Willy's case, sat. Tito, about to take a shot, landed on the table top, his blood pooling on the green felt. Peter and Paul each had a drink in their hand and dropped them a millisecond before they themselves dropped. As it turned out, their blood was even redder than the red carpet.

Willy never even looked up from his work when the three men entered the office. He died with his head down on the desk, with a pen in his hand, and he bled on his pristine ledger.

The whole thing took about five seconds. Maybe 10. When the police found the bodies the next day, that was all they found. There was no ledger and there was no money, not a centime — just four dead bodies. Well, six if you counted Marc and the manager of the store. The safe had been cleaned out, but the Schmid Company would be pleased to know that their guarantee was intact. The lock and tumbler system had not been breached by an unauthorized intruder — because when the shooting started, the damn thing had been wide open.

Henri ate lunch at Gartner's pretty much every day he was at the uniform company, mostly because it was just around the corner — La Rue Uniforms faced onto Avenue de Clichy, Gartner's onto Boulevard de Clichy. He was pretty sure the two establishments shared at least part of a wall, and that the part was back where Henri's office was. He used to joke with Old Mr. Gartner about knocking a hole in the wall so that he could have a private entrance. Old Mr. Gartner, whose first name was unknown to Henri, was actually willing to consider it — such was the business Henri brought to the place because he almost never ate alone.

This day, he was waiting for Willy and his meticulous ledger. Willy was late, which was unusual, but whatever. Old Mr. Gartner always served Henri's party himself, leaving the stool next to the small bar in the back and hustling his 80-year-old body out to greet him when he arrived, and then taking care of everything after that. After about 10 minutes, the old man came over and asked Henri if he wanted to get started. He hadn't picked up the menu.

"Why not?" Henri said.

"The current usual?" Gartner said.

Henri nodded. Gartner called it the "current usual" because Henri had a habit of eating his way through the lunch menu and repeating the same order until he was sick of it — at which point he would begin ordering something else until he was sick of that. The current "current usual" was the Salad Niçoise without the hard boiled eggs. Henri thought it was filling without being too fattening. As soon as he put on five pounds, Sylvie was all over his ass — so he watched what he ate, at least to a degree. And whatever Henri ordered from the menu, Old Man Gartner knew that he was to bring only two slices of bread and one pat of butter to the table.

Henri got halfway through the salad, and Willy still had not shown up — and while he was not a stickler for punctuality, being more than a half-hour late was a sign of disrespect. He got madder with each forkful and with each glance at his wrist-watch. Finally, he muttered "fuck it" loud enough that a couple eating at a table 20 feet away could hear him. Then he got up and stormed out the front door. He didn't need to pay — Old Man Gartner ran a tab, and submitted the bill to the uniform company every month.

It was when Henri was back in his office, fuming, that the telephone rang. It was Chrétien. He was standing when he picked up the call and slumped in his chair when he ended it. Between sitting and standing, his paid cop read off a list of six names, starting with Willy's. He didn't recognize two of them. He also heard Chrétien use the terms "very professional" and "very purposeful," but Henri couldn't focus on most of the rest.

The last thing Chrétien said was, "There's no reason to go. The safe's empty. The detectives are all over it — and I wouldn't even be able to explain why I was walking you through if you did come. It's not like you're next of kin to do the identifications."

"But—" Henri said. It was half-hearted. If Chrétien hadn't jumped in to interrupt, Henri realized later, he had no idea what he was going to say.

"Besides, it's been on the police radio and the newspa-permen are already outside," Chrétien said. "Just stay away."

PART IX

A NIGHT AT THE ONYX

The La Rue family actually had a procedure in place for such occurrences. Whoever found out first was to call Gérard, who then would call the next oldest, who then would call the youngest. This was how Henri spread the word of the massacre in the 10th.

The other part of the established procedure — established back when Henri's father was still alive, and maybe even before that — was that there would be a meeting way over in the 6th, a place on Rue du Four called Café Klein, and that the meeting would take place exactly 90 minutes after the first call in the chain. That would give them all time to notify their underlings about what was happening, and about the precautions they needed to take. The choice of Café Klein was a bit of an inside joke, if you were a student of such things because it was in that café that Paul Cardone, the boss of the 6th back before World War I, was shot at by a husband who objected to Cardone's regular presence in his wife's bed. The shot missed, but there was still a bullet hole in the wall of the main dining room.

When he called Gérard, Henri wasn't sure what the reaction would be. The old man had warned him about taking over the 10th, after all, warned him for the millionth time about hogs getting slaughtered. But when he got him on the telephone, Gérard was quiet and then almost mechanical in his response.

"Same plan, right?" he said.

"Yep, yep," Henri said. He still hadn't really caught his breath.

"So we'll meet at, let me look at my watch, let's call it 3 o'clock."

"Okay, okay," Henri said. Gérard didn't answer. His reply was a click and then a dial tone.

Henri looked at his watch, and then ran his fingers through his hair, and then walked to the office door and shouted into the din of the sewing machines: "Passy!"

Henri was back in his chair when Passy arrived at a half-trot.

"Shut the door," Henri said.

"Oh, shit."

"Yeah," Henri said. "Oh, shit."

He had been determined to be as businesslike as he could, but as it turned out, in the next five minutes, Henri would shout and throw a pencil cup and then cry as he told Passy what had happened to Willy and the rest. It was just one or two tears, and because it was Passy, he wasn't worried. Because Passy was out-and-out bawling, and then after he managed to catch his breath and wipe his nose on his sleeve, he picked up the cheap wooden chair that sat next to Henri's desk and smashed it into a half-dozen pieces with one mighty thwack.

"Motherfuckers," Passy said. He was on his knees, picking up the pieces of the chair. He looked up at Henri. "The Levines, right?"

"That's my first guess," Henri said. "And to be honest, I don't think I have a second guess."

Henri helped him with the chair, and then he said to Passy, "So, you know the drill, right?"

"Jesus, Henri — when was the last one?"

"Shit, I forget — 1950?"

"Maybe 1951," Passy said. "Yeah, definitely 1951. Hélène was pregnant with Claudia. Summer."

"Hot as balls, remember?" Henri said.

"Pregnant wife in the heat — yeah, I remember," Passy said.

Back then, it was a fight with the Dumonts in the 17th over bullshit. Two members of his brother Jean's crew were having too much to drink at a bar on Rue des Dames, and one of the guys grabbed the ass of the wrong girl, and the fight spilled out onto the street, and somebody pulled a gun, and Jean's guy with the roving hands got shot and killed.

It was the kind of thing that should have been settled with an apology for the entire situation — from the grabbed ass to the fired pistol — and a cash settlement for the dead kid's new wife. Except that the Dumonts didn't quite see it that way because the ass in question belonged to one Marie Dumont, daughter of the boss of the family.

The way Gérard told the story, the old man kept preaching in the meeting about "a matter of honor," and Henri's father kept answering that "the kid is fucking dead, and his family needs to be compensated." And then Dumont said, "That scum defiled my girl." And then Henri's father said, "He grabbed her ass, he didn't fuck her." And then Dumont began screaming and left with his people. And then, when Henri's father told his sons about the meeting, Jean looked at Henri and his father and said, "Defiled? I'll show you fucking defiled." At which point, he stormed out of the room. A few minutes later, Henri was deputized to find his brother and rein him in — but he couldn't find him. In fact, he didn't see him for weeks after they all heard the news on the radio that the Dumont soldier who had shot Jean's man had himself been shot as sat on the toilet in his apartment on Rue de Bizerte.

"Fucking crazy times," Passy said. "Do you even remember how it ended?"

"Nope," Henri said. "We all just got a call that it was over. Remember, we were in that fucking rat trap that we all stayed in on Rue Letort — remember that shithole?"

"To this day, if I ever find myself on Rue Letort, I retch a little bit," Passy said.

"Oh, fuck," Henri said. He looked at his wristwatch again. "You have calls to make, and a new fucking rat trap to find for you and the other guys."

"You coming with us?"

"No," Henri said. "We still have to meet. I have to hear everybody out first. Just take care of our main guys — we definitely don't have to worry below that. But you make sure you get Timmy, and make sure that Timmy calls Freddy — this is mostly just for you guys. Make sure the three of you are safe — no Trinity One, no whorehouses for Freddy. You guys stay out of sight. Let your guys run things for a few days. Hopefully, that's all it will be."

"How can you be sure?" Passy said.

"I'm not," Henri said.

Gérard was already at the table when Henri arrived. He had ordered a bottle and four glasses, and he began pouring when he saw Henri approach the table. Michel was next and Martin, not surprisingly, was last. He was last and he was borderline hysterical. They drank a toast to Willy and the rest, and then he was off, just raving. It went on for about a minute, or at least it seemed like a minute.

"This is fucking bullshit, and it demands an answer, and it demands an answer immediately," Martin said. "We cannot allow this to stand. The disrespect here, it's fucking disgraceful. That's what it is, a disgrace. The lines exist for a reason. We respect their lines, for God's sake. You don't think I could sell plenty — I mean, fucking plenty — in the cafés in the 3rd? Or the 2nd for that matter? But I respect the lines. There is no way this can be permitted to go unanswered, to go unpunished."

On and on he went, and Henri quickly realized that — given Martin's long history as a physical coward — this must have been the envelopes talking. Their share of the after-expenses money from the 10th, from the train stations, had just begun to flow to Martin and Michel, and it was substantial.

While Martin talked, Henri made a point of looking at Michel. He didn't bother to look at Gérard because his uncle never betrayed what he was thinking. Michel was different. And what he saw there was not a man fixated on his raving cousin. What he saw, instead, was Michel looking at Gérard, looking for any kind of a clue about what the old man was thinking.

When Martin finally ran out of steam, Henri said, "You all know that we have to, well..." He didn't finish the thought, but he didn't need to, either.

Martin and Michel nodded. Michel said, "I've got a place. It's easier because I don't have the organization that you do."

Martin nodded. "I'll be fine — it's being arranged."

Henri told them that Passy was working on a place for his people. They all looked at Gérard and asked without asking. He said, "I'm not going anywhere. Nobody's coming after me — nobody's that stupid. The question is, after you're all settled, are we going to do anything about this?"

"How can you even ask?" Martin said. "Of course we fucking have to do something about this." And then he was off again, loud enough this time that Gérard shushed him with raised hands. With his voice lowered, he still needed to channel the emotion elsewhere, though, which meant his arms began waving. He actually knocked over the bottle after about 15 seconds, and Michel caught it before it crashed.

"Everybody needs to calm down," Gérard said, again shushing Martin with two raised hands. Then he looked at Henri. To his credit, Gérard was not second-guessing the takeover of the 10th. Maybe that would come later, in a private conversation. But in the here and now, in the middle of the crisis, the old man's eyes were focused only on the present and the future.

Gérard looked at Henri, and then the other two did, too. Because while Gérard was the titular boss, they all knew — even Gérard — that Henri was the operational boss, the day-to-day boss. And while they all ran their own ends of the business without much interference, both Martin and Michel also knew that Henri's nod was required for any expansion or any coordination efforts. It was why Martin came to him about Gus Parent's trucks, why he wouldn't act without Henri's consent.

So, they all looked at him and waited, and then Henri said, "There needs to be a response, I think."

"Fucking right there needs to be a response," Martin said.

And then his mouth was off again, just running, and then Gérard was shushing him again, and then all eyes reflexively turned to Michel. He was an equal partner in this by virtue of the job Gérard had given him. It was ridiculous — he was only about 35 and only a cousin — but it was the reality.

And Michel said, "I'm not so sure."

Martin erupted. What came out of his mouth at that point, the words spitting out so quickly that they sounded like gibberish, caused Gérard to say, "Enough!" And then he pointed a finger at Martin and said, "You don't talk again — got it?" At which point, Martin slumped back in his chair and took a big slug from his glass. He must have been exhausted.

"Look," Michel said. "I get it — I really do. But sometimes, I also try to sit in the other guy's chair and see it from his perspective. Old Joe Levine thinks you stole the 10th from him."

"But that's bull—" Henri said, but Michel held up his hand.

"I hear you — I do," Michel said. "But sit in his chair. The 10th became available, and you took it rather than approach him with a negotiation. He feels victimized. He—"

"Fuck his feelings," Henri said. "I've got six dead men because of his fucking feelings? That's supposed to be an acceptable trade-off? Six men for some hurt feelings? No."

"I'm just trying to point something out," Michel said. "You made the big, smart, bold play, and Levine feels like he lost. So now, he feels like he's getting even — maybe even getting back what he feels like he deserves."

"Fuck deserves," Martin said. "Fuck Levine."

"I'm just saying," Michel said. "So here we are now. The first shots of a war have been fired — although Levine probably thinks the first shots were when you blasted the salmon croquettes all over Morel's three idiots in that café along the canal. Anyway, where's it going to end? Be logical. You hit them back, then what happens? Do they just give up? Where does it end?"

"Six of my men are dead," Henri said. "End of discussion."

They all looked at Gérard. He didn't say anything, but he did nod, and they all got it. It was understood, without a word being said, that this was now Henri's operation and that he would keep them informed. They all agreed that, since Gérard wasn't going into hiding, he would be the conduit through which all information would flow. Henri's plans would be communicated to the rest through their uncle. All communications from their hiding places would go through their uncle.

"Last chance to say anything," Henri said, looking each of the others in the eye. No one said a word. Henri reached into his wallet for a bill and slapped it on the table, and then he got up and left. They all knew to leave in five-minute intervals after he did. That, too, was part of the protocol.

Gina's apartment was on Rue de Saint-Quentin, in a particularly crappy part of the 10th — which was saying something, in Henri's mind. He loved the train stations in the 10th and the revenues they provided. He liked the Place de la République and the canal. He pretty much thought the rest of it was somewhere between tattered and torn, which wasn't fair, but what he believed nonetheless. And Gina's apartment was doing nothing to change his mind.

He called her at work, and she met him outside and down the street from the restaurant and gave him the key without asking for an explanation. He had never been to the apartment — they had never been alone together anywhere other than the little hotel on Place Émile Goudeau — but Gina said nothing, other than that she would be home after her shift, in about 90 minutes. Henri drove down the butte and was at her building in less than 15 minutes. There was trash in the street outside, and the smell of rotting vegetables in the air, and a guy sitting on the curb and drinking from a pint bottle. It was, by any measure, a shithole — and if the building itself appeared clean enough to perhaps qualify as a polished shithole, it was a shithole none-theless.

Gina lived on the third floor, and Henri's right knee barked ever so quietly as he took the last few steps to the top. The knee was like that now on the stairs. The apartment itself was fine — a big-ish room with a bed and a dresser in one corner, a sofa and chair in another corner, a rickety table and two chairs in a third corner, and the kitchen in the fourth corner. Actually, it was a cabinet on the floor, next to a sink, next to a gas cooktop, next to a commode. The bathtub must have been down the hall.

Henri was hungry, and he opened a can of vegetable soup and set the pot on the cooktop. When he sat down to give the commode a test drive, he realized that he could reach over and stir the soup while seated, and that made him laugh out loud.

"Multi-tasking," is what Willy would have called it. It was a term he liked to use, something he said he read one time in some kind of business magazine. The last time Henri heard him say it was months earlier — before the 10th and the train stations — and it was immediately following the punchline of a joke Timmy told about a guy who insisted on eating a sandwich while having sex. Multi-tasking. Fucking Willy. Goddamn.

The guilt that Henri felt about putting Willy and the rest of them in a position to be killed — but mostly Willy, if he was being honest — was fleeting, but it was there. It was there, and then it wasn't, and then it was. Because, on the one hand, Henri had given Willy a tremendous opportunity in this business of theirs, an opportunity to earn a lot of money. At the same time, it wasn't as if Willy was a virgin or didn't know what he was getting himself into. The business was the business. Their suit jackets were a size bigger than the pants for a reason, and everybody knew the reason. The guns they carried were not props. They were for protection, and they sometimes needed to be used, to be fired in anger, and they all knew it. Willy certainly did. And all of those were Henri's dominant thoughts in the hours since the phone had rung in his office behind the uniform store.

But then, there were those other, fleeting thoughts. Five minutes an hour. No more than 10. And those were the thoughts that could be summed up by Gérard's three-word mantra: "Hogs get slaughtered." Those were the guilty thoughts, the ones where Henri beat himself up for not taking the proper precautions, for putting Willy into too dangerous a situation, for not recognizing — as Gérard had so aptly pointed out when they were at the football game — that the Levines bought their sport jackets a size bigger than their pants, too. They were the thoughts that it was all his fault that Willy and the rest had been killed, his fault that six families were grieving, his fault that they were now at war with the Levines, or something just short of it.

It came and it passed. Henri was just finishing the soup when there was a knock on the door. He immediately reached for his gun. There was no way anybody would know him in the neighborhood, and he was positive he wasn't followed, and his car was parked two blocks away, and nobody — nobody — knew about him and Gina. That's what he told himself as he stood and crept toward the door. The floorboards were loose, though, and they squeaked with each step he took — and in the silence, at least to Henri, the squeaks sounded like wails.

He got to the entrance, gun in hand, and pressed his ear to the door. He heard nothing, and then there were two more knocks that were more like flat-handed bangs, and then he backed away from the door, startled.

And then: "Henri, it's me. You've got my keys, remember?"

He let Gina in, and locked the door behind her with the keys. Without a word from either of them, they were naked within a minute and finished within five. As they lay in bed, Gina lit up a cigarette while Henri tried to catch his breath. I took him longer than it used to, as with a lot of things.

"Aren't you even going to ask me?" he said, once his heart rate had dropped back to its normal range.

"I figured you'd tell me if you wanted me to know," she said.

"It's just, well, I needed a place for a while that nobody knew anything about," he said.

"I figured," Gina said.

This time, it was Henri who sent the message to Chrétien: "Mr. Brown, 5 p.m." The meeting was to be at the same little park on Rue Burq where Chrétien had told him about Guy and the clown masks. Henri was taking a chance by returning to the butte, but not really. The park, at the end of a street that went nowhere, was one of the least likely places in Montmartre to be spotted accidentally, which was why they had chosen it in the first place.

Henri had spent two days and two nights in Gina's apartment and the experience had begun to wear him down — and not just from the sex. The truth was, he enjoyed being with Gina even as they barely spoke to each other. He was comforted by her touch, and by the silence that allowed him to think. The family was counting on a plan — this whole thing belonged to him, for better or for worse, and everybody who worked under the La Rue banner knew it. Henri had made them money, and he had put Willy and the rest in a position to be killed, and it was now up to him to craft them a resolution, be it with negotiations or with handguns. And after two days of thinking about it, he felt even more strongly that the La Rue family had to hit back, to make the Levines understand that their actions could not go unanswered. It wasn't because he was a dinosaur or a Neanderthal. It was because he was both a realist and a student of human nature — and there was no way to allow this to stand, if for no other reason than that a potential negotiation down the road would be tilted severely toward the Levines if the La Rue family did not respond.

So, Henri called Chrétien. As it turned out, the cop arrived in the park on Rue Burq before he did.

"How much do you know about the Levines?" Henri said.

"I'm not sure I want to be involved in this conversation," Chrétien said.

"I'm not sure you have a choice," Henri said. "In fact, I'm just about certain that you don't have a choice."

Chrétien had been leaning forward, but then he slumped back on the bench. He slumped back, and he extended his arms out to his sides and rested them on the back of the bench. It was a physical sign of surrender, which he followed up with an actual surrender.

"All right," he said. "Okay, Henri. Fuck me. What do you want to know?"

"How good is your information, your intelligence, about the Levines?"

"Better than it was three days ago."

"Better how?"

"It's all anybody is talking about," Chrétien said. "I've had a couple of beers with some detectives from the 10th. And when we were on our third beer, a couple of detectives from the 3rd showed up. Call it an unofficial police task force. So, my knowledge of the Levines is better. It's a lot fucking better."

At which point, Henri and his paid cop began trading names — not Joseph and Daniel Levine, but names from the next rung down, the rung analogous to where Willy had sat in the La Rue hierarchy. Henri knew three names, and Chrétien was able to confirm them but also add a fourth.

"Harry Pearl," Chrétien said. "A little younger than the others — probably not 35. A little younger and a little more reckless. He does street collections, mostly — well, he's in charge of them. At least that's what the cops in the 3rd think — they're not exactly sure how the Levines organize things. But they do know that young Harry's specialty is the broken leg."

Henri grimaced. "And they know this how?"

"They know this because, behind his back, his men apparently refer to him as 'Limpy.' It's quite charming."

"Harry Pearl," Henri said, rolling the syllables around in his mouth. This was a possibility. The names Henri had known were old pros — like Passy or Timmy. They weren't going to do anything stupid. But Harry Pearl, the leg breaker, Limpy, a little reckless — this, Henri might be able to work with.

"There's something else about Harry," Chrétien said. "He has a reputation for his, well, his proclivities."

Henri raised an eyebrow.

"The dark meat," Chrétien said.

"Whores?"

"No."

"So, a girlfriend?" Henri said.

"No one steady — at least no one the cops in the 3rd know about."

"Then?"

"A bar, The Onyx Club," Chrétien said. "Black strippers. Back rooms. Like, five nights a week."

"Still? I mean, isn't he in hiding?"

"Don't know," Chrétien said. "I think the Levines are like you — Old Joe is still in his own house, like Gérard—"

"How the fuck do you know—"

"We're not deaf and dumb," Chrétien said. "If you didn't expect a little extra scrutiny after something like what happened at the luggage store, you're really not thinking straight."

"Then what do I pay you for?" Henri said.

"You pay me for information," Chrétien said. "And I'm giving you information right now. We know that Gérard is at his home, and we know that Old Joe Levine is at his home. We know that you and a couple of your men are, shall we say, out of pocket, and the detectives in the 3rd know that those names we discussed earlier, they're also out of pocket. So is Harry Pearl."

"But—"

"But, the dark meat," Chrétien said. "The Onyx Club. If there's an opening, that's the most obvious one."

Freddy sat in his car, outside The Onyx Club and down the street. He had worried when Henri had called him with the details of the job — not because of the danger, or because Harry Pearl might recognize him because he had never met Pearl or any of his people. He was worried about being the only white face in the black club, but Henri told him there would be at least one other, Harry Pearl, and that it was a chance he would just have to take.

"Why can't I just do it on the street?" Freddy said. "I'm a good enough shot with a rifle."

"Inside is better," is what Henri told him.

"Better how?"

"Just better," Henri said. Freddy understood, but he still wanted to hear Henri say it, that inside meant a more embarrassing scene for the Levines to deal with. Inside with a black stripper would be part of every newspaper story. The La Rues would have their eye for an eye, and the Levines would have red faces besides.

Freddy sat in the car for an hour, as it turned out. As he watched men walk in at varying intervals, he realized that his concerns had been for naught because almost half of the customers were white. As he sat there, Freddy was half consumed by pride and half by rage — pride because Henri trusted him with such a delicate bit of business, but rage because he was being brought in to clean up Willy's mess. Henri had insisted that Willy was ready, that he nearly had a business degree, but there was a difference between book smarts and street smarts, and for all of his book smarts, the fucking idiot still managed to get himself and five others killed. They obviously didn't have a chapter in the business management book about protecting your ass from armed rivals. And while Freddy was sure that Willy's ledger was pristine, well, exactly how pristine was it now that he had just bled all over the goddamn thing?

He could actually feel his heart beating faster as he thought about that dead idiot. And then, just like that, Freddy snapped out of it when he saw a tall thirtyish guy with blond, shaggy hair look both ways at the door and then enter The Onyx Club.

Freddy counted to 60 and then followed Harry Pearl into the club. It was like a dozen other places Freddy had been in in his life — a horseshoe-shaped stage with a bar at one end and seats all around, with booths along the perimeter of the rest of the room and a curtained entrance to what was undoubtedly where the real business was done. A gigantic black guy in a tuxedo stood by the curtain, arms crossed. The girls came in and out of there, sometimes alone, sometimes hand in hand with a client. When they weren't dancing on stage, they were working the men sitting in the booths. It was all pretty standard.

It took a second for Freddy's eyes to adjust to the overall darkness of the place — only the stage was well lit. As casually as he could, Freddy scanned the seat around the bar and saw no shaggy blond hair. He had to squint a little as he scanned the booths, but he saw Harry Pearl pretty quickly. He hadn't been inside for two minutes and there already were two girls sitting on either side of him.

Freddy decided on a booth on the other side, where he could keep an eye on Pearl. He was joined quickly by a curvy but very young-looking dancer. He bought her a ridiculously expensive drink, which was the minimum requirement for the random, intermittent rubs and tugs that she would be performing beneath the table. Her name was Candy, and she was cute, and Freddy was enjoying the attention he was receiving beneath the table, despite the fact that he was fixated on Harry Pearl the entire time. And when Pearl got up with one of the girls and walked with her through the curtain, Freddy closed his eyes and again counted to 60 before standing up and taking Candy's hand and walking past the giant in the tuxedo and into the back.

It was actually just a long hallway, and the rooms were just curtained-off cubicles. Candy led him to her cubicle, and she reached the buttons on her front, and Freddy said, "Toilet?"

"Make a left, end of the hall," she said. "Don't be long."

"I won't, baby," Freddy said.

There were about 10 cubicles, and only five were occupied — at least, from what he could hear. He could peek into each cubicle through the tiny slit where the curtains didn't quite meet. It was in the third cubicle where he looked that Freddy could see, from top to bottom, the back of a shaggy blond head, and then a suit jacket that half covered a naked ass, and then a naked dancer on her knees, and then the pants of the suit gathered around Harry Pearl's ankles.

Freddy fired two bullets into the back of the shaggy blond head with his silenced revolver, and then he ran the five steps down the hall and through the exit door next to the toilet.

PART X

AN EYE FOR AN EYE

Henri and Freddy had agreed ahead of time that they would have no further contact, at least in the short term. Freddy was to do the job and then disappear — really disappear. He had some family outside of Lyon and that was where he drove, directly from The Onyx Club. He was to stay there until contacted by Henri. Whatever happened at The Onyx, it would appear in the newspapers, and that was how Henri would find out.

The next day, Gina brought him a copy of France-Soir to the apartment, and the story was on the front page. The headline: "Reputed Gangster Slain at The Onyx." The photo was of the body being carried out of the front door of the club, beneath the marquee. The stretcher was covered by a white sheet, and a couple of cops watched in the background.

The story went through all of the splendidly gory details. It said that Harry Pearl had been shot twice in the back of the head while "visiting with one of the club's Negro temptresses in a back room designed for such assignations." The story said that the temptress in question, one Nina Boileau, "was covered in blood but otherwise unhurt." It said that, "because she was on her knees and otherwise occupied," she did not get a look at the shooter.

Henri laughed out loud. It was perfect, as good as he had hoped. Pearl was dead, the Levines were undoubtedly mortified, and a measure of balance had been returned to the relationship between the two families. Now, some kind of accommodation in the 10th could be worked out.

Henri kept reading. The story said that no one saw the shooter, and that he had escaped out a back door before Miss Boileau's screams brought club security to the scene. Police were certain that the shooter had used a silenced weapon, given that no one said they heard any gunshots. Another temptress, Miss Candy Ruel, said that her back-room client had fled about the time of the screams, but that she did not know his name and could only describe him as "average height, average weight, just average and white."

Henri turned the page to where the story jumped to the inside of the paper and read a few paragraphs wondering if this was somehow related to the killings at the luggage store at Place de la République. This was the only mention of the La Rue family — the raising of the possibility that all of this might have something to do with control of the 10th arrondissement now that the Morel family had disintegrated.

Really, Henri could not have been more pleased. It was clear that Freddy had done his work and escaped without anyone having a clue who he was. The whole thing was perfect, he believed — until he read the final paragraph of the story:

"According to police sources, Mr. Pearl was married last week to the former Ida Levine in a private ceremony. Mrs. Levine is the daughter of Daniel Levine, the son of Levine family kingpin Joseph Levine."

The subsequent screaming match with Chrétien was as loud as it was unsatisfying. Henri called him from a pay phone at the end of Gina's street, called him right in the precinct — which violated their understanding, but he didn't care — and the cop answered every shouted question with some variation of the same shouted reply: "Henri, I didn't fucking know."

The marriage changed everything, of course. To take out one soldier of equivalent rank to Willy — forget the other five — was, in Henri's mind, an even-enough trade. The truth was, any objective observer would say that Henri had been entirely reasonable, that he had not insisted on a six-for-six trade or anything close to six-for-six. One man of equivalent rank to Willy was enough to make his point. Harry Pearl, with two slugs in the back of his head, was enough to restore the La Rue family's honor.

But the fact that Pearl was married to Old Joe's granddaughter changed the calculus, changed it dramatically, and Henri knew it as soon as he read the final paragraph of the newspaper story. However unintentionally, Henri had turned a conventional war into a nuclear war — because Harry Pearl was not just a dead soldier anymore. He was a dead member of the family.

There would have to be another meeting, Henri knew. When he called Gérard to set it up, his uncle answered the phone himself, which was unusual. Before Henri got a word out, the old man indicated that he, indeed, had read all the way to the last paragraph.

"A son-in-law? Really?" Gérard said.

"I didn't know," Henri said. "They've only been married for a week."

"Like that matters," Gérard said.

Henri began to offer a half-hearted protest, but Gérard cut him off.

"And it's not just that," he said.

"Not just what?"

"Not just a son-in-law."

"What are you talking about?"

"Think about it," Gérard said. "Who gets married in a private ceremony?"

Henri thought for a second and said, "Oh, shit."

"Oh, shit is right," Gérard said. "She's almost certainly pregnant. So not only did you kill his granddaughter's husband, you also killed the father of his granddaughter's child — oh, and you also embarrassed the hell out of his granddaughter in the bargain. A Negro temptress with blood all over her in the back room of some strip joint. Christ."

Henri had known it was bad when he dialed the phone number, but now he knew it was worse. The final tell was when Gérard said he would not be leaving his house to come to a meeting.

"Tell me what you decide," Gérard said, and Henri couldn't figure if his uncle's decision to step away from any further deliberations was because he was legitimately afraid to leave his house or because he wanted to distance himself from the pile of shit that Henri had created. Probably both, Henri reasoned.

The new meeting place, Henri decided, would be in the Luxembourg Gardens — kind of in the back part, or at least what Henri considered to be the back part. It was where the old men and the younger boys with greasy hair played chess. Just by happenstance, the three of them approached the meeting place from different directions — and since Henri got there first, he was afforded a long look at both of their approaches. Neither Martin nor Michel had been followed.

Still, he asked them the perfunctory question about precautions, and their answers were an accurate reflection of their mindsets.

Michel arrived first, and he said, "Yep, yep, no worries there. I took the Metro, overshot by a stop and took a different train back. I'm clean."

Martin arrived a few minutes after Michel. He said, "Yeah, I was careful. Not everybody in this family is a fucking idiot."

It was a remark designed to sting, and it did. It was role reversal time for the La Rue brothers, and Martin was relishing the notion that Henri was the irresponsible one, the unthinking one. Of course, relishing is one thing and being able to play the part is another thing altogether — and the idea of Martin taking charge and navigating the family through the shit-filled rapids was inconceivable.

So, Henri just took it. He swallowed hard, and he stared at them, first Martin and then Michel and then Martin again.

"You guys go first," Henri said, and Michel jumped in before Martin could react.

"Look, for whatever reason, we are where we are," Michel said. And despite Martin's half-harrumph/half-sigh, he ignored the distraction and continued his analysis. And that is exactly what it was — an analysis.

"The theory was a good one — one man equivalent to Willy, one for that one, just restoring some equilibrium to the relationship. And after that, well, what? You figured there would be a negotiation?"

Henri nodded.

"So, the way you were plotting it, we weren't winning a war but trying to get in a position to win a fair peace?"

"Pretty much," Henri said. In his heart, he had always hoped that the Levines would fold and the La Rues would keep most of the 10th, but it would have been a long shot. A more equal negotiation was always the likely result.

Michel looked at both of them for a second. Henri looked tired. Martin looked crazed.

"Okay, so that was the goal then," Michel said. "With the son-in-law dead, is that still the goal now — some kind of equitable split of the 10th?"

"Fuck that," Martin said. "Fuck some kind of equitable split. We're in a war now, for better or worse, and we need to fucking win it. Screw the peace. Win the war."

So, there were the two positions. On the one hand, the La Rues could try to find a way to open a back channel to the Levines, eat some shit, and carve the 10th into two pieces. On the other hand, the La Rues could continue to blast away until the Levines folded.

"I'm not taking a position yet," Henri said. "I'm just thinking out loud. But we're definitely bigger than the Levines, right?"

"Way fucking bigger," Martin said. "And that's without taking into account the Morel people in the 10th who are on our payroll. They just add to our advantage."

"Are we sure of that?" Michel said.

"It's a good number of men," Martin said.

"I mean, are we sure they still work for us?"

Michel's question was a fair one, and even Martin knew it. Since Willy and the rest had been blown away in the luggage store, there had not been any communication with the Morel people they had inherited. They didn't know if the Levines had already moved in and co-opted the Morel people. They didn't know anything, given that they all had been hiding.

"Okay — but even without them, we're still bigger, yes?" Henri said.

"Yes," Martin said. "Rough guess, 30 to 50 percent bigger."

That's what Henri had figured. They had the manpower to win a war with the Levines. What they might not have had was the will to win it.

"Tell me something," Michel said. "I don't know the history. Tell me about the Levines."

"Tell you what?" Martin said.

"Tell me, I don't know, their history. Do they fight? Have the La Rues ever fought them? Have they ever fought anyone else?"

"Not in our time, right?" Martin said. He looked over at Henri.

"I don't remember one," Henri said. "But Old Man Joe, he's older than Gérard, I think. So, maybe? I don't know. When their money is on the street, they protect their interest — I know that. They might be rougher on deadbeats than we are — I don't know, I've heard stories. They supposedly called Harry Pearl by a nickname, 'Limpy.'"

"What the hell—" Martin said.

"Because he liked to break legs," Henri said.

"But that doesn't mean—"

"I know, Martin," Henri said. "Breaking legs isn't going to war."

"Exactly," Martin said. "And I don't think they will."

"Not even over a son-in-law?" Michel said. "And don't forget how they killed Willy and the rest of those poor fuckers. If that's not war—"

"So, what side are you on here?" Martin said.

"I'm not on a side," Michel said. "Other than trying to help figure out what's the best and smartest thing for the La Rue family to do."

"We don't have a choice," Martin said.

"No, we might not," Henri said. And then they all were quiet again, the only noises coming from the thwack of tennis balls on the courts a hundred yards in one direction, and the muted conversations of chess players 50 feet in the other direction.

"I don't want to insult you," Michel said. He was looking directly at Henri. "I don't want to do that and I'm sure you've already thought of this, but Guy…"

Henri nodded. It was almost the first thing he thought of when he read the last paragraph of the story of Harry Pearl's murder in France-Soir. The Levine and La Rue families were different, and there wasn't a perfect comparison. But seeing as how the La Rues had just killed a lower-level son-in-law, a lower-level family member who was not a civilian, if there was to be a retaliation of a similar kind — an eye for an eye, as it were — all indications pointed to the same place. They pointed to Guy La Rue, the only lower-level family member who was not a civilian. Guy La Rue, son of Henri and Sylvie, now wore a target that he had no hand in affixing to his back.

"I know, Michel, I know," Henri said. He ran his fingers through his hair and sighed more loudly than he had intended, and then Henri told Martin and Michel to get their families out of their apartments, at least for a little while, and to check with Gérard at least twice a day for messages and instructions.

"You need to decide," Martin said.

"I will," Henri said. "And I won't be long. I just need a little more clarity. A day or two."

Place des Vosges was surrounded by big houses on all four sides. Somebody had told Jean Lemieux that they were from the 17th century, but he had no idea. All he knew was that they looked old — not bad old, but expensive old. Solid old. Lasting old. Like the church — or, at least the church of Father Lemieux's dreams. That was the church in France from before Lemieux's birth, a time when the church and the priesthood were respected throughout the nation, respected and powerful. It was the church he had read about but never experienced.

The square was ringed by trees, with benches beneath. There were four fountains, one in each corner. He had never been there when all four were functioning. It was three on a good day. That day, it was only two. Like the church, like the country.

Gérard had been cryptic on the phone when he called to cancel their appointment, but Lemieux understood the subtext. It was very clear. He had read the newspapers, too. He knew about the man who had been killed in The Onyx Club, and about the men who had been killed before that in the luggage shop at Place de la République. He knew what the La Rue family was about, and he understood that this had become a time of heightened security for Gérard.

"Maybe next week," Gérard had said, when the priest asked about when they might get together for another look at the family ledgers. "I'll call."

"And the 7 at Sacré-Coeur?" Lemieux said.

"I'll call," Gérard said.

"If there's anything—"

"Father, I'll call," Gérard said. And then he hung up.

Their relationship had grown closer in recent months — and

Lemieux's agreement to help in the scheme to spring young Guy La Rue from the jail had made it even closer. And if the rest of the family had wondered about the relationship, that bit of subterfuge at the police precinct went a long way toward allaying whatever concerns they might have. He was a friend — a good friend, a real friend. And that was enough.

A five-year-old boy ran by Father Lemieux just then, carrying a stick and banging it on each tree trunk in succession. A woman pushing another child in a pram did her best to keep up. Lemieux always came to Place des Vosges, always found a bench, always permitted his mind to wander. And through the wandering, along the random path, he always ended up in the same place and asking himself the same question: why did he hide it?

Lemieux knew at least two other priests who had mistresses. One was Father Lyon, the pastor at Saint Stephen. His woman didn't live in the rectory, certainly, or even in the parish. But they had gone out twice a week for years, and Father Lyon lived in her apartment on his days off and during his vacations. For appearances, she was introduced as his cousin if the need arose. One time, Father Lyon ran into Bishop Latrec at Tour d'Argent — yes, with his mistress. It was their anniversary. But as Father Lyon told it, the meeting was brief, as the bishop was at the restaurant with a woman of his own. Latrec introduce her as his niece.

So, why hide it? He didn't want a relationship, didn't want the bother. And besides, this way attached less meaning to the whole thing. It was just a physical act. A sin, yes, but maybe less of a sin.

He always said a prayer, just the same. It wasn't a prayer to help him avoid the temptation because while he had a strong spiritual side, Lemieux also had a strong realistic side — and the realistic side of him knew that avoiding the temptation just wasn't happening. It was simply a prayer for forgiveness. In the church, you become comfortable with ritual, and that was his.

After the little prayer, he always left Place des Vosges by the same exit, and then his legs carried him pretty much without thinking. It was about a 10-minute walk, the lefts and rights through the narrow streets taking care of themselves. It was like that feeling Lemieux got sometimes when he was driving, lost in thought, and the car somehow found its way home even as the priest could not remember any of the driving maneuvers it had taken to get there.

At the front door, there was always a slight hesitation — very slight, maybe a second, maybe less, before he grabbed the knob.

"Mr. Morin, so nice to see you again."

"Is Patrice available?" the priest asked.

"Yes, yes. Have a seat, and I will call up to her room."

Henri got to the apartment by parking three blocks away and making his way to the building's back entrance through the alley, slaloming between the garbage bins. He had gotten word to Passy, who had gotten word to Guy. They were to meet in the apartment — a meeting that was mandatory and urgent. Passy said the message had been received.

First, though, there was Sylvie. She was surprised to see him when he unlocked the door and offered a hug for a greeting. Henri tried to read her face, and he did not sense fear. This was good. It meant she hadn't yet figured it out, and that they could have a normal, non-hysterical conversation before Guy arrived.

"I'm sure you saw the paper," Henri said, as he poured them both a Pernod. It was early, but what the hell.

"Do you think it's over now?" Sylvie said.

"I don't," Henri said.

"Why not? Eye for an eye, right?"

"It might be more complicated than that," Henri said.

"Meaning?"

"Meaning, I think it might be best if you change residences for a little while."

"But, they don't go after wives," Sylvie said. "What the hell is this all about?"

"Just a precaution," Henri said. "So, I can think of two places that make sense for you — either the house in Normandy, or maybe the Ritz."

Henri reached into his jacket pocket for the envelope that he had picked up from the uniform store — again, entering through the alley and staying only five minutes. It was enough cash for a month at the Ritz or a year at the Normandy house. Sylvie took it from him and nodded. She admired its heft.

"Not Normandy, not the Ritz," Sylvie said. She opened the envelope and peeked inside and said, "The George V."

She looked intently into Henri's eyes when she said it, said "The George V." She looked and saw what she was hoping to see — the quickest inability to look back into her eyes, just a blink of discomfort. Good.

"Um, sure," Henri said. "George V. Wherever."

The unspoken message — delivered by the wife, received by the husband — was that she knew where the mistress had her apartment, that it was on the Champs-Élysées and that if you looked out the window and directly across the street, you would be looking at The George V.

She had known for months. Sylvie had found a scrap of forgotten paper in the pants pockets of one of Henri's suits that was headed to the dry cleaner. The paper was an invoice from the manager of the apartment building where the lovely Marina lived, an invoice for damages caused by her dog's unfortunate piss on a lobby sofa. Sylvie knew the address, then, and after a disguised call to the manager, she knew what a similar apartment in the same building cost.

In the time since, she had made sure to let Henri know that she changed the tearoom she and her friends visited whenever they shopped on the Champs. She had chosen a new place — a shiny, modern place that happened to occupy the ground floor of the building right next to the lovely Marina's apartment building. She would sit there with her friends and wonder if any of the young women walking by the front window was the lovely Marina — and they always sat at a table in the front window, a fact that she made sure to relay to Henri every time she was there. She could tell it made him uneasy. You're married long enough, you don't need words. A little crack in his voice, a sudden shifting in his chair — she could tell. She could tell that he knew that she knew.

Sylvie weighed the envelope in her hand again. Good.

"Tell me what's going on," Sylvie said.

"Just a precaution is all," Henri said. "Like I said."

"The truth, Henri."

"You didn't read the whole newspaper story, did you?" he said.

"I thought I did."

"You still have the paper?"

Sylvie stood up and walked across the room to the desk in the corner. There was a small stack of newspapers there, and she found the France-Soir near the top.

"The very end," Henri said.

Sylvie opened the paper to the jump page and scanned down.

"Last paragraph," Henri said.

"Shhh," Sylvie said. She laid the paper on the desk and traced down the column of type with her finger. Then she stopped and read. She read for a long time, a lot longer than it should have taken. But Sylvie knew the business, and she knew the implications.

"Henri, how could you be so stupid?" is what she finally said.

"We didn't know. It was only a week."

"But, damn it—" Sylvie's voice was raised, and she was preparing a verbal onslaught that would have made Martin sound tame by comparison. Henri steeled himself for it, but then he saw the look on his wife's face change from anger to fear. The final connection in the circuit had just been made.

"Oh, Henri," she said. "Where is he? Tell me he's safe."

"He's on the way here," Henri said. "Passy got him the message. He knows to come up through the alley."

As they spoke, a key turned in the lock. Sylvie rushed across the room to hug her son, who was part surprised and part put off by the unexpected display of affection.

"So, what's this about? Where's the fire?" Guy said.

"Did you read the paper?"

"About Harry Pearl? Sure," Guy said. "Poor fellow. At the same time, if you've got to go, there are worse ways than with a pair of luscious black lips around your—"

Guy didn't finish the thought because his father interrupted him with a backhand across the mouth. At which point, the son said, "What the fuck?" And the father said, "Will you be serious for five minutes?" And the mother said, "Listen to your father, Guy." That last bit got the son's attention, seeing as how his mother normally took his side in a typical family argument, or at least humored him.

Henri showed him the newspaper and pointed to the last paragraph. Guy read it quickly and said, "So?"

"Read it again," Henri said. "Think about it."

"I still don't get it," Guy said. He looked at his mother when he said it, and the concern on her face caused just a smidgen of the edge to drop from his voice.

Henri and Sylvie looked at each other, and she decided to tell him. She used the word "maybe" three times, and also threw in an "on the off chance," but there was no sugarcoating the truth. As she finally said to her son: "If the Levines look for revenge, you're the one who's in danger. In this world we live in, you are to the La Rues what this Harry Pearl was to the Levines — a young family member, just starting in the business."

"He wasn't their family," Guy said.

"Son-in-law is family," Sylvie said.

"It's not the same as blood," Guy said.

"It's not the same, but it's close enough," Henri said. "You need to go to Normandy."

"When?"

"Now."

"I'm not hiding," Guy said.

"You're going to Normandy," Sylvie said.

"I'm not afraid," Guy said.

"This isn't up for discussion — you're going," Sylvie said.

"Because he fucked up, I have to run?" Guy said. He was looking directly at his mother. This was their discussion now. Henri was a bystander, just the guy who had fucked up. He said nothing.

"It's just common sense, and it's just temporary, and you're doing it," Sylvie said. Her face was hard, but she also felt the need to flick away a tear from the outside of her left eye.

"This is bullshit," Guy said. "I can take care of myself."

"Nobody's saying you can't," Sylvie said.

"Then I'll stay and take care of myself," Guy said.

"Be reasonable," Sylvie said.

"Fuck this bullshit," Guy said.

He began to make his way to the door, and Sylvie rushed to stop him. But she was too slow, and barely touched his sleeve with her reach before he squeezed his way through the doorway, out of the apartment and into the hall.

When the door shut, and Sylvie dropped to her knees and wailed his name, Henri said, "Calm down."

"You have to go after him," she said.

"I will, after I get you to The George V."

"But how will you find him?"

"We know his bar," Henri said. "And Passy — I've been in contact with him, and he had somebody follow Guy here. At least, that was the plan. I'll catch up with him as soon as I get you to the hotel."

"I don't need—"

"Don't you start," Henri said. "I'm taking you. Five minutes. One small suitcase. You can buy whatever else you need after you get there."

She stared at him and wiped another tear.

"I'll watch him — I promise," Henri said. "Come on, now. Five minutes — and then I'll show you the delights of the back alley. Come to think of it, you might want to wear an old pair of shoes."

PART XI

THE LONGEST NIGHT

The bar was called Sally's. That was the place Passy had told him about, the place where Guy and his crew hung out. But with the entire crew in jail — except for one young kid, whose father apparently knew someone who knew someone — they weren't sure if it was still Guy's place. They weren't sure until the guy Passy had following Henri's son tailed him back to the bar.

Just to be sure, Henri parked a borrowed car — a little Renault shitbox driven by one of Passy's guys — about a half-block from the entrance to Sally's and across the street. The view was good, and it also was in the opposite direction to where Guy's car was parked — meaning he wasn't likely to look that way when he came out.

Just to be sure, Henri crossed the street and walked by the door to the bar. He stopped for a second and peeked through the little diamond-shaped window. The place was decently lit and not very crowded, and Henri had no trouble picking out his son at the far end of the bar. He was sitting there and talking to two other young kids.

It is hard to determine someone's true feelings in a second of observation, or even less. It is hard to tell what somebody is thinking from that kind of animated snapshot. Still, you can get something. You can sense a mood, be it morose or celebratory, angry or joyful. And what Henri sensed when he looked at his son was, well, normal. He did not look like a kid who felt his life was truly in danger. He saw Guy and two buddies in a bar. Guy was making a point with his finger tip, jabbing it into the chest of one of the others, but he didn't look scared or angry or even particularly insistent. He was just telling a story. He just looked like himself, like a 25-year-old who thought he knew everything.

Henri got back into his car and settled in. He couldn't

remember the last time had been on a stakeout, and he wasn't prepared. He had nothing to eat and, more importantly, no jar in which to piss. He solved that by unscrewing the bulb from the overhead light, sliding over to the passenger side, quietly opening the door a few inches and pissing out on the sidewalk as he sat. He didn't get a drop on his pants and hoped that this would be his greatest accomplishment of the evening.

He couldn't remember the last one, but he couldn't forget the all-timer. It was the night that his father and brother were killed. It was a nothing kind of caper, a load of tabletop radios — but the expensive kind with real mahogany cabinets. When he sketched it out, Henri actually said to his father, "Isn't this kind of small potatoes for you to be involved."

His father laughed. "There are no small potatoes, only small men," he said.

"What the—"

"Just want to keep my hand in," his father said. "It's a muscle, and you need to use it. If you don't, it becomes weak and useless."

"You should use it on something other than a truckload of goddamn radios," Henri said.

At which point, Henri's brother stage-whispered, "Some fathers take their sons out to a ballgame. Ours takes us out for a heist."

"You see, he gets it," their father said. And then he laughed in a way that Henri had rarely heard, long and loud and genuine.

The radio factory was on Rue de Berne in a corner of the 9th. It was an unremarkable setup, a smallish building with a parking area on one side. There was no fence around the place, no gates, no nothing. The plan was for Henri to park down the street in an unmarked panel truck about 9 p.m. He was to find a spot with a view of both the front and side doors on the south side, which wasn't hard. He was to sit there and make sure that there were no lights on inside, no signs of movement. They hadn't expected to see any — four nights of observation had turned up nothing, not a night watchman or a special police patrol, not a soul between 9 and 11. But if Henri did see something, and it was before 9:45, he was to return to the butte and warn off his father and brother, Big Jean and Little Jean. If it was after 9:45, and too late to catch them before they left, he was to open up the hood of his car and stand in the street and act as if he was making some kind of repair to the engine. If Big Jean and Little Jean saw that, they would know there was trouble and just keep driving.

Henri was on time, and he was parked in the proper place on the south side. He could see both entrances, front and side. He could see them the whole time — as well as the window in the front. And there was nothing, as he told Gérard later that night. He had sat there for an hour and there had been nothing — no light, no movement, no watchman, no police patrol, nothing. In the 60 minutes he sat there, exactly three cars had driven down the street, three civilians headed to wherever.

When his father and brother drove up, they went into the parking lot and right next to the side entrance, as if they owned the place. The plan was for Henri to remain in place until they were inside, and then back in the panel truck so that it could be loaded. Big Jean picked the lock — it was his specialty. Uncle Gérard sometimes called him "Fingers" when he was in a playful mood. It didn't take two minutes for them to get inside, and that was when Henri drove out of his parking spot and began to back in to the parking lot. He was not much of a driver in reverse, and the truck was bigger than he was used to handling, so it was an extra-slow process — but he did it, and managed not to scrape a fender against the side of the building or the concrete steps leading up to the side entrance.

Henri had just gotten the truck into park when he heard the first of the gunshots. Because he would have to tell the story so quickly to his uncle, not a half-hour after it all went down, he felt confident in his memory even after seven — no, eight years. Christ. Eight years.

Henri heard the shots, drew his pistol, and moved quickly, up the concrete steps and to the side door. As he got inside, he saw his father sprawled on the floor to his left, half of his head blown off. On his right, wedged into a hiding spot behind a cabinet of some sort, Little Jean was holding his gun with both hands and, well, just hiding.

Henri took one more step into the room — it was the radio assembly area, he guessed, with long wooden tables and work stations piled with parts, things like tubes and dials and whatever. He took a second step, and then he heard a man scream one word, "Assholes." And then he heard the punctuation, a single shot. He thought it was from a rifle, and it must have been aimed at him, seeing as how he felt a spray of wood chips from behind him where the bullet must have struck the wall.

And then it was all very fast, but Henri could still close his eyes and see it in slow motion. Little Jean, reacting to the shot, leaped out from his hiding spot and fired in the direction of the man who had just yelled "Assholes." He missed, though — and now he was exposed. The next shot was from the man with the rifle. Little Jean, too, had part of his head blown off.

Then, Henri fired — one shaky shot with his pistol. He didn't know if he found his target until the man with the rifle cried, "Shiiiiiii..." He never got to the T at the end. He fell, and Henri approached him, and he was still breathing a little, and then Henri fired a second shot. It was another head shot.

He went back to his father and his brother, to Big Jean and Little Jean, and he crouched down next to each of them, first his father, then his brother, just to make sure. He knew they wouldn't be carrying identification because you never carried identification on a job — but, really, what was the difference? They were dead, and the police would recognize them immediately, even with the injuries. Their faces were still intact, and everyone knew Big Jean and Little Jean La Rue.

Henri collected their weapons, although he wasn't even sure why. He moved the car from the parking lot and put it in a spot on the street — somebody would pick it up the next day. He drove the panel truck up the butte, directly to Uncle Gérard's house behind Sacré-Coeur. It was there that they grieved, and they planned, pretty much simultaneously.

The bodies would not be found for a day. The newspapers would surmise about a robbery that went wrong, about a hail of bullets — the newspapers loved that phrase — and three dead bodies. Workers at the radio factory would be quoted as saying that the owner kept a small windowless apartment in the back, that he never seemed to leave the premises. He even had one of the female workers bring his groceries every week, and another who cut his hair.

"He was like a recluse," one of the workers said. "Nice man. Odd man."

Dead man. Three dead men. And suddenly, the La Rue family was being run by a second son who never thought he would be in charge and assisted by a second son who never thought he would occupy that place. They were second sons, Gérard and Henri — born that way, trained that way, genetically predisposed to take orders, not give them.

Suddenly, a flash of light caught Henri's eye as he slumped down in the front seat of the shitbox. It shook him out of his reminiscence. It was the door of Sally's, opening and closing, with the light splashing on the sidewalk. Through the door came Guy, who looked neither to his left nor his right. Instead, he walked straight to his car, gunned the engine and sped away.

Henri didn't know where Guy was headed, but he had little trouble following him. It was late enough that the traffic was light, and the car was nondescript enough and his son was oblivious enough that Henri felt little need to camouflage his intentions. He was right on Guy's bumper at a stop light, more than once, and part of him wanted to honk his horn so that his son knew he was watching. But Henri didn't honk, and he eventually backed away so that there was at least one car between them. Stealth was better for now. There was no telling how Guy might react if he saw Henri covering his flank.

Guy pulled over and parked, and Henri was able to ease into a spot three cars behind him. The one bit of preparation he had done was to bring a pair of miniature binoculars, and he was able to focus on his son as he climbed the steps to an apartment building and then leaned on one of the buttons that buzzed up to the apartments. He could see that it was the top button, but the binoculars weren't good enough to read the name next to it.

Guy stood with his hands on his hips and then backed away as the door opened. On the other side was a girl, a brunette with shoulder-length hair. The hair, though, was not what caught Henri's attention. It was the pink bathrobe that did that, the thigh-high bathrobe that fell open as Guy leaned in to kiss the girl, to kiss her and then to caress what had fallen out of the wide-open silk.

"Christ," Henri thought. His son really was not worried about anything other than leaving that robe in a pile at the bottom of the bed. The idea that he might be a target of the Levine family, if it was even in his head, was quite obviously not the first priority — unless, of course, this was Guy's place to hide out. All right, maybe he wasn't an idiot.

After all, part of Henri said that he should just leave and head back to Gina's apartment, to his own hideaway with its own pleasures. But the rest of him thought he had to stay, that he couldn't take the chance. A father staking out a son to protect him from assassination was not a long-term solution to anything, he knew — but he also couldn't leave, not yet, not in the first hours of the first night.

He looked at his watch when Guy went inside and waited 10 minutes. The street was quiet. Exactly one car went by — not stopping, not slowing down, just cruising past. After the 10 minutes was up, Henri did his one bit of reconnaissance — down the street, up the apartment steps to the front door, not to ring a bell but instead to read a name. It was the name next to the first buzzer: G. Delacroix, 1-Rear. He registered that, and then he looked down at the door. It was old and ajar. Henri was back in the car within a minute.

For some reason, Henri wasn't tired. He settled back into the front seat of the shitbox — but on the passenger side, next to the curb — and slithered down so that he could barely see over the glove box. Luckily he was parked under a tree and nowhere near a streetlight, so there was little chance of anyone seeing him if they drove by. Perched as he was, almost reclining, he should have become sleepy — but, for whatever reason, it never happened. He saw the headlights of cars on the cross street far ahead, and he heard a couple of drunk guys yelling about whatever in the next block, and he never lost focus on the apartment steps. He never slept. He never even rested his eyes.

He did daydream, though. For whatever reason, he thought about the days and weeks after his father and brother were killed. After the bodies were found, there was the inevitable newspaper story — but it was less of a big public deal than Henri had expected. There was only the one story, the one where they died in a hail of bullets and the man who owned the radio factory was a recluse. Big Jean and Little Jean were identified as "the father and son leaders of the La Rue crime family." But that was it — no follow-up story, no speculation about what might be next for the La Rues, no photos or words from the service at the cemetery.

After the burial and the lunch, Gérard and Henri went back to Gérard's house on Cité du Sacré-Coeur. Henri thought about it and realized that Gérard had just bought the palace, that he had moved in only weeks earlier. The rooms were still mostly bare, as were the walls — and the two of them sat in the midst of that emptiness, accompanied only by a bottle of Armagnac.

"That they did not die in vain," Gérard said, in his first toast.

"Meaning?" Henri said.

"Just what I said," Gérard said. He downed his drink in a single swallow, and then he poured another.

"I don't get it," Henri said. "I'm not trying to be dense here, but what the hell are you saying?"

"Just this: we need to learn from what happened," Gérard said.

"What is there to learn? It was a bullshit robbery, and they got killed by an unknowable risk factor — an old recluse in the back room. What is there to learn?"

Then it was Henri's turn to down his drink. His uncle leaned over and filled it again, and then he stared at Henri until Henri noticed. Their eyes stayed locked for a full second, and then Gérard sat back in his chair and began talking.

"You said it — you said it exactly — but you don't realize what you said," Gérard said.

"What did I say? That it was a bullshit—"

"First, though: it was not an unknowable risk," Gérard said. "It was hard to know, but it wasn't unknowable. They could have taken longer with the reconnaissance. Maybe they would have seen the person who brought in the groceries and wondered what that was all about. Or maybe they could have worked to get a source inside rather than just observing from the outside. So, not unknowable. Hard to know, but not unknowable. Agreed?"

Henri nodded.

"Okay, then," Gérard said. "So that's one thing to learn — to work as hard on the reconnaissance and the planning as you dream about the payoff. And not to be blinded by the payoff."

"But, like I said, the payoff was going to be shit," Henri said. "It was a bullshit job."

"And that's the real point," Gérard said. "Because it was a bullshit job. Because the payoff was going to be a pittance in the grand scheme of things. Why the hell were your father and brother even involved? You take risks for a reason — and a pile of fucking mahogany radios were not enough of a reason for men of that stature to take the risk."

"My father said—"

"That he was just keeping his hand in?" Gérard said. "That he didn't want the muscle to atrophy? Jesus — I heard him say that a dozen times over the years when he got involved in something below his pay grade. He liked to think he was still one of the men, but he wasn't. He was the leader of the men — and leaders do not brush against those kinds of dangers, do not pull those kinds of menial jobs because however hard you work on the planning, there is always — your word — an unknowable element of risk. The risks have to be calculated, and the risks have to be worth it — for the leader most of all."

Gérard was mourning his brother while simultaneously criticizing him, praising his memory while cursing his recklessness. That he was now in charge of the family was unquestioned. That he would be cautious from the start — and increasingly more cautious with each year — was foretold in that conversation.

"Are you okay?" Gérard said. They were pretty drunk at that point.

"Fine, fine," Henri said.

"Don't give me 'fine, fine,'" the uncle said to the nephew.

"Really," Henri said.

"None of this was your fault," Gérard said.

Henri began to tear up and said, "I mean, I even told him the radios weren't worth his time. And when that first shot, when I heard it, I ran as fast as I could. And then I almost got hit, and then Little Jean leaned out, and..."

He stopped telling the story he had already told Gérard at least three times.

"You followed the plan," Gérard said. "You killed the old man. You survived. Jesus, you survived."

They drank some more, talked some more. Henri didn't remember a lot of the rest of it, except for one thing. In that mostly empty sitting room, their words echoing just a little in the vacant space, it was the first time he heard his uncle say, "Hogs get slaughtered."

PART XII

THEY DIDN'T EVEN LOOK JEWISH

Henri realized he had a tear rolling down his cheek, and he was wiping it away when he saw the headlights behind him. He slithered down a little farther — his head was now completely below the seat back, and he couldn't see over the glove box — but he could still see the headlamps that illuminated the darkened street. As the car rolled by his, Henri sensed that it was traveling a little slower than it should have been. Maybe the driver was drunk and navigating more carefully than was typical. Maybe the driver was looking for an address to drop somebody off — except, that made no sense because the person being dropped off would point out where they lived. Unless, maybe, the passenger being dropped off was the drunk one.

Whatever. As the car rolled past the shitbox, Henri straightened up a little. His eyes were above the glove box, and he could see the car rolling past the apartment where guy and the short pink robe had gone inside. The car never stopped, not completely. The brake lights did not flash red. But the foot was off the gas, and Henri could see two heads in the car, two heads turned toward the steps of the apartment building. When the car had rolled past the apartment, Henri could hear the engine gun just a little, and the car resumed driving at a normal speed. At the end of the street — maybe 300 feet ahead, the car made a right turn.

Henri didn't like it, but he wasn't exactly sure what to make of it. A car rolling past an address. An address with 10 apartments. The likelihood was that it meant nothing. Still, he was worried. He looked at his watch. He checked the pistol. He scrunched down in the seat. There was no chance he would begin daydreaming again about his father and his brother and his uncle. Suddenly, he felt the urge to piss.

Low down, eyes focused on the apartment steps, he was distracted again by headlights approaching from behind — first from a distance in the rear-view mirror, then flooding the dark street. This time, the car seemed to be traveling at a more normal speed. Henri figured it must have been somebody different. Still, he got down lower, so his head was again behind the rear of the seat and his eyes were below the glove box. He couldn't see anything as the car traveled past the shitbox. The first thing that registered was the red brake lights that filled the darkness — the red lights followed immediately by the grinding of brakes that needed new shoes.

He slid up in the seat. The car was parked in front of the apartment building — not parked, but completely stopped in the middle of the street. The person on the passenger side rolled down his window — it was a he — and leaned out of the opening to have a look. Three, four, five seconds — it seemed like more. And then the head disappeared back inside the car, and the engine gunned, and it traveled the 300 feet to the corner and made another right turn.

Once was meaningless. Twice was meaningful. Henri felt for the pistol, and then he looked at his watch. It had been three minutes since the last time.

Three minutes. Henri did a quick calculation, all wrapped up in a single question: where was the proper place for all of this to happen? Inside or outside?

There was probably a 25 percent chance that the two men in the car were harmless idiots — which meant that there was a 25 percent chance that he would be killing two innocents on the front steps of the apartment building, if indeed they returned. Twenty-five percent was too high. But if he went inside and hid somewhere, and waited until they reached the apartment, he could reduce that 25 percent to near zero percent. That was far preferable, even if it was more dangerous for him.

He looked at his watch. One minute had gone by.

Henri felt for the pistol one more time, and opened the passenger door. He was at the steps in a few seconds, and he took a look over his shoulder. No headlights. He leaned on the door, and it opened on noisy hinges. He made sure to close it tightly behind him, but the door was a piece of shit — and ancient to boot. A school kid could force it open with his shoulder.

G. Delacroix, 1-Rear. Henri said a small prayer as his eyes got used to the darkness. He prayed that the building was like every other building of the same type — one apartment in the front, one in the back, with the stairs in the back. As his eyes focused, he saw that it was so.

He made his way back — past the concierge's apartment with its glass door — and found the stairs, and went up to the first floor. He leaned over to the rear door and saw the name tag: G. Delacroix. As quietly as he could, he climbed to the next landing, halfway to the second floor. From there, he could see the bottom half of the door to 1-Rear. He squinted at his watch. One and a half minutes since the last time. He moved one step below the landing, which afforded a more complete view of the door. He sat down, and took the pistol out of his pocket, and clicked off the safety. He sat down, and he waited, and just for a second, Henri thought back to the night when he was sitting outside the radio factory. That night, he had to wait an hour. This night, he feared, would not be as long.

The first thing Henri heard was the rattle of the doorknob — the rattle and then a thud, a shoulder into the door. The first thud was followed by a second, and then by the sound of wood splintering and the hinges groaning. They were in. Twenty-five percent had dropped precipitously — and, for one fleeting second, Henri wondered if he could have hit the two of them as they stood on the front steps of the apartment building, hit them from about three car lengths back.

No matter. No time for second-guesses or recriminations. He heard two sets of footsteps — cautious footsteps, quiet footsteps, the kind you might hear if somebody was trying to sneak up on you. He heard them on the hallway below, and then he heard them on the stairs up to the first floor. If Henri had this wrong, and the two sets of footsteps continued on up to the second floor, they would run into him halfway there. It would be an awkward situation but likely not fatal. Sitting on the stairs, sitting in the dark, Henri could just play drunk and allow the two of them to pass him on the way to wherever.

As it turned out, though, Henri had not been wrong. From his perch on the stairs, he could see the two of them. One of them leaned over to read the name tag, and then he turned back and nodded to the other guy. And then, as they turned to face the door more directly, he could see them, even in the dark. He could see the two handguns that each of them held in their right hands.

Then the one guy turned to the other and theatrically raised one finger. One.

And then he raised two fingers. Two.

One...

Two...

The guy was about to raise a third finger while simultane-ously leaning into the door with his shoulder. He was about to, and then Henri fired. One, two — and both of the men were down in a heap. One, two — and the hallway was filled with the smell of a discharged weapon. The sound of the shots was louder than Henri ever remembered from a pistol. Then again, it made sense because the hallway was a pretty cramped space.

Someone from a higher floor screamed, "What was that?" At the same time, the door of 1-Rear opened up. Guy was standing there in his underwear, holding a pistol of his own.

"Holy—" he said, and then he stopped himself when he saw his father, still holding his own pistol.

"Jesus Christ," Guy said. "I mean, what—"

"We've got to go now," Henri said.

"What... I mean..." Guy could not complete a thought. Appearing behind him was the girl, except she wasn't wearing the short pink robe anymore. She wasn't wearing anything. She was just screaming.

"We have to go, like right now," Henri said. And then he looked at the naked woman and said, "Does she know your name?"

The woman stopped screaming and said, "Marcel, who the hell is this guy?"

Marcel. Finally, a break.

"Get your clothes — just carry them," Henri said.

Guy was frozen in place.

"Now," Henri said. Guy turned back into the apartment, and the screaming naked girl followed him in, and then he was back in 10 seconds, his clothes and shoes in his arms.

"Later, baby," he said, and then he slammed the door in the naked girl's face. Henri stepped over the fallen bodies first, followed by his son. When Henri's eye fell, he noticed some-thing. If the dead men had been Jewish, it wasn't obvious — not that he was planning on hanging around for a more thorough examination.

There were more people shouting from upstairs as they began to run, but the concierge must have been drunk or deaf or both because they got past the apartment with the glass door and out the front door without anyone seeing them. They were in the shitbox and on the move within about 30 seconds. Guy dressed as they drove, and the father explained to the son what had just happened.

Silent Moe did the driving and, as was typical, said nothing. Gérard La Rue sat in the passenger seat and embraced the silence.

It had been maybe 30 hours since the business on the apartment stairs. The whole thing had spun completely out of control. Goddamn hogs. It had to stop. For Gérard, that was the only certainty. Whatever the intentions at the beginning — good, bad or indifferent — the business was too far off the rails to salvage. The dangers had grown exponentially — not that they would ever touch him, not directly, but nephews and grand-nephews were close enough. They were too close. Goddamn hogs.

Moe pulled up at the Mazarine Library.

"Just park up there," Gérard said. He waved indifferently with his right hand.

"Come inside?" Moe said.

"Stay with the car," Gérard said.

It took him a couple of steps after sitting in a car — after sitting anywhere, truth be told — before Gérard loosened up and felt relatively normal. He was almost in the building before the aches in his hips disappeared. He walked past the information counter used by civilians, and the girl sitting behind him offered a nod. She knew him. He walked a few more steps and knocked on the door jamb of an office whose door was open.

"Ah, my American friend," said the man behind the desk. Roger Cornette was the head librarian at the Mazarine. Cornette had known Gérard since they were teenagers, two bookworms who ended up, as Cornette liked to say, "at different ends of the worm."

"So, which one of us got the ass end?" Gérard said, the first time his friend said it.

"My paycheck suggests that I did," Cornette said.

"Don't kid yourself," Gérard said. "You don't know what I would give to live my professional life in this place, to dedicate my working hours to... to... this."

"You've seen my car," Cornette said. "You wouldn't trade."

For the better part of their adult lives, the two men had broadened their reading horizons together, in a kind of book club all their own. Cornette would choose the topic — say, 19th-century Russian novels — and they would work their way through the titles that the librarian selected until they were tired of the area. Cornette would read the book first, then Gérard — and then they would discuss what they read, normally after hours on Thursday nights in the main reading room.

The current area of study was the early 20th-century American novel — hence, Cornette's reference to his American friend. Gérard handed the librarian his copy of Babbitt.

"What did you think — no, save it for Thursday night," Cornette said.

Gérard responded with a face and a thumbs-down gesture.

"No, no, save your disdain," Cornette said. "Disdainful Gérard is the most entertaining Gérard."

Cornette handed him a copy of the next book, Winesburg, Ohio, and the two agreed that Thursday night was still on. Gérard took the book and walked into the main reading room. God, he loved it — the polished wood tables, the brass lamps with the green shades, the stacks of books like a mountain over your shoulder when you sat there. He scanned the faces of the scholars and wondered what they were studying. He thought he could tell sometimes, but he knew it was a stupid exercise. Still, there was that old man at the third table on the right, bent over three open volumes, reading one, marking the place with his finger, and then reading the next one. What could still engage his attention so late in his life — he must have been 80. He probably fought in the first war and lived through the hell of the German occupation during the second war. He undoubtedly lost friends and maybe sons, and carried unspeakable emotional burdens. Yet, he was excited as he scanned from the second book to the third, his finger still marking his place in the first — and almost triumphant as he found what he was looking for in the third book, his two fingers now marking two places. Gérard envied that feeling. He truly did envy Cornette and his scholar's life.

Gérard looked farther toward the back of the room. He saw Old Joe Levine sitting in the back row, all by himself, hands folded in front of him, seemingly staring at nothing. Gérard walked over and took the seat next to him.

"Thanks for coming," Gérard said.

"It's time," Levine said.

"It's spun out of—"

"Out of control," Levine said. "Completely out of control."

Gérard sat silently for a few seconds. If Levine was going to air any grievances, this was the time for them. His argument, which Gérard had heard the last time, was that the whole thing started only because the La Rue family was greedy when it took the 10th from the Morels. That Gérard did not disagree — well, Levine knew that, too.

"But in the here and now," Gérard said.

"In the here and now, I have two more dead men."

"Who were going to kill my grand-nephew."

"Because you killed my granddaughter's husband."

"Ahh," Gérard said. He raised his hand weakly as if the whole discussion exhausted him, which it did. "We're getting nowhere this way."

The two old men were quiet again. Gérard looked around

the big reading room at the rows of tables, concerned that their conversation had drawn attention. But it had not.

Finally, Old Joe said, "How could we not have foreseen this?"

"Well, for starters, you killed six men in the luggage store. Christ, six!"

"You gave the okay," Levine said, quietly.

"The okay for some action, not for mass murder," Gérard said.

This time, it was Levine's turn to raise his hand and wave weakly. He, too, was exhausted.

The two old men met three times a year in the Mazarine, on the last Friday in January, May and September. Younger men handled a lot of the daily details, but Gérard La Rue and Joseph Levine still ran their families — and they were of like minds. They had seen a lot, seen the consequences of conflict. Gérard never told anybody, but it was decades earlier when he first heard someone use the phrase "hogs get slaughtered." The someone was Old Joe Levine.

The last meeting came several weeks after Henri's move to take out the Morels and take over the 10th. Old Joe was disappointed, and he said flatly, "You had nothing to do with this, right?"

"I advised against it," Gérard said. "Because I knew that this conversation would be coming, and I knew what the long-term solution was going to have to be."

At that meeting, Gérard allowed the notion of a counter strike by the Levines to be floated. He knew they had been embarrassed, and that they could not allow the usurping of the 10th and its two train stations to stand. But he also knew that Henri would never negotiate. He believed he had won, and that the Levines would just eat it and stay where they belonged, in the 3rd and the 2nd.

"We must be permitted to get your nephew's attention,"

Levine said that day. Gérard answered only with a nod. Unspoken was the notion that there would potentially be bloodshed, but Gérard understood that. He didn't understand six dead bodies — he never would have guessed that was coming — but he did understand, and he did accept that something was going to happen. And it was more than understanding, to be truthful. It was sanctioning. Gérard was sanctioning another family to make a move against his own.

But then the attention-getting turned out to be six dead bodies, and then the granddaughter's husband was killed with his pants around his ankles, and then the two men were shot before they could shoot Guy, and the snowball traveling down the hill was growing bigger and moving faster and threatening to flatten all of them — all of the Levines, all of the La Rues.

"I think this is our last chance to stop it," Gérard said.

"I agree."

"I mean, if we don't—"

"I know, I know," Levine said. "We could end up crippling each other to the point where somebody else comes in and takes the whole thing. Those goddamn Delacroixes are always sniffing around. It wouldn't take much."

"That girl with my grand-nephew," Gérard said.

"Yeah, Delacroix. We saw and we checked it out. There's no connection. Just a name. But—"

"Yeah, I know," Gérard said. "Those bastards wouldn't hesitate if they saw an opportunity."

"So, it ends, yes?" Levine said.

"Henri and David will handle the details, yes?" Gérard said.

Levine nodded, and Gérard nodded in reply. He looked around the reading room again, and the dozen or so heads were down in their work. No one was looking to the back of the room, to where the two old crime bosses were sitting.

In their silence, Gérard knew what he was thinking — and

he was pretty sure that Old Joe was thinking the same thing. There was one last detail, after all.

"So, who makes the approach?" Gérard said.

"Henri," Levine said.

"Why Henri?"

"He had my granddaughter's husband killed."

"Which was an accident."

"He still did it."

"There was no way to know."

"He was still my granddaughter's husband, and he's still dead, and it was still a most embarrassing death," Levine said.

Gérard sighed, and he didn't care if Levine heard him. Everything was a negotiation, every last thing, and it was tiring.

"David needs to make the approach," Gérard said.

"Why David?"

"Because he's going to be the beneficiary," Gérard said. "He's going to win the negotiation in the end. You can't ask Henri to lose the negotiation after first making him crawl to the table. He won't do it."

"You can make him do it," Levine said.

"I won't make him do it, not that," Gérard said. "And I can't make him do it because this meeting between us today, and any previous meetings, never happened."

They were silent again. Gérard scanned the reading room one more time. The old man with the three books had closed one of them, but he was still reading the other two. The print must have been especially small in one of them, and the old man's nose was nearly touching the book as he read.

Old Joe Levine stood up.

"David will make the approach," he said. And then he shuffled toward the door.

Whenever he went to Montmartre Cemetery, Henri always stopped to see Zola first. Even on that day, he saw no reason to change. He had instructed Passy and Timmy to go on ahead, and to take a quick stroll, and then to park themselves on benches a couple of hundred yards from the meeting point. If they saw anything particularly egregious, anything more than just a couple of other men parked on a couple of other benches, they were to leave the cemetery and intercept Henri before he arrived. Except that wasn't going to happen.

"Weapons?" Timmy said. It was almost a tradition that he always asked that question before any kind of a meeting or operation. It was almost like a trope in a movie script. There were two things the La Rue family could not do without a comment from Timmy. Whenever they entertained a group of strippers in one of the back rooms of Trinity One, Timmy invariably said, "You all worry about the carpet matching the drapes, but I love the shine on a bare floor." And whenever they went out on a more mundane business excursion, Timmy always asked, "Weapons?"

"Just pistols," Henri said.

"Are you sure?" Passy said. He had looked somewhere between worried and dyspeptic since Henri told him about the meeting.

"It's not going to be like that," Henri said. "Pistols will be fine. They called to set it up."

"Could be a trap," Timmy said.

"No," Henri said. "Just pistols."

It wasn't going to be a trap. One of David Levine's men had made the call to Passy to set the time, and Henri picked the place. It was the ending that, if it wasn't preordained, was certainly more than predictable. As soon as the massacre in the luggage store took place, this meeting was almost inevitable. That's what Henri told himself. That was his miscalculation — that the Levines would strike back after he took over the 10th, and that they would strike back so hard. That was what he had not seen — that the Levines would risk an all-out war between the families rather than just negotiate for a piece of the old Morel territory. Henri had been ready for that negotiation. He had been ready to offer the Levines the gambling and the whorehouses in the 10th while the La Rue family kept the train stations. It would be a negotiation from a position of strength, with the La Rues firmly established in the 10th. It would be a negotiation where the La Rues kept both train stations and, as a result, about three-quarters of the revenue from the 10th. That's what Henri had always mapped out in his head, a negotiation that Gérard would have blessed for its wisdom and its financial acumen.

That was no longer going to be the conversation, though. And Henri well knew that, too. The only lever he had to pull was that David Levine had made the approach about the meeting, that the Levines were as ready to stop the bloodshed as Henri was.

"All right, go," Henri said, and Passy and Timmy left the uniform store. The cemetery was an easy walk. Henri waited 15 minutes and then made the walk himself, up Boulevard de Clichy toward the Moulin Rouge, up and then down the steps to the left. The roads overhung the cemetery in places.

The Zola family grave was pretty close to the entrance. The author's remains were moved to the Pantheon at some point, but the rest of the family and the memorial remained in Montmartre. It's hard to describe — a bold red stone thing with a bronze bust of Émile Zola framed in more red stone and overlooking the graves themselves, the metal oxidized to green by the years. Henri knew the basics of the story, of course, but he never read much about Zola and never read anything he wrote. Still, he stopped and looked every time because his brother Jean had always stopped and looked — stopped and looked and said the same thing every time, adding a quick salute as punctuation. And so, Henri said it as he looked up at the wild-looking bust. Just as his brother always had, Henri said, "J'accuse, mother-fucker," and then he saluted.

Walking along the cinder path, Henri looked up and saw a man sitting on a bench about 150 yards ahead. It looked like Passy. About 20 yards past him, on another bench, was another man he did not recognize. It must have been one of the Levine men. He did not see David Levine.

He turned right and made his way gingerly between the graves to the biggest building in the section, marble with a sizable cross on its roof. He always thought it was too big, just a bit out of place for the surroundings, and when he said it once to Gérard, his uncle replied, "It's perfect." And then, with the two of them standing there, standing there and looking up at the word LA RUE etched in the marble above the entrance, Gérard pointed his finger and scanned the immediate neighborhood, a true hodgepodge of memorials of different sizes and shapes all crammed together. "It's perfect, and they all know it's perfect," he said.

There was room inside for six graves and four of them were filled by Henri's grandmother and grandfather, and by Big Jean and Little Jean. The fifth spot belonged to Gérard and everybody knew it without saying it. That left one final grave for one final La Rue. At family holiday get-togethers, there was inevitably a riotous, usually drunken, always hilarious discussion about the final grave. Henri and Martin would laughingly make their case for why they deserved the spot. Of course, Henri never said what he really thought about his brother, and he never said what he was really thinking whenever he visited the graves. He looked at his father and his brother, Big Jean and Little Jean, and then he thought about the night they died, and about how Martin was not involved in any of what happened. While Henri really didn't feel guilty — he knew it wasn't his fault — and while he also knew that Martin's presence would not have made a difference either way, he envied the fact that his brother had not been there. Martin had not had to see it. Martin had not had to spend hours, then days, then years, convincing himself that there was nothing he could have done. Martin did not see the scene, the bodies, the blood, just for a second whenever he closed his eyes.

So, they would jokingly argue about superficial reasons why each of them deserved the final spot — like who was the better dresser, or who had lost the most weight that year, or who could tell the funnier joke. Stuff like that. Their wives would hoot them down sometimes and advocate for their husbands at other times. Because, as Sylvie said pretty much every year, "The last thing I want to do is spend eternity with you. A mortal life will be long enough, thank you."

Henri smiled as he navigated his way back through the jammed-together graves, some leaving only a foot or so to walk between them. Henri had never done it drunk — or, rather, really drunk — but you could legitimately hurt yourself if your balance was even a little impaired. The last thing he needed that day was to face-plant onto some asshole's grave, so he walked extra carefully back to the cinder path. A few steps farther along, he found David Levine sitting on a bench.

"I didn't want to disturb your moment," Levine said. He stood and offered his hand to Henri, and they shook.

The pleasantries were pleasant enough. Henri did not know David Levine well, but they were of the same generation, and Henri knew that David had also fought in the Resistance, and had always been cordial. One other thing they shared was a double burden — they did all of the work and dealt with all of the headaches while, at the same time, still had to answer to the second-guesses from an elder. There also were the envelopes that they had to kick up, Henri to Uncle Gérard, David to his father. Henri actually smiled when he wondered if the Levines used envelopes.

"You're smiling," David said.

"I was just thinking, we're not that different, you and me," Henri said.

"Yeah," David Levine said, and then he nodded. "Yeah."

David made the phone call to Henri because his father told him to make the phone call. His inclination was not to do it. The Levines had just lost two more men on the staircase outside of the apartment where Henri's son had been banging that Delacroix girl, and it was not the time to waver.

"It's the perfect time," Old Joe said.

"How can you say that? It makes no sense," David said.

"It makes perfect sense," the father said. "We could fight for longer. We might be able to beat them. But think. We want something that they have taken. The truth is, we're willing to split it. We've always been willing to split it. But now they have it. The best way to get our piece is to move now. The La Rues will see it as a sign of weakness, asking for the meeting."

"Because it is a sign of weakness," the son said.

"Think," Old Joe said. He tapped his index finger on his temple — once, twice, three times, and pretty hard.

"I don't get it," David said.

"That's the only way they'll take the meeting," Old Joe said. "And don't you get it? As soon as they take the meeting, we win — because it means they want to make a deal, too. And then, in the negotiation, they'll be giving us something that they currently possess. They take the meeting, we win."

So, David had one of his guys make the call to Passy. Everybody's blood was up in the office behind the uniform store. Six dead in the luggage store. Guy almost killed at the apartment door. Fuck some meeting. Fuck the Levines. That was the sentiment in the office, and Henri shared most of it.

But he felt as if he needed to take this decision to Gérard, and so, he climbed the butte and knocked on the door of the house on Cite du Sacre-Coeur. Gérard poured him a drink and listened to everything, to the facts and the emotions. And then, the old man said, "Fuck the Levines, but take the meeting."

"That makes no sense," Henri said.

"They're coming crawling," Gérard said. "It makes perfect sense."

"If they're crawling, we should fucking step on them," Henri said.

"Which is fine if your boot is big enough — if you're sure you can win," Gérard said.

He poured them each a second glass, and they sipped in silence. That was always the question, the one that Henri managed to keep submerged whenever the adrenaline was gushing but that always resurfaced in the quiet times. Could they win? He honestly believed that they could, but it wasn't just a question of numbers and tactics.

"Be honest," Gérard said, breaking the silence. "What you did the other night — I've never been prouder of you. You saved your son. You saved the family, in some ways — the present and the future. If they had gotten Guy, the down-spiral of this thing would have been — I don't know. I don't like to think about it. But how long can you protect him? How long can Passy and the rest of them live in hiding? This is not a game, as you well know. This is not generals moving miniature artillery pieces on a map and then sipping cognac hundreds of miles behind the lines. It's real. Imagine if they had gotten Guy — how you would feel, how Sylvie would feel about you and your marriage. Imagine."

They were quiet again. For Henri, that imagining was really what happened when the adrenaline ebbed. Things would never have been the same if the Levines had killed Guy, even if the La Rue family won in the end.

"You saved your son," Gérard said. "You saved the family's position in this, the La Rue position of strength. And now the Levines are on bended knee. It's time. It's the only thing that makes sense."

And so, each manipulated by his elder, David Levine and Henri La Rue shared a bench in Montmartre Cemetery. The negotiation wasn't that difficult in the end. Henri opened with an offer of the gambling casino, the two whorehouses and the street money in the 10th arrondissement. David said that would not be adequate, as Henri knew he would, but he did not get up to leave or show any strong displeasure. They were not leaving the bench without a deal, and both of them knew it.

It came together within about 15 minutes. The La Rues would take the Gare du Nord, the bigger and more lucrative of the train stations — although it wasn't clear to Henri if the Levines knew that. The Levines would get the Gare de l'Est. The La Rues would take the whorehouses and the Levines would take the casino — all of which were shit, and almost more trouble than they were worth. As for the street money, the Levines wanted it all — which would have come closer to balancing the financial split of the 10th pretty evenly. Henri insisted that they divide the arrondissement and the street money. The dividing line would be Rue Lafayette, which left the Levines with the bigger territory but which, based upon the meticulous ledger that Willy had kept, gave the La Rues the bigger financial share.

Those ledgers told Henri that the whole deal left his family with at least 60 percent of the money from the 10th, and maybe 65 percent. David Levine could only be guessing at his share of the split, but he seemed satisfied. In the end, David had one more demand — a payment to his daughter, the pregnant widow of the recently departed Mr. Pants-Around-His-Ankles. Henri quickly agreed.

"An honest bargain," David said. He extended his hand, and the two of them shook on the deal, and then they stood up. Each of them took a step in the opposite direction, and then Henri said, "Well, there is one obvious winner here."

"Who?" David Levine said. His face hardened, but then he smiled when Henri said, "The cops. They're the biggest winner. Now we both have to pay them off."

PART XIII

UP THE BUTTE

Julian Broussard couldn't pay, again. What he was even doing in Trinity One was another matter altogether. When Henri shouted into the telephone, "He was fucking banned," Passy replied with what amounted to a lot of gibberish. The way Passy ended up telling it, it was his night off, and his guys didn't know about the ban, and Broussard came with at least some cash, and they let him in, and then he started losing, and then they gave him more credit, and then came the commotion.

Passy and Henri arrived at Trinity One at almost exactly the same time. They went upstairs and saw Paco, who filled in for Passy on his nights off. He was actually shaking when Henri and Passy approached the office. As he closed the door, Passy began screaming, but Henri cut him off.

"Jesus," Henri said. "He actually tried to make a run for it?"

"Honest to God," Paco said. "Fool."

"He's 50-something, and he thought he was going to outrun you and the rest of the 20-something tuxedos out there?"

"Fool," Paco said.

The three of them trudged down to the alley, the same alley where their previous conversation had taken place. This time, Broussard looked a lot worse than he had before. There were still no visible bruises that could be seen beneath the single overhead light fixture, but Broussard was beyond shaken.

"You're a goddamned idiot," Henri said. Then he pulled up a crate and sat next to Broussard.

"I'm going to have to tell your wife," Henri said.

"No, no, you can't," Broussard said.

"It's the only way to get you to stop," Henri said.

"You can't," Broussard said. "Not Jen. No, you can't. I'll lose her. I'll lose everything."

"I'm against leg-breaking as a business practice," Henri said. "But that's where we are in the operations manual. That's the chapter we have reached, you and I. But short of that, I can't have this. This has gone too far. It's the only way I can get my money — to tell your wife, and to tell her everything, and to make her realize that a family financial sacrifice is the only way to clear this up."

"Everything?" Broussard said. His eyes were down, and he was almost whimpering.

"The casino, the third floor — yes, everything," Henri said.

The whimpering turned to crying, and Broussard said, "Henri, you can't. I'll lose her, lose my family — God, the third floor, especially. I'll lose them. They're my whole life."

"Well, not your whole life," Henri said.

"There has to be another way," Broussard said. At which point, Henri told Passy and Paco and the others to leave him and Broussard alone, that he would handle things from there.

A week or so after the meeting in Montmartre Cemetery, the mechanics of the agreement were still being worked out with the Levines. Introductions needed to be made, lists of men — the ones the La Rues had inherited from the Morels after they interrupted that salmon croquettes lunch — had to be handed over. How the Levines would handle the manpower in their part of the 10th was their own business, but it was only right to make the introductions and give the current men a chance at further employment.

Gérard suggested a drink at his house as a way to update him on what was happening. To Henri, it seemed as if his uncle was spending more time at home than before — or maybe it was just that Henri was being invited more often than before.

When they sat down, Henri noticed a book on Gérard's side table.

"What's the latest?" he asked. He pointed to the book.

"'Winesburg, Ohio,'" Gérard said.

"Of course," Henri said. He had never heard of it and his tone — as it always was when he asked about Gérard's little book club — was half mocking. Over the years, Gérard managed to ignore the tone, although Henri could tell that it always registered.

"It's by Sherwood Anderson, an American," Gérard said. "It's not a novel, not exactly. It's a group of separate stories about people who live in a small town. Christ, they're a miserable bunch."

"Sounds like fun," Henri said.

"It wouldn't hurt to broaden your horizons a little," Gérard said.

On the floor next to Gérard's chair was another book —

bigger, sturdier, obviously a ledger of some sort.

"And what's that, if I may ask?" Henri said. He pointed again.

"Just my accounts," Gérard said.

"You don't actually—"

"They're disguised," Gérard said. "No one but me would know that 'Groceries' was the money from Trinity One, or that 'Clothing' was the money from the general pot."

"But who buys that much clothing?" Henri said.

"It's not that much — I just knock off the last two zeroes from all of the entries."

"And you just leave it lying around?"

"Well, we've been going over the figures," Gérard said.

"We?"

"Jean Lemieux and I," Gérard said.

"You have that priest in our business?" Henri said. "What are you thinking?"

"He's an accountant — well, like an accountant," Gérard said. "He does these kinds of things for the archdiocese — that's his day job."

"But he's not family," Henri said.

"He's just helping me tidy things up a little bit," Gérard said.

"But he's not family," Henri said. "What aren't you hearing? He's not fucking family."

Gérard poured another small drink, took a sip, and said, "It's not a big deal."

"The hell it isn't."

"It's not a big thing," Gérard said. "And it's like confession — he can't tell anybody. For him, it's a solemn oath."

"That's bullshit, and you know it," Henri said. "This is crazy. There're no names in that book, right?"

"No real names," Gérard said.

"Jesus."

"And the family thing, you're forgetting," Gérard said. "We

had Izzy, forever. Since he died, I haven't had a real accountant. And Izzy wasn't family — not unless there is Jewish blood in there somewhere that none of us knows about."

"Izzy was ancient," Henri said. "Izzy was grandfathered in. This priest, though—"

"He's helping, that's all," Gérard said. "I need another set of eyes."

"But—"

"Enough, it's done," Gérard said. "Now, tell me about our piece of the 10th."

When Henri ran through the personnel details, Gérard nodded. When he told him the last part, though, he grinned.

Henri told Sylvie the night before — and she did more than grin in bed that night, and it wasn't even his birthday. He told Freddy the next morning — and he thought that Freddy might have blown him, too, if the office door had been closed. Freddy was going to run the Gare du Nord in the new setup — and if it wasn't quite as much responsibility as Willy had been given, it was a big step up, financially and otherwise.

Which left the whorehouses. And while some families discuss politics at the breakfast table, or current events, the whorehouses were what Henri and Guy talked about over coffee and croissants. Sylvie made each of them an egg and then sat down to join the conversation.

"It's time," Henri said. Guy's reaction was a fist pump, and then a quick look at his mother, and then what seemed to be a sincere look at his father, followed by, "I won't let you down."

Since that night in the apartment hallway, Guy had been different — at least, a little different. There was an unspoken admiration for his father, something that Henri just sensed as they sat around the house and watched television. That was the other thing — Guy was around the house a lot more, even in the days since the deal with the Levines had been struck. Henri didn't know if he was lost, or scared, or just humbled. He was praying for humbled.

"How does it all work?" Guy said.

"Well, the girl pulls down her knickers, and—"

"The money," Guy said. Then he muttered the word "asshole" under his breath, and the three of them broke up laughing.

"I'm going to tell you everything," Henri said. "This is more than the rest of the guys know, and it stays within the family. Got it?"

Guy nodded. He was trying to keep a straight face, but he couldn't camouflage his eagerness. He was inside now. He was part of it. It was his goddamn birthright, but it also was a signal that his father believed he had earned it. He had always been a part of the La Rue family, but now he was truly a part of it. The moment was undeniable — and then, Henri laid it out.

Every month, Guy would give his father 10 percent off the top, before expenses. Two percent went to Gérard in the envelopes in the back room of Vincent's, and Henri kept the other 8 percent. With the other 90 percent, Guy paid himself and his men, paid the whores, and paid for the upkeep on the business. What was left over went into a pot that was split four ways between Gérard, Henri, Martin and Michel.

Guy took it all in, and his first comment surprised Henri.

"Two percent for Gérard?" Guy said. "Two percent of everything? Plus his share of the split? Nice life if you can fucking get it."

"With age come its privileges," Henri said.

"That's a lot of cash for an old man who already owns his house," Guy said. "I mean, what does he spend it on other than diddling that priest?"

Sylvie and Henri reflexively looked at each other. Gérard and Father Lemieux? Guy saw their faces, the surprise.

"What, it never crossed your mind?" Guy said.

"You don't actually know something, do you?" Sylvie said.

"No, but, come on," Guy said. "You don't really believe it's just spiritual counseling, do you? I mean, seriously?"

"He's lending a hand with Gérard's ledger, his accounts," Henri said.

"That's not all he's lending a hand with," Guy said. "I mean, open your eyes."

This was a possibility that Henri had never considered — and, from the look on Sylvie's face, neither had she. Gérard had never married, true enough, but there was a story of a young love of his who died of something-or-other during World War I. The idea that, well, no — it had never crossed Henri's mind. If nothing else, Gérard was too old for all of that.

Guy changed the subject. He was full of questions. How much should his salary be? Ten percent, Henri told him. As for the expenses, anything within reason was okay — but there would be a lot of scrutiny if the money he kicked into the pot was shy of 10 percent. Fifteen percent was more like it.

"Here's the thing," Henri said. "The two places, they're both shitholes. They need work. You can do it in stages over the first few months, if that's the way you want to go. But there is a question you'll need to answer."

Guy looked at him, waiting.

"Shitty clientele, shitty whores, shitty facilities, shitty revenues," Henri said.

"So if I upgrade, the clientele will improve?" Guy said.

"Exactly," Henri said. "What comes first, the chicken or the egg?"

"Better paint job, better pussy, better profits?" Guy said. Then he looked at his mother and apologized. She swatted him with the back of her hand, and the three of them laughed some more. Family time for the La Rues, then.

The address of the house was 25 Rue du Mont-Cenis. If the café where Sylvie liked to sit with Henri and bitch about her living circumstances was at the bottom of the endless series of staircases, 25 Rue du Mont-Cenis was at the top. The very top.

It was less than a five-minute walk from where Henri and Sylvie had gone to lunch. They were on the top of the butte, at a no-name bistro on Place du Tertre, taking a table outside and watching the world go by — tourists being sketched by the local artists, writers nursing a single glass of wine and scribbling for hours, people just moving about. The sun felt wonderful on their faces. They were basking, both literally and figuratively.

"You have any doubts?" Sylvie said. The waiter had brought a second bottle of Bordeaux, and they were in no hurry.

"About what?" Henri said.

"About Guy"

"Sure. I wouldn't be a businessman if I didn't have doubts. I wouldn't be a parent if I didn't have worries. That's just human nature."

"Still," Sylvie said. "You know how excited I am for him — for both of you. But—"

"You're worried about the danger?"

She nodded.

"Whorehouses aren't dangerous, except for the diseases," Henri said, and she elbowed him gently, and he continued. "But the way I figure it, if Timmy can survive a lifetime sampling the wares, anybody can. God bless penicillin."

"That's not what I mean."

"I know, I know," he said. "I've accepted the risks of the business for myself, and so have you. I get that this is different. But, well, I wasn't kidding. Whorehouses really aren't very dangerous

— and that's all he'll be doing. He won't have any money on the street, and he won't be called on for any — how should I say this? — for any enforcement activities. I promise you that, at least for the foreseeable future."

"But stuff happens," Sylvie said. "Stuff you can't predict. Stuff like the Levines — and then, everything changes."

"There's nothing on the immediate horizon," Henri said. "You can look at this as the La Rue family entering a period of consolidation. We're not looking to get bigger. We're just looking to get richer."

The walk, as it turned out, took only two minutes — a half-block in the direction of the basilica and then a left onto Rue du Mont-Cenis. It was probably 500 feet from Place du Tertre, 500 feet of small shops and cafés and then the big water tower on the right. Just past there was the first of the cascade of staircases that led down, down, down to the street where Henri and Sylvie lived.

"What do you think?" Henri said. He was facing No. 25.

"About what?"

"About that."

"What are you talking about?"

Henri reached into his pocket and pulled out a set of keys. He walked over to the door of the house and inserted the key and, as he turned it, he looked over his shoulder at his wife and said, "The very top. No steps. Not one."

Sylvie was speechless.

"Close your mouth," he said. "And follow me."

Julian Broussard and his family had moved out the week before, and the place was empty. Truth be told, their current amalgamation of apartments was bigger, but this one — on the fourth floor, with an elevator — was more than big enough. It would have cost Henri half again what their current place was worth, if he had bought it at the market price.

Instead, Henri paid about 50 cents on the dollar. That was the deal he had cut with Broussard after the other had left the two of them sitting on crates in the alley behind Trinity One.

"That's robbery," Broussard said, after several seconds of fumphering.

"It's my offer," Henri said. "You'll be free and clear of your debts here, and your wife will be none the wiser."

"It's a lot more than I owe," Broussard said, attempting to make a logical argument in the alley behind a combination casino/whorehouse.

"It's my offer," Henri said. "You're free and clear, but you're out of the fucking house."

"And if I say no?" Broussard said.

"Then I go to the operations manual," Henri said. "I break your legs. I tell your wife. Then I have the negotiation over the lease with her. How do you think that might go — not that you'll really give a shit, seeing as how she would have divorced your ass, how you would be living in a cold-water flat somewhere in the 10th."

"But what will I tell her?" Broussard said. If there had been a hint of bravado before, there was none now that the topic of broken legs had been raised again.

"Tell her whatever you want," Henri said. "Tell her you need to downsize. Lots of couples do it when they get to be your age. But I really don't give a shit."

Henri had no idea what Broussard ended up telling his wife. All he knew was that the deal went through, and the apartment was empty and that, once he sold the place on Rue Caulaincourt, there would be a nice profit that Sylvie would have no idea about.

As they toured the place, Sylvie's mouth still never really closed, especially when she looked out the windows — and looked down, down, down the staircases.

"Is this really—"

"All yours — well, ours," Henri said. He tossed her the keys. "Painters are all lined up for a week from today — all you have to do is pick the colors. The movers are reserved for two weeks after that. It's all done."

She kissed him, and hugged him, and kissed him again. As they backed away from each other, he smiled and wondered to himself what Sylvie would have to bitch about now that she lived on the top of the butte. Probably Marina.

"What are you smiling about?" Sylvie said.

"Just happy," he said. "Although there is one problem."

"What?"

"Gérard."

"How's that a problem? Sylvie said. "You think he'll be mad that we've joined him on the top of the butte?"

"No, not that. I don't think he thinks that way. It's just that he's... he's right fucking there," Henri said. He pointed out the living room window. It was another two-minute walk to his uncle's house, maybe three minutes. Then Henri walked Sylvie to the other window and pointed at a café, Le Cenis.

"I'm pretty sure that's his local," Henri said.

"Don't worry about that," she said. "There are about 10 places to get a glass within five minutes of here."

"Like I could ever avoid him."

"Have you ever considered that he might want to avoid you?" Sylvie said.

ENJOY THIS BOOK? YOU CAN REALLY HELP ME OUT.

The truth is that, even as an author who has sold a quarter-million books, it can be hard to get readers' attention. But if you have read this far, I have yours – and I could use a favor.

Reviews from people who liked this book go a long way toward convincing future readers of its worth. It won't take five minutes of your time, but it would mean a lot to me. Long or short, it doesn't matter.

Thanks!

I hope you enjoyed *Conquest*, the first book in my La Rue family crime thriller series. The second book in the series, *Power*, will be available in August 2023.

My main series features Alex Kovacs, an everyman who tries to do the right thing as the Nazis are preparing to invade his home in Austria in 1938 and ends up as a spy, and then in the French Resistance, and then as a spy again during the Cold War. The first book in the series is *Vienna at Nightfall*.

My other series, beginning with *A Death in East Berlin*, features a protagonist named Peter Ritter, a young murder detective in East Berlin at the time of the building of the Berlin Wall.

Those books, as well as the rest of all three series, are available for purchase now. You can find the links to all of my books at https://www.amazon.com/author/richardwake.

Thanks for your interest! And here is a free sample from the second book in the La Rue crime family thriller series, *Power*:

SUNDAY AT VINCENT'S

Sunday afternoon, the first Sunday of the month, the back table at Vincent's. For Henri La Rue and the rest of the La Rue family, this was the other holy day of obligation. There was nothing particularly warm or loving about the gathering, and nothing spiritual about it — other than that money was the family religion, and that the first Sunday of the month was Gerard's envelope day.

For years, Sylvie had been threatening to forego the family style roast pork or roast chicken (on alternating months) and order off of the card, but she never did. This was true mostly because, in the end, she got a lot more pleasure out of the complaining than she would have out of the brisket, or the pig's knuckle, or whatever else was on offer. They had been married long enough that Henri knew this intuitively. It just wouldn't be the first Sunday of the month if Sylvie wasn't bitching about how cheap Uncle Gerard was.

As in, "I mean, what is the old fossil saving it for? It isn't as if he can bury the loot with him when the time comes — and it's coming quick. Christ, look at him."

Gerard sat at the head of the table, his face in shadow, but it was still easy to see that he looked like hell. His oldest friend, Maurice — Silent Moe to everyone, for obvious reasons — sat in his customary spot to Gerard's right, and Father Lemieux — Gerard's priest — sat in what had more recently become his customary spot to Gerard's left. The three of them at the end, the priest carrying the conversation, Silent Moe nodding a lot, Gerard in the middle, Gerard deteriorating a little more every month. His health had been the topic of sub rosa family conversations for a while — and whatever was wrong with him, it wasn't getting any better. Sylvie was incorrect, though. It wasn't coming quick. Gerard's decline had been slow — months long, six, eight, maybe 10 months long. And unless something had changed in recent weeks, Gerard still had not been to see a doctor.

The man was a creature of habit — Mass every morning at Sacre Coeur; toast and jam and coffee for breakfast; suit jacket one size bigger than the pants to accommodate the holster he always wore and the pistol he never fired; platters of roast pork or roast chicken at Vincent's. All of that, and no visits to doctors, whom the old man referred to as "well educated charlatans" when he wasn't calling them "nicely dressed thieves."

The last time he went on his "nicely dressed thieves" rant, Henri nearly spit out his coffee and said, "Pot, kettle?"

"Meaning what?" Gerard said.

"Meaning exactly what you think it means. Come on. Nicely dressed thieves? Have you looked in a mirror lately? Are you that lacking in self-awareness."

"I'm perfectly self-aware. The difference is, I come by my theft honestly. There is no pretense. I am what I am — and I am not a well-educated charlatan who sometimes pretends to hand you an answer but always wraps his bullshit in an invoice."

The memory was interrupted by a coughing fit coming from the end of the table. It sounded as if Gerard was hacking up a lung, and Silent Mo and Father Lemieux were each poised for action, Moe with a glass of water and the priest with a napkin. At one point, Henri's wiseass of a son theatrically wiped at his cheek, as if Gerard had nailed him with some spittle from 15 feet away.

"Christ," said Guy, the son. "He's more dead than alive."

At which point, Guy poked Henri with his elbow and nodded toward the platter of pork. Henri handed it over and the 26-year-old refilled his plate. Sylvie watched and tut-tutted quietly, but her son heard her.

"Better than your cooking," he said. At which point, the mother picked up her knife and menaced it at her oldest. Of course, this — the brandished knife — was something Guy saw on a monthly basis at the two brothels that he ran for the family.

"Take your best shot," Guy said. Then he leaned over, kissed his mother on the cheek, and swiped the roll from her bread plate.

Getting Guy into the business had been good for all of them. Much of the surliness was gone. That he still drank too much and stayed out too late was true, but at least he managed to shave and put on a fresh suit most of the time. And if he and Henri weren't exactly close, father and son were somehow a bit tighter now that "employer and employee" had been added to their relationship resume.

Then, there was Clarice. If Henri had been reluctant to bring Guy into the family business — and he had been, never trusting in the boy's competence — he was adamant that his 23-year-old daughter would not get within a million miles of the La Rue family enterprises. He was proud of her brain and her initiative

— she had gone to school for a degree in finance in Zurich, one of only two women in her class, and was finishing up an extra bit of post-graduate coursework at the Sorbonne. She was too smart, too good, with too much potential, and she was not going to be handing anybody an envelope — not as long as Henri had anything to say about it. And that would be for quite a while, seeing as how he was essentially the family's managing partner as it was — and if Gerard continued to decline, he would be more than that.

The fights between father and daughter over this issue had been fierce — and, in this one case, Sylvie tended to side with her husband. She was more old school than Henri in that she didn't think there was a place for women in the business, other than as unofficial counselors to their husbands. Henri was less a traditionalist than Sylvie was that way. He wasn't against a woman taking a seat at the table — just this particular woman, his daughter. The result of the arguments had been, and continued to be, a condition of permafrost in the house, with Clarice often finding an excuse to stay with various friends who had apartments near the Sorbonne.

Still, she had come to the last couple of lunches. And even if she mostly pushed the food around her plate, and whispered conspiratorially to her brother, and pretty much ignored her parents, it was something.

———

It was in the little back room behind the back table at Vincent's where Henri always took the best measure of his uncle. After dessert, Gerard would get to his feet and go through the door, accompanied by Silent Moe. That was where the real business of the afternoon was conducted, in age order: first Henri, then his brother Martin, then his cousin Michel. Guy and Clarice would follow after that, but theirs were only quick social visits. They didn't carry sealed white envelopes in their breast pockets.

The mystery this day was Michel, his chair empty. His wife, Romy, was there, but not the man himself. She had announced when she arrived that "Michel has been detained on a work matter. He'll be here soon." But the coffee was being poured, and still no Michel. Henri looked at Martin, and they both shrugged, and the older brother began the parade into the back room.

"Sit, sit," Gerard said, pointing at the small arm chair. Silent Moe handed him a small glass of brandy, and Henri took a long sip. Then, he reached into his pocket for the envelope. It was all a part of the ritual — sit, sip, serve the master.

And then, Gerard held out his hand.

There were three main business arms to the La Rue family enterprises — four, if you counted the street money that everyone was permitted to lend out within specified territories. Even Gerard still had a small street operation — although, as Martin put it, "His guys are as old as he is. Tough to break someone's legs when you have a 70-year-old trying to chase the guy down."

So, three arms. Henri handled the bread and butter — thefts from the train station as well as whorehouses and gambling, especially Trinity One, the combination casino/brothel in the 9th, down near the opera, that attracted only the wealthiest clients and was the crown jewel of the operation. Martin handled alcohol in all of its forms, running a legitimate wine and liquor importing business that covered for the real operation: supplying bars and cafes with beer and wine whether they wanted it or not. Then there was Michel, the cousin who grew up in Marseille and brought the heroin smuggling business with him to the La Rue family in Paris. Heroin had become the most lucrative part of the operation and also the most controversial —

at least to Henri and Martin, who very much liked the additional income but very much hated that their younger cousin had control over so much cash.

Henri handed the envelope to Gerard, and he weighed it in his hand. If it felt light, he tended to say something. If it felt appropriate or heavy, he tended to nod but say nothing — not a "thank you," not a "good job," nothing.

That day, Gerard weighed it for what seemed like an extra long time, but he said nothing. Just a nod.

In their envelopes, Henri, Martin and Michel each delivered two percent of their gross revenues for the previous month. That was Gerard's take, and it involved the simplest math — two percent was two percent — but it wasn't all that the old man received for, as Sylvie said, "Sitting on his ass and getting in the way." Because there was another financial reckoning that usually took place on a quarterly basis, the distribution of profits after salaries and expenses. It tended to be about 15 percent of the gross, and that amount was split four ways between Gerard, Henri, Martin and Michel.

Gerard handed the envelope to Silent Moe, then took a sip of his own brandy. His hand shook.

"You feeling okay?" Henri said.

"Fine. Getting old is a bitch, but fine."

"You sure?"

"Stop," Gerard said. "I'm fine."

"But, a doctor —"

"Will you fucking stop — I'm fucking fine."

"Well, you don't —"

"I'm not going to warn you again."

"It's just —"

Gerard glared at him, and Henri stopped.

The envelopes he had brought Gerard were smaller than they had been six months earlier, but the old man was fine with that. A year earlier, the La Rues had taken over control of both the Gare du Nord and the Gare de l'Est from a rival family that was in the midst of a crisis. Six months later, the La Rues were forced to make a deal with another rival, the Levines, to give them the Gare de l'Est in exchange for ending what was very nearly a full-on war.

It was a deal that Gerard had quietly brokered with Old Joe Levine, although neither Henri nor Levine's son, David — Henri's counterpart — knew all of the details.

"Better this way," Gerard said. He seemed to know what Henri was thinking without his nephew saying anything.

"Lighter envelopes are never better, uncle."

"Better than a shooting war."

"I guess," Henri said.

Martin followed Henri into the back room. Michel's chair was still empty. Henri disliked both of them but for opposite reasons. The problem with Martin was that Henri knew him too well. The issue with Michel was that Henri barely knew him at all.

Martin always spent the least amount of time with Gerard — five minutes, tops. There was no grand strategy to be discussed with the youngest La Rue brother, and Gerard had little time for fools, and Martin was, if not a full-fledged fool, at least fool-ish. While he was in with their uncle, Sylvie said, "Anything?"

"Like what?"

"Deathbed confession? Revised will and testament? I don't know."

"He's not dying," Henri said.

Sylvie arched an eyebrow.

"At least, he's not dying tomorrow. I mean, he looks like shit, but if I had to guess, there are miles to go."

Just then, Father Lemiuex crouched between their two chairs and whispered, "I heard what you were saying."

"And what of it?" Sylvie said. She had no time for the man she referred to as "the briefcase priest" because of his job working with the cardinal on the archdiocese's finances. The way he told it, Lemieux had never been a pastor anywhere, just an assistant. But he lived in the big rectory near Notre Dame and had the cardinal's ear, and that wasn't nothing.

"It's just, I'm also worried," the priest said. "This has been going on for too long, and he won't see a doctor, and..."

His voice trailed off. Henri said, "Can't you convince him?"

"About the doctor? Impossible. Such a smart man, but such an imbecile about the medical profession."

"So, what?" Sylvie said. The tone was beyond disrespectful. Henri felt like grabbing her by the hair and reminding her that, if it hadn't been for a bit of subterfuge engineered by Lemieux a few months earlier, her son might have been imprisoned following a bank robbery. By Henri's reckoning, his wife's gratitude could have been measured in mere hours — and no more than days.

"I don't like it and I don't like him," is where Sylvie always ended up. "What the hell is he up to?"

"He's Gerard's friend," Henri said.

"So why did he move in? You know what Guy says."

"Guy has sex and conspiracy on the brain. Gerard's too old for that — even if he was interested, which I don't believe. I mean, there was always the story about that girl who died —"

"A story," Sylvie said.

"He's a friend to an old man, and we're lucky for it," Henri said. "I mean, Moe still has his wife to go home to for dinner, and the nights alone for Gerard must be ... Christ, do you want to spend time with him?"

"Like he'd ever invite us over — and don't start with the almighty annual Christmas drink. Some goddamned invitation."

That's how the conversation went every time the subject of Lemieux came up. Sylvie didn't like Gerard and she didn't like anybody who liked Gerard, and that was that. It was her transitive property of relationships, and it was immutable. Lemieux would have had to have been brain dead not to sense the hostility, but he never shied away from a conversation.

"I don't know what to do at this point," Lemieux said. "He won't listen to me. I've gotten Maurice's ear, but he doesn't seem to be making a lot of progress — not that he says very much. Part of me thinks I should just bring a doctor around to the house, but, well, no."

"He deserves his dignity," Henri said.

"Yeah, that's what I keep coming back to, even if he is an imbecile."

Lemieux smiled weakly, stood up, and went back to his seat. Henri looked at his watch. If the past was an accurate predictor, Martin would be out in two minutes.

———

Michel had taken off his jacket and tie, his shirt and his undershirt, his shoes and socks and trousers. He stood there in his boxer shorts, on the dirt floor of a garage that was maybe four blocks from Vincent's restaurant, and swung the tire iron he held in his right hand, swung it in a wide arc that ended precisely in the center of Frankie Briere's left kneecap.

Briere screamed, and not for the first time — but the rag stuffed into his mouth and tied into place managed to muffle most of it. Michel had a system when it came to this kind of thing, starting by flattening the subject's nose and frightening him with all of the blood, and then proceeding as necessary. It was why he stripped after tying up Briere — because he still had plans to attend the family lunch, and there would be no time to go home for a fresh change of clothes.

Based on what he knew about Briere, Michel thought the broken nose might be enough. But Briere surprised him. The broken nose produced only a "fuck you" in reply. Next, Michel pulled down Briere's trousers, put on his right shoe, and kicked Briere in the balls as hard as he could. There was no "fuck you" that time, only a first and then a second spew of vomit.

When Briere's breathing approximated normal again, Michel asked him for the fourth time — all four times without raising his voice — "Frankie, I need the delivery details."

Then came another "fuck you." Then came the gag, and then the tire iron that shattered the knee cap. That did the trick — that and a gentle massage of Briere's right knee cap with the tire iron. The details — a vegetable truck with the stencil of a tomato painted on the side, at Les Halles, on Thursday morning at 2 a.m. — were accompanied by tears, and that was the only disappointment Michel felt. Because he admired Frankie's toughness and bravery, and the tears diminished them. It was what he was thinking about, that disappointment, as he finished Frankie's final Sunday afternoon with one, two, three blows to the head with the tire iron.

One, two, three. Michel washed his hands in a nasty sink, and got dressed, and walked the four blocks to Vincent's restaurant. Romy greeted him with a hug, and Henri with mock applause. It wasn't a minute after he walked in that Martin emerged from the back room, signaling that it was Michel's turn.

———

Henri: "So, what do you think about him?"

Martin: "Looks like shit, same as always."

Henri: "Not Gerard. What do you think about Michel?"

Martin: "The fucking golden child? Same as ever, I guess."

Henri: "But, he missed ..."

Martin: "He missed the crap food but he made it for the main event. I'm sure, whatever his excuse, uncle will weigh the slight with one hand and the envelope with the other hand, and ..."

Henri: "I guess."

Martin: "You don't guess. You know. You've know for as long as you've had hair on your balls. Hell, you coined the phrase."

Henri: "In the La Rue family, it doesn't matter what's in your head or what's in your heart as long as there's something in the envelope."

Martin: "Here he comes. That was quick."

Henri: "Smug little prick."

Martin: "In his case, he could wipe his ass with the envelope and Gerard would still accept it happily."

Henri: "Smug little prick."

Michel came out and Guy took his place in the back room. There was no envelope involved. Guy kicked up only to his father — 10 percent of the gross revenues from the two brothels. He kept another 10 percent for his own salary. After paying all of his expenses — from the girls, to the bartenders, to the security men, and the rest — Guy had to find a way to kick 15 percent into the big pot that Gerard, Henri, Martin and Michel split on a quarterly basis. It was almost never a problem. And in the months when there was more than about 18 percent left after expenses, the rest went into Guy's pocket by means of some creative accounting. Plumbing emergency one month, electrician another, and on and on.

This wasn't a business meeting, then, even if everything about the La Rue family was business.

"You look like hell," Gerard said.

"That's supposed to be my line."

"Meaning?"

"You own a mirror?"

"I'm fine," the old man said. "But you, every time I see you, you're hung over. Or worse."

"I work nights in a whorehouse — how do you expect me to look."

"It's not the work that exhausts you, it's the play."

Guy saluted. His uncle smiled.

"Any complaints with my performance?"

"That's your father's department, and if he has any, he hasn't expressed them to me. But, you know, I worry."

"No need."

"I can't help it. I just worry —"

"That I'm not cut out for the family business?" Guy said. "Aren't we done with that?"

Gerard took a sip from his drink. Guy had already downed his and help up the glass for Moe to refill.

"I don't know," Gerard said. "It's just, for the longest time ..."

"With all due respect, that's bullshit. For the longest time, I was a kid. Granted. Guilty. But my father was a kid once, and you were a kid once — you know, before we had electricity or toilet paper ..."

"I could wipe my ass with your face if you're not careful," Gerard said, and then he laughed.

"And you know my father is watching," Guy said. "And you know he can feel how heavy his envelope from me is, and you know that all of you pay pretty close attention to what I throw into the pot every month because I'm my father's son. And there's nothing to bitch about. And the reason there's nothing to bitch about is that I'm pretty fucking good at this, as it turns out."

"You sound surprised."

"I am, a little — but don't you ever tell my father I said that."

The two brothels he ran catered to different clientele. The one on Rue Lepic, farther up the butte in Montmartre, was a bit higher class — not like Trinity One, but not bad. The other whorehouse, on Boulevard de Clichy, was universally known in the family as "the skank place." But Guy had made the decision, despite some skepticism from above, to spend some not-insignificant money to class-up the skank place, at least a bit — and it was beginning to pay off.

"I still don't know, putting money in that, in that shithole," Gerard said.

"That's the whole point," Guy said. "Working men have a right to clean, disease-free dicks, too — and to a relaxing complimentary drink after they've put their clean, disease-free dicks away."

Gerard laughed and waved at Silent Moe. He poured them each another half shot of the brandy.

"We're both working men, right?"the old man said, raising his glass. "In that case, I drink to clean, disease-free dicks."

Guy emerged from the back room and Clarice was on her feet before he reached the table. They shared a whisper and a laugh — "Did Moe say anything ... Nope ... So, how long since ... Three years, easy ..." — and then she was in the back room. She leaned over and kissed Gerard on the top of his head. Silent Moe poured her something from a different bottle — sherry, not brandy.

"So, when ..."

"Husband or degree completion?"

"I'll leave the husband to your mother," Gerard said. "I was asking about your studies."

"Two credits to go — a few months."

"And then?"

Clarice had practiced her speech a dozen times in the three days since she had become aware of the information. There was no question in her mind that Gerard shared every bit of her father's chauvinism when it came to the idea of her becoming involved in the family business. At the same time, she also knew that Gerard was allowing the priest, an outsider, to care for his personal books and likely the books of the family — which meant that he was at least a little open to non-traditional thinking. But what she was counting on most was much more basic: that Gerard had never been known as someone to turn down a payday.

"It's simple," she said. "I have come into possession of some rather lucrative information."

Gerard stared back at her.

"Very lucrative information," Clarice said.

Gerard continued staring, and then he said, "You cannot. It's impossible."

"Listen for two minutes without interrupting. After that, if you want to pat me on the head and send me away, fine. I might have other options."

"It's inconceivable," Gerard said. "I mean, your father ..."

"Two minutes," she said. "Two minutes, yes?"

The stare was harder this time. There was something on the old man's face that she couldn't quite decipher.

"Two minutes," he said, and then Gerard actually looked down at his watch. So did Silent Moe, from his seat in the outfield.

In the end, it didn't take 90 seconds. The information that

she had obtained from one of her professors at the Sorbonne — a man with government connections — was that the French franc was about to be devalued. There was significant money to be made from this information, and it was a sure thing. The La Rue family profits would only be limited by the amount of money the family was willing to risk — and it wasn't a risk. The information was rock-solid.

Gerard was now leaning forward in his seat.

"Explain," he said. "Slowly."

Sometime in mid-to-late December, the franc would be devalued, she said. The country would make the announcement, and as if by magic, the amount of gold or foreign currency that a franc could purchase would be lowered by a certain percentage. From her information, that amount was about 15 percent.

"Why would they do such a thing?" Gerard said.

"It has to do with getting into the common market they're talking about with Europe and England," she said. "There's a need to, I don't know, equalize the values of the different currencies. You don't make them exactly equal, but get them in a kind of range of equality."

The old man nodded.

"OK, how does this help us?" he said.

Clarice went on to explain the basics of the futures markets when it came to currencies. You could place a bet, essentially, on whether you thought the value of the franc was going to go up or down during a specific time period.

"So you can bet it's going to go down?"

"Exactly," she said. "Except, in our case, it won't be gambling because we already know what's going to happen."

"And this is illegal?"

"Quite."

"So, how do you not get caught?"

"By placing your bets somewhere else," Clarice said. "You can't do it in the bourse here. You have to go to a foreign country, you have to use cash, and you have to pay off the broker you use to place the trade so that there is no paper trail."

"And this is doable? By who?"

"By me, dear uncle. I suggest we do it in Zurich, where I have some connections because of school. I travel there with the money in my suitcase, and I make the arrangements, and I return after the devaluation with the profits. The guaranteed profits."

"Your suitcase? Really?"

"We could wire the money to an account, and I could withdraw it there, but why complicate things? The banks there are very secret when you want them to be, but why create a record when there is no need to create a record? Smuggling the money in and out is just neater and cleaner. I mean, have you ever seen any of the border guards open a single piece of luggage when you make the crossing? No less, a young girl's luggage?"

Clarice stopped talking. Gerard went from leaning forward to leaning back, arms folded, eyes closed. He sighed, and then he was quiet, and then he sighed again, deeper than the first time.

And then, he leaned over his shoulder and said, "Maurice." Silent Moe came over, and Gerard whispered something in his ear. Then, Gerard grabbed the pencil and notepad from his little side table, and scrawled something on it, and folded it, and handed it to Clarice. It was a larger amount than she had expected — not that she really expected anything.

"Come by the house in a few hours and Maurice will give you the money," Gerard said. "You will handle the investment as you see fit and keep 20 percent of the profit for yourself. The rest will be mine. This is my personal money, not La Rue money.

This is a business arrangement between you and me and no one else is to know — not your father, not anyone. Understood?"

"Understood," Clarice said. "But there is another way to play this if you're willing to involve Martin. He makes a lot of foreign wine and liquor purchases, I believe. Well, if you told him to pre-pay some of his accounts, before the devaluation was announced, he would save a lot of money."

"No," Gerard said.

"But ..."

"No. This is private, just between you and me. It has to be that way, and if you can't accept that, we're done with our two minute conversation."

"No, no, I accept," Clarice said.

Gerard raised his glass, and Clarice raised hers. Gerard finished his, and Clarice barely wet her lips. She couldn't stand sherry.

Another kiss on the head, and they were done — except for Gerard placing his hands on Clarice's shoulders, and pushing her back a bit until they were just beyond nose-to-nose, and saying, "Don't let me down, baby girl."

They had been drinking since it got dark, if you didn't count the beers at lunch. It had been that kind of a day, nothing much happening, just shit-talking and drinking. It was the kind of day that made Jerzy Lewinsky antsy, which is why he seemed to drink more than the rest of them. It was something he was aware of, too, the antsy-ness. "Self-medicating" is what he called it when he found himself downing three ryes to everyone else's two.

In the Levine family, Jerzy and his crew were known as the Young Bucks. As often as not, on days like that, they ended up in the informal Levine clubhouse, a big room in the back of a butcher shop off of Rue de Rosiers. The butcher had used it for cold storage at one point, apparently, but refrigeration had somehow reduced the amount of space they needed, and there had been a debt owed at some point, and the Levines ended up with a key to the back room, and a refrigerator of their own, and a card table, and a little bar — but it was such a shithole that mostly the Young Bucks used it. The older soldiers in the family had better places.

Jerzy was there that night with three of his crew members, and they were making fun of David Levine, the boss. It was what the Young Bucks did, especially when fueled by alcohol. They never mentioned Old Joe Levine when they got like this because they assumed that the technical boss of the family was pretty much a technical corpse at that point. David, his son, really ran things. David was the guy who took the envelope from Jerzy every month. David was the guy who always bitched about family standards not being met, and "rules and decorum" being important. David was the one who told Jerzy in their most recent conversation, "If I can smell the alcohol on your breath at 11 a.m., there's a problem. A big fucking problem."

"Because the envelope is light?" Jerzy said. Then he belched, and was fortunate that no one in the vicinity was lighting a match.

"The envelope isn't everything," David Levine said. "At some point, you know, a young buck has to grow up — because if he doesn't, if he doesn't start to observe the rules and decorum, if he doesn't start to take care, he ends up a dead buck."

Jerzy was reciting the speech to his boys, doing a bad imitation of David's deep baritone, and they were pissing themselves. Then, each in turn, they tried the imitation, and one was worse than the next, and the laughing was convulsive.

And with every fresh drink, the toast was the same:

"Young Bucks ... Dead Bucks ... Fuck it."

Jerzy could barely feel the tip of his nose when they locked the door behind them at the butcher shop. The rest had girl-friends to see, but Jerzy was free — "between snatches," as he told his mates. There was a regular bar a few blocks away, though, and he had some civilian friends who figured to be there — and, maybe some snatches. He figured he would stop for one more.

As it turned out, it was just two other guys he knew and no women. One more became two, and two became three, and Jerzy's finger tips were also becoming numb, and then one of the civilians said, "There's a new casino on Rue Pierre Dupont. Let's go check it out."

"Where did you say?" Jerzy said. His hearing was fine, but his attention span had shortened considerably through the evening.

"On Pierre Dupont."

"That's not possible?"

"Fuck you — it's right there. I've seen it."

But it was not possible. Jerzy knew where Rue Pierre Dupont was, and while it was tucked into a corner of the 10th, it was clearly within the boundaries of the Levines' territory. Everybody knew the line between Levine territory and La Rue territory was Rue La Fayette. That was the line that had been brokered in the peace treaty. And if there was a new casino on Rue Pierre Dupont, it had to be a Levine casino — except that he knew there was no new Levine casino. He knew it because, while the Levines did do some casino work, David hated the casino business — "shitty people, shitty profits, not worth the effort." David said that as often as he said "rules and decorum"

And as they grabbed their coats, and one of the civilians got the bartender to call a taxi, Jerzy reached into his pocket. It was such a small pistol that sometimes he forgot about it, but it was there.

And 10 minutes after that, they three of them were piling out of the taxi. There was no sign out front of the building, just a gorilla bundled up against the cold. The gorilla asked what they wanted. One of the civilians said, "To try our luck in the best new place in town." The gorilla sneered but opened the door. They were drunk enough to be big losers and quick losers — that is, the best losers of all.

Inside, up one flight of steps, the casino was, in fact, there. Jerzy couldn't believe it. He looked around, and there were about a dozen punters in the place — three at the roulette table, five playing craps, the rest at a poker table. He could feel the heat rising in his face, even if his nose was numb. He put his hand in his coat pocket and fingered the revolver.

There was a bar along the far wall. It took Jerzy a second to focus, but he knew one of the bartenders. It was a La Rue kid who one of his crew once got into an argument with over a girl in a bar. It ended with a lot of fuck-you's and nothing worse.

A La Rue casino, then.

He fingered the gun and felt the safety.

This was a clear violation of the rules. The treaty had been brokered. The boundary was Rue La Fayette. This place was on the Levines' side of Rue La Fayette — just barely, maybe two blocks over, but it was definitely on the Levines' side.

Against the rules. Clearly fucking against the rules. The goddamn La Rues. They caused all of the trouble in the first place by grabbing both of the train stations when the Morels fell apart. Greedy fucking pigs. There should have been a negotiation from the beginning, and after they did what they did, there should have been an all-out war. Why David made peace after the Levines had them on the run — fucking pussy. It was what he thought when it happened and it was what he thought as he stood there.

With his thumb, Jerzy clicked off the safety. He did that, and he mumbled, "Fucking pussy."

This could not be allowed to stand. Rules and decorum insisted that it could not be allowed to stand.

Rules and decorum.

Fucking pussy.

Young Bucks ... Dead Bucks ...

"Fuck it!" Jerzy Lewinsky shouted, and then he said some other stuff while yanking the revolver out of his pocket. It caught on the fabric, though, and it took two yanks to get it out, and then Jerzy aimed the gun wildly toward the bar and squeezed the trigger.

The single bullet he fired lodged in the ceiling. The single bullet fired in reply lodged in his brain.

"Who the fuck is he?"

"Don't know."

"What did he say again?"

"'Who the hell do you La Rues think you are? There are rules to this arrangement.'"

"What does that mean?"

"Don't know."

"When do you tell the boss?"

"Not sure I have to."

"Freddy, I think you do."

"There won't be any publicity. No body for the cops to find. Not sure anybody outside of here as to know."

"Freddy, the boss would want to know."

"Yeah, maybe. It's late, though."

"Saturday night."

"Yeah, I was out with him earlier."

"Tomorrow, then."

"No, maybe Monday. No newspapers, no cops — there's no need to ruin Henri's weekend."

They bent over to drag the body off of the casino floor. The customers had long scattered, and the four of them were alone. When they turned the body over, they saw that one ear was partially blown off. Freddy stared at the face, though, and then observed, "Shit, he looks Jewish, doesn't he?"

Saturday night, like every Saturday night, was wives' night for the La Rue family. Henri wondered if it was like that for all of the families sometimes. He kind of liked David Levine — as much as you can like the operational head of a family who was trying to kill you not that long ago, and vice versa — but they almost never talked, and Henri never thought they were close enough for him to ask. You know, if Levine was wining and dining his side piece on Friday night and repeating the gesture for his wife on Saturday night. Come to think of it, he wasn't even sure if David Levine was married.

They tended to rotate the places, and this week was the Moulin Rouge. Henri hated the Moulin Rouge. He sometimes thought about putting his foot down and removing it from the rotation, but always backed off. Passy liked it because he was fucking one of the cigarette girls, and Passy was his right hand, and, well, the hell with it.

Still, that didn't mean he wouldn't bust Passy's balls about it.

They all had girlfriends, and their wives knew they all had girlfriends. They knew that, and they knew that Friday nights were reserved for the girlfriends, and they knew it from before they were married, and they accepted it. Accepted. The exact word. It was part of marriage to a gangster — fur coats, fancy vacations, Friday nights alone.

The cigarette girl was different, though. Both his wife (Carolina) and his girlfriend (Yvette) would have his nuts for lunch if they knew, for instance, that Passy once did the cigarette girl from behind in the alley while she was on her break — and while Carolina was out at the table watching the floor show.

That night was like most of them in that, after dinner, the women tended to cluster together toward the front of the table, nearest to the entertainment, while the men sat in the back and talked shop. At a certain point, Freddy and his wife begged off early — something about a babysitter problem, same as the week before. Then, Carolina was watching a juggler and then a comic and gabbing with Sylvie and the rest of the wives, while Passy bought his Galousies from his girl, followed her into the back, and returned 10 minutes later with a barely suppressed smile.

"Well?" Henri said.

"Christ, really?"

"Yes, really."

"I finished on her face."

"Always the gentleman."

"She's redoing her makeup."

"As one must."

The two of them, old friends and old co-workers, burst out laughing — loud enough that Sylvie turned around and stared. Apparently, the comic was in the middle of a joke.

"Between you and me," Henri said.

"What?"

"We're not kids anymore. You going to be able to take care of Carolina when you get home?"

"Bah, separate rooms these days," Passy said.

"Because she's mad about —"

"Because she's mad about growing old is the best I can figure. I mean, whatever."

Henri shrugged and poured a couple more from the open bottle. The truth was, he and Sylvie were on an upswing in that department — not young and frisky like when they were in their 20s, but not dead and desiccated, either. It was all kind of nice. It is fair to say that theirs was a contentious marriage, but the two of them were partners, lifelong partners. She was a crucial business counselor for him, not only keeping her eyes and ears open when it came to the wives of his soldiers — the best source of information about their husbands — but also with a great sense of how to deal with Gerard. So there was that, and also, well, Sylvie's bitching in the background was, if not soothing like a concert played low on the radio, at least familiar. It was what he knew.

And then, with the sex lately, Henri smiled, and Passy caught him.

"What?"

"Nothing," Henri said. "Except the cigarette girl. I can't tell from here which side of her face she had to re-touch."

Only one of the four fountains at the Place des Voges, which was about how it went. He'd never seen the full complement in operation, not in all of his years in Paris. One, two — that was normal. And the few times when he saw three, he thought it was a cause for celebration.

On this day, though, one. It wasn't too cold in the darkness, beneath the leafless trees and the dim street lights, and Jean Lemieux chose a bench with the wind at his back, and it wasn't too bad. The cassock and collar were back at the rectory. Lemieux wore what he sometimes called his Saturday clothes —

dark brown slacks and shoes, camel-colored sport jacket, black overcoat. There was no getting away from that black garment, seeing as how it was the only warm coat he owned.

Lemieux came to Place des Voges to think. It was not necessarily to examine his conscience, not like that, but just to close his eyes — or, sometimes, just have them go out of focus — and to inventory both his thoughts and his emotions.

On this day in mid-December, with the tree lights shining from dozens of windows all around him — the centuries-old apartment buildings that surrounded the square were owned by those well north of well-to-do on the economic scale — the out-of-focus tactic resulted in a gauzy kind of glow.

And, he thought: it's working.

And, he felt: then why am I so scared?

He watched Gerard closely and he could tell that he was succeeding. Slowly, slowly, the old man was crumbling. Part of him wished he didn't have to rely on his memory, but Lemieux did not dare keep a notebook. Besides, without photographs, well, photographs would be the best record of Gerard's decline — but there was no way to accomplish that.

So, the priest was stuck with his mental snapshots. Gerard's skin had gone from old and mottled — but still capable of pink cheeks on a cold day or after a brisk walk — to permanently sallow. After nine months of this, it was almost gray on some days — and he complained about hard patches on the soles of his feet besides. As for pink cheeks and brisk walks, they no longer existed. Gerard got himself to and from church in the morning, and out for lunch on Sundays, and that was about it.

Nine months. Good God. But it had to be that way. It had to be so gradual that it seemed natural, the decline. That part was working perfectly, and it would leave Gerard where Lemieux needed him to be when the next steps were taken.

Still, the priest worried. What if he was pushing things too far? What if he was miscalculating somehow? It wasn't as if he was trained to assess the old man. His eyes were not medically educated eyes, after all. There was no way to know what was going on inside Gerard's body. Lemieux saw how much bicarbonate he was drinking, and heard him say pretty much every day, "What I wouldn't give to take a solid shit." But the complaints were not increasing. It had been the same for at least four months. Gerard seemed to be slipping away very, very slowly. It was as if he was living on a hellish plateau with just the slightest downward tilt.

Another month.

Not much more.

Another month, and the next step.

Not much more.

Father Lemieux stood up and began wandering through the warren of streets to fed off of the Place de Voges. He always arrived at the same destination after he'd had one of these conversations with himself, but he always took a different, meandering route. Left, right, left again — he didn't even think about it as he walked. His head was stuck where it had been stuck, worried but hopeful.

Another month.

Not much more.

"Ah, Mr. Morin — so good to see you," said the man who worked inside the door that he always managed to arrive at.

"Is Patrice available?" the priest said.

"Yes, yes, take a seat — won't be a minute."

Clarice had two boyfriends — not that she would ever tell her mother about either of them. Sylvie had stopped even asking because of the fights that followed every question. The fact that her mother took her father's side in the ongoing argument about working in the family business — that Sylvie seemed even more adamant about it than Henri, somehow — caused the rupture that was unbridgeable, at least from Clarice's perspective. The way the daughter had the relationship figured, her mother neither loved her nor liked her. Worst of all, her mother was jealous of her — the education, the potential, all of it. She was jealous of her daughter and she felt threatened by her.

During their most recent fight, Sylvie had yelled, "You can have influence. You just have to do it behind-the-scenes. There is power in whispering."

"So, why are you screaming?"

"You know what I mean."

"I do know," Clarice said. "You and your whispers. You don't have the balls to be at the table. You hide behind your own skirts. You're afraid of the risks. You're afraid to be heard by more than one man. Afraid to make your own way. Afraid to be rejected. Afraid of the consequences. Afraid. It is no way to live."

After that one, Clarice began spending even less time at the family house in Montmartre and more time near the Sorbonne — on the couch of one of her girlfriends, or with one of her boyfriends. There were two of them.

One of them was her age. Pierre. He was a graduate student in history, which left him with decidedly dismal prospects when measured in francs. That didn't matter, though, because Clarice and Pierre didn't talk about the future — not a him-and-her future, anyway. They were buddies more than lovers — although the sex was an integral part of their relationship, especially the thing that Pierre did with his finger. For the two of them, Saturdays were for laying around naked all day. They only left his tiny apartment to eat.

When they weren't fucking, they were laughing and arguing and existing so comfortably. They would have had a future if he hadn't been Jewish, a reality that would have sent both sets of parents into the kind of state that often resulted in not only screaming, but also cutting off financial support. And that couldn't happen, especially not for Pierre.

Then, there was Clarice's other man. Louis. He was a professor of economics and finance. He was as old as Henri and had a daughter exactly Clarice's age. His family lived outside the city and he kept a pied a terre where he slept most weeks during the semester from Monday to Thursday. Sometimes, he would come to the city on Sunday afternoon "to grade these goddamn papers." Those were the Sundays when Clarice missed lunch at Vincent's. When she was still bothering to inform her mother, she sometimes said she was going to see her "girlfriend" on Thursday night to start the weekend early. Louis on Thursday. Pierre on Friday and Saturday. Louis on Sunday.

The sex with Louis was great, too, but she was the aggressor. With them, it was her finger that did the work. And as it turned out, the old man had more stamina that she expected, and memorable equipment besides.

It was after a second go-round one Thursday night — he was leaning on an elbow and smoking a cigarette, she was washing her hands in the basin — when Louis told her about the drink he'd had the previous week with an old school chum, now a fairly senior official in the ministry of finance. During the conversation, the friend explained about the upcoming devaluation of the franc. Louis actually whispered when he told her.

After the mini-war against the Levines over the train stations — that is, after Willy and his men were slaughtered in the office that fronted on the Place de Republique, slaughtered by the Levines — Freddy was put in charge of the Gare du Nord. It was a significant promotion for Henri's youngest lieutenant — other than his son — but he made the most sense. Among other things, Freddy was by far the handiest La Rue man when it came to the use of any and all firearms. His predecessor had been a genius of organization — but, as Passy said, "Look where all of those neatly-kept ledgers got our Willy. His brains were blown all over his perfect fucking penmanship."

So, if Freddy was a little young and a little scattered, Henri figured he could mentor him and that the kid would grow into the job. Boys became men in their 30s, Henri believed, and he would guide Freddy and maybe accelerate the process. It was going well, too. The envelopes were of the appropriate weight, and the headaches seemed to be nothing beyond the usual bullshit of their business: cops who suddenly materialized with their hands out, employees who drank too much or spent too much time with their pants around their ankles, stuff like that. Freddy was dealing with the headaches after seeking some advice from Henri — and so, a fatter envelope for this cop, a backhand and a threat for this young lunkhead on the staff. Henri had been attentive at the start — or, as Freddy said to him, "so far up my fucking ass" — but the boss had begun to back off in recent months.

It really felt like the La Rue operation in their half of the 10th arrondissement was humming. The truth was, the whole thing was humming. The traditional La Rue base was in Montmartre (the 18th) and below it in the 9th, and there hadn't been a hiccup there in forever. Guy was working out better than his father ever expected with his two brothels, and Timmy and Passy kept Trinity One operating like a goddamned printing press for francs. They had been in charge for more than a decade — Passy of the Trinity One casino, Timmy of the brothel one flight above — and the returns were big and consistent. It was safer than owning a bond in Electricite de France.

Every month, the La Rues clipped the fucking coupon and collected.

Henri knew less about Martin's end of the business, the liquor, and knew almost nothing about Michel's heroin trade. Well, he knew the profit sharing envelope he received every quarter, and it, too was consistent and growing. The whole thing seemed too easy sometimes.

"I had just said to Passy, 'It's been too quiet, some shit is coming.' Goddammit, Freddy. God-fucking-dammit."

There were in the back room of the uniform company on Avenue de Clichy. It was the legitimate arm of the La Rue family, a company that made school uniforms. It existed to break even — which it did, barely — and to provide pay stubs to everyone under Henri's purview, so as to keep the tax authorities happy. Passy ran the thing — a complete pain in the ass, but a fair trade off for the huge income he received from Trinity One. Henri kept an office — his only office — in the back.

It was Monday morning, and Freddy had arrived with the news of the punter who ended up dead on his casino floor on Saturday night.

"Who —"

"I did," Freddy said.

"Of course, you fucking did."

"Boss, he took at shot at one of my guys working the bar."

"Which guy?"

"Tommy."

"Fuck me. The one who —"

"Yeah, drank too much and spent too much time sniffing his fingers. But I took care of that, like you said. He's been good. He was just working the bar, minding his own business."

"And which casino was this? Wait a minute."

It just dawned on Henri that the La Rues were no longer in the casino business in the 10th, that the Levines had taken the single shitty joint in the arrondissement as part of the deal that split up the train stations.

"Freddy," Henri said. He wasn't screaming anymore. His was snarling, quietly.

"Boss, it was perfectly legitimate."

"The fuck it was. Nothing's legitimate if I don't know about it. Motherfucker. How long?"

"Two weeks."

"Babysitter problems, my ass."

"It's been good," Freddy said, desperate to steer the conversation toward the envelopes.

"It can't be good if I didn't know about it," Henri said. He was yelling again. He couldn't believe how often he found himself repeating the Uncle Gerard line about how "hogs get slaughtered." He always made fun of Gerard for that behind his back, and sometimes to his face.

"I was just trying to show some initiative," Freddy said.

"Fuck you and fuck your initiative. So where exactly is this shithole?"

Freddy told him it was on Rue Pierre Dupont, and Henri opened the door to the office and walked over to the enormous map of the city that was tacked up outside. The uniform delivery people used it in setting up their routes.

Henri looked around, and everyone — Passy at his desk, the seamstresses, all of them — had their eyes down and were concentrating on what was in front of them, or pretending to concentrate.

Henri checked the map again, squinting, just to be sure. Then he slammed the door and screamed, "On the other side of Rue La Fayette?"

Freddy nodded.

"What makes you think —"

"It's in the agreement, Henri. It's completely legitimate."

"The hell it is. It's on the other side of Rue La Fayette."

"It's legit."

"Bullshit."

"You made the deal, and you explained it to us. It's legitimate. I swear. I wouldn't have done something to violate the agreement. Henri, I swear."

Henri's mind immediately went back to the peace treaty that he and David Levine had negotiated that day, sitting on a bench in Montmartre Cemetery. It's not as if anybody wrote anything down, but the understanding seemed clear enough to Henri. The big part of the deal was the division of the train stations — the bigger and more lucrative Gare du Nord to the La Rues, the Gare de l'Est to the Levines. The La Rues took the two crappy whorehouses that were more trouble than they were worth. The Levines got the crappy casino that also was more a pain in the ass than anything.

Then Freddy began talking.

"I can repeat that conversation word for word — that's how meaningful it was to me," he said. And then he did repeat it, word for word, and Henri listened to his recitation. Train stations, check. Brothels, check. Casino, check.

"Then, the street money," Freddy said. "You said that the Levines wanted it all, but that you negotiated a split. The dividing line for the street money was Rue La Fayette."

"Like I said," Henri said.

"The dividing line for the the street money — that was it," Freddy said. "There was no dividing line for anything else, right? There was no mention of a dividing line before you came to the street money, right? Boss, I listened. It was the first big conversation I'd ever been a part of, and I listened. It's fucking imprinted on my memory. The Rue La Fayette line was about street money and only street money. That's how you explained it. Am I wrong?"

Henri closed his eyes and rubbed his temples and thought back to Montmartre Cemetery. And when he did, he realized that Freddy was right, and that there was indeed a loophole in the deal, and that the little fucker had jumped through it with both feet.

"Boss," Freddy said, and Henri opened his eyes. Freddy explained that there were no police and no newspapers that night. He said that the customers in the place were all in the wind, which wasn't ideal. That included the two guys who came in with the dearly departed, which was even less ideal.

Henri said nothing. His head suddenly seemed full of static.

"There's one more thing, Boss," Freddy said. "Tommy looked at the dead guy and, well, he's not 100 percent sure — I mean, I got him in the head after he took the shot at Tommy, and it was kind of messy."

"But ..."

"Not 100 percent, but Tommy thinks the stiff looked like a Levine guy who was there this one time when he got in a beef over a girl."

At which point, the static cleared — or, rather, morphed. Because what Henri was feeling then was his heart beginning to beat faster, and by an overall ache in his gut.

———

Thanks for sampling *Power*. You can buy it here: https://www.amazon.com/author/richardwake

Printed in Great Britain
by Amazon

45852752R00169